BARD
TIDINGS

War & Peace

Paul Regnier

Bard Tidings

For Phil Wickham,
your music is magic.

BARD
TIDINGS

PAUL REGNIER

CHAPTER 1

THE LIFE OF a castle bard isn't as glamorous as the lute crafters make it sound. When music is your trade, you learn that people are a fickle bunch. All it takes is one bad song to lose your audience. And when you play for the king, one bad song and you could lose your head.

I sat on the edge of the straw bed in my chamber, shivering under the threadbare blanket wrapped tightly around my shoulders. Of course, to call it a chamber was generous. It was more of a glorified closet. Just enough room for my squat chest of clothes, a wash basin, a stool by a small desk, and my bed.

A lone candle burned on the desk, painting the cold stones around me with an orange light. I pretended it was a hearty fire, thawing my bones.

Some might say I had a window. Others would more accurately call it a long crack in the castle wall. Late at night, the wind coming through that crack felt like the breath of a frost giant. Still, I was lucky to have fresh air and a thin ray of sunshine peeking in at times. Life was full of give and take.

A hideous scream rose up through the stone floor, making

me flinch. The dungeons were located directly beneath me. Apparently, I'd drawn the short straw when it came to bed chambers. Either that or the king employed cruel reminders to castle entertainers of the pain a bad performance could bring. Whatever the case, it was a foul place to lay one's head... I spent a lot of my free time outdoors.

On the plus side, I'd never spent more time playing the lute. Plucking out a merry tune did wonders to mute the moans and wails ascending from the dungeons.

Up until six months ago, I'd lived the carefree life of a traveling entertainer. The money was terrible, but at twenty years of age I figured some grand opportunity was just around the corner. And suddenly, there it was. A chance to play before royalty.

Grandelon Kingdom had need of castle entertainment. Sometimes the wrong opportunities roll out before you like a royal carpet, teasing the fulfillment of your dreams. My best friend and fellow entertainer, Elrick, said it was the chance of a lifetime. So, we rushed right over like lambs to the slaughter. And now, after six months of performing as the castle bard under the iron fist of King Mulraith, all I could think about was how to get away.

Three heavy thuds shook the wooden door of my chamber. A rat scurried across the floor at the sound.

"Ho there, bard," A gruff voice said. "The king summons you."

"I have a name, you know," I said.

The door squeaked open on rusty hinges, and a large silhouette filled the entrance. The wild red beard and protruding mead belly were the distinguishing marks of Sir Glimdrigul. A strong whiff of unwashed warrior assaulted my nostrils.

"You mocking me, vermin?" Glimdrigul frowned and adjusted his belt.

Bards got little respect in King Mulraith's castle. I was just a hair above a jester in the pecking order.

"No," I said. "I'm just saying you can call me Jonas. Do I call you Knight?"

His meaty hand rested on the hilt of his broadsword. "Not unless you want a good thrashing."

I sighed. A free exchange of ideas was a foreign concept within the castle walls. I ditched the blanket and stood up, grabbing my trusty lute. My prized possession. The candlelight flickered across the rich wood of the beautiful, eleven-string instrument.

My lute was an original Clarg. He'd earned a reputation among local musicians as a master craftsman. Not only had he made it rich and resonant, but the wood carvings were like a fine tapestry. Clarg had only made instruments for five years. There was little doubt that he would have been a legend in the musical world, had King Mulraith not executed him. No one knew exactly how he upset the king. There were rumors about an unflattering depiction on one of his harpsichords. These days, executions over the king's petty grievances were all too common.

"So." I slung the lute across my back. "The king has had some wine, and wants a song?"

"Sir Archinlanks has returned from battle," Sir Glimdrigul said. "And it is his birthday. The king is throwing a royal feast to celebrate his son. You must sing of his conquests tonight after the feast."

My shoulders sagged. Songs about Archinlanks were the worst. Endless poems of his exploits had been penned throughout the kingdom of Grandelon, songs of his victories were sung, dances were danced in his honor, yet his cup was never full. The man never met a mirror he didn't love.

The problem was, he was a true champion. Unlike the slobbish Glimdrigul who currently darkened my doorway, Archinlanks was a force to be reckoned with. He was undefeated in kingdom tournaments, and he generally returned from battle with nothing but a few bumps and bruises.

"Take note, dog." Glimdrigul pointed a threatening finger at me. "They say Archinlanks defeated a dozen ogres with nothing more than a dinner fork."

It was foolish to question a knight's tale of conquest, however ridiculous, but sometimes my lips moved before my brain could catch up. "Ogres? With a dinner fork?"

His fists clenched. "You dare question Sir Archinlanks' veracity?"

I shook my head vigorously.

"Then mind your tongue, boy, and prepare a song. You and the jester will perform in the great hall after the feast. And you'd better sing well, or it's your head."

My mind ran through potential lyrics. What on earth rhymes with ogre?

The red-bearded oaf left and slammed my door shut. Thankfully, he took his smell with him.

"Fat fool," I muttered.

Something pounded against my door.

"I didn't say anything," my voice quivered.

The door squeaked open and there stood Elrick, the castle jester and my best friend. His beanpole of a body leaned against my door frame.

Elrick ran a hand through his shaggy blonde hair, clearing it from his brown eyes. "What'd you say?"

"Nothing. You know we're performing tonight, right?"

He glanced over both shoulders, checking the hallway behind him. "Yeah. Our farewell performance."

I put a finger to my lips.

"Come on." He motioned to the hallway. "The feast won't start for a couple hours. Let's get out of here for a while."

I perked up. "The Slaughtered Boar?"

He nodded.

"Finally, some good news."

I grabbed my cloak, and we headed out of the castle into the common lanes of the kingdom.

Grandelon wasn't a large kingdom, as kingdoms go. Half a day's travel could take you from the edge of Fetrell Forest to the farmlands on the outskirts of town. But under King Mulraith's rule, the borders were ever expanding, as neighboring towns fell under his power.

Slipping away from the oppressive thumb of castle life requires finding a place where nobility fears to tread. Of the three taverns in Grandelon kingdom, The Slaughtered Boar was the smallest, the dirtiest, and had the worst food. Situated among the commonest of commoners, it generally attracted the least desirable members of the citizenry. And beside the benefit of attracting fewer nobles, it had one thing the other taverns did not – the lovely Bree, Elrick's older sister.

The tavern was dark and cozy, with thick wood beams, and a humble stone fireplace on the western wall. Flickering candles danced like fireflies above the wooden tables. It was suppertime, and a handful of the usual patrons were scattered throughout the room. Farmers and tradesmen huddled over their pints in earth-toned, well-worn pants and tunics. Oddly enough, the aromatic blend of wood smoke, ale, and sweaty farmers was almost pleasant.

Stumpy Jake manned the bar, eternally filling and cleaning glasses of ale and mead. Contrary to rumors, Jake did not have a wooden leg. But for some reason he enjoyed the nickname and did nothing to dispel the myth. In fact, he attached a wooden block to his heel so he'd make a clomping sound when he walked across the floor. He thought it added character to his establishment.

It always amazed me that Stumpy Jake, the cantankerous owner of The Slaughtered Boar, was Bree's uncle. Given that he resembled a squat swamp troll, and she had the allure of an enchanted wood nymph, family heredity was really straining at the borders.

Time seemed to slow down, and a warmer glow spread across the tavern as I spotted Bree weaving through the tables. Candlelight on her copper hair was like a sunset over fields of wheat. Her bright blue eyes glanced over at me and she gave a small wave. The heavy weight of my ill-fated decision to be a castle bard melted away.

I waved back to Bree, unable to keep a childish smile from my face.

Elrick patted me on the shoulder. "You okay, Jonas? You want to sit down? Maybe throw a bucket of ice water on your head?"

I frowned at him. "I have to sing a song about Archinlanks tonight. Let me have a few moments of joy."

He rolled his eyes. "Suit yourself. I'm grabbing a booth."

The nights when I could get away from the castle and see Bree were the best parts of my life during these difficult days. She was smart and playful, with a fire in her eyes that promised she could endure a lifetime of storms. Not to mention her unique ability to create illusions, which was as much an art as it was a magical gift.

At first, Elrick wasn't too thrilled about my infatuation with Bree, given that she was his sister. Thankfully, my competition for her affections consisted mostly of drunk tavern riff-raff, so he'd come to accept me as the better option. These days he mainly teased me for admiring her from afar, and not having the courage to profess my love.

When I thought about it, it was hard to believe she even paid me any attention at all. Not that I was some wart-covered toad by any means. Some had even likened my appearance to that of Sir Perticul, who had an unusual combination of boyish good looks and broad-shouldered might. Elrick said the comparison was generous, but then again, I don't remember him being compared to a knight.

Wyatt, the local ale maker, sat on a stool in the corner, playing a somber tune on his wooden flute. His chord progressions could bring you right to tears if your guard was down.

Wyatt nodded at me without missing a note. I slung my lute in front of me and simulated plucking a few strings. He winked, indicating he was open to a flute-lute arrangement. I could certainly use some musical redemption before selling out with my horrific Sir Archinlanks songs.

Besides our kinship as fellow musicians, we also shared a skill with the quarterstaff. Wyatt's mastery of this weapon was the stuff of legends. Before I met him, I thought my abilities with the staff were quite good. After months of being disarmed and knocked about during our sparring sessions, I had a whole new appreciation for the weapon. Thankfully, he was a patient teacher and kept the bruising to a bare minimum.

My aversion to blood and carnage were the main reason I wielded a staff rather than the sharper alternatives. Wyatt assumed the choice was due to being clever and refined like he was, so I let him believe it. He always said swords were for mindless slaughter, whereas staves were for teaching lessons. And he was quick to add that you could employ it as a walking stick, and if challenged by some lout with a sword, most opponents would never see it coming.

I strolled over to Wyatt as he finished his weepy flute tune. "Up for some music tonight?"

Wyatt smiled, his gray beard lifting in the process. "Of course… You all right? You look a bit down."

"I have to sing songs about Sir Archinlanks tonight."

He winced. "Mercy. Condolences, lad."

"Yeah. When I started playing the lute, this isn't where I expected to wind up."

"Indeed. The life of a musician is a twisting road. But it's worth it, eh?"

I shrugged. "I suppose."

He shook his head. "Nothing to suppose about it. Music is precious. A gift from the Eternal One. It lifts people up. Haven't you seen what it can do?"

"Well, I'm stuck playing battle songs for the king's arrogant son. Pretty sure I'm on the wrong musical path."

Wyatt smiled. "It's not all roses, lad. But the music rises above it all. One of the transcendent gifts from above. When we play, we get to be a part of that transcendence."

I sighed. "It sounds beautiful when you talk about it. But when I'm singing about slaying ogres with kitchen implements, all the beauty dies."

He chuckled. "Keep at it, young Jonas. You have been gifted. And your music will have its moment. Rest assured it will find the ears of those who need it. Focus on them. Ignore the rest."

Wyatt had reached that enviable level of existence where he seemed to walk above the daily grind. Or perhaps his head had received one too many blows with the quarterstaff. Either way, whenever I spoke with him I found myself jealous of his outlook on life.

"Thanks," I said. "Listen, I need to speak with Elrick, but maybe we can play a song in a bit if you're up for it."

"Of course," Wyatt said. "And perhaps some staff training tomorrow."

I couldn't bring myself to tell him I was planning on leaving the kingdom. He'd been an unexpected friend during the last few months, and I just didn't know how to say goodbye.

"Perhaps. Listen, Wyatt. Thanks for helping me with the staff and playing music with me and… Well, thanks for everything."

Wyatt arched a brow. "Now hold on a minute. You're headed back on the road, aren't you?"

"Oh. Well, you know, the thing is—"

He held up his hand and grinned. "Say no more. The wanderlust of the traveling musician. I understand. You want to experience adventure beyond Grandelon and share your songs across Ashrellan. I did the same thing at your age."

Wyatt made it sound far more glorious than fleeing from a tyrant under the cover of night.

"Something like that," I said.

"Then may the Eternal One guide you." Wyatt put his hand on my shoulder. "It's been a pleasure knowing you, Jonas. I wish you safe journeys."

I gave a tight grin and turned away before my lip started trembling.

I headed through the tavern as Wyatt resumed the otherworldly sounds of his wooden flute. The music was a beautiful counter to the clanking utensils and gruff conversations of the tavern.

Elrick reclined in a dark wooden booth near the fireplace. I slid into the booth, propping my lute up by the wall.

He shook a small leather bag, making a clinking sound. "You up for some goblin bones?"

"Nah."

"Scared?"

"I beat you the last three games."

Elrick mumbled under his breath and returned the bag to his pocket. My mind drifted back to potential lyrics for my farewell performance at the feast.

"Do you know what rhymes with ogre?" I said.

Elrick paused for a moment. "Badger?"

I shook my head. "I have a bad feeling about my song tonight."

"Well, at least the king likes your music. A few nights ago, during my backflip finale, he threw a plate of peach pits at me. Peach pits, Jonas. Still slimy from his serpent tongue. How did I come to this?" Elrick threw up his hands. "How did we end up here?"

"You said we should come here, remember? You said castle entertainment is the ultimate goal of any performer."

"Oh, sure. Throw that back in my face."

"Look, it doesn't matter. Soon we'll leave this wretched

kingdom and go back on the road. We only have to endure this for one more feast, right?"

"Speaking of which, as a special gift for his wretched son, the king told me to juggle six candlesticks while dancing tonight. Six! He's trying to make me crack."

"Can you juggle six?"

"Not while I'm dancing."

I frowned. "This might not be the best farewell performance."

He nodded. "Either way, I can't wait to get away from here. Archinlank's birthday feast promises the drink will flow freely. Once night falls in earnest, and the soldiers are sleeping it off, we pack up and leave. Free once more."

At the thought of escape, a tingle of nerves spread through my skin. "Hopefully, we don't get caught. The king expects us to stay through winter, you know. If he finds out, we're really poking the bear. Except the bear is an angry sorcerer with a legion of soldiers."

"We won't live through winter in that castle. If we're ever going to get out of here, this is our best chance. Mulraith's a boiling kettle burning everyone around him. Sorcery has poisoned his mind. And now we have that cursed dragon Baldramorg to deal with. He gets closer every day. Once the farm animals run out, he'll come for the town, mark my words."

Sometimes tough situations go from bad to worse. Case in point, a green-scaled dragon known as Baldramorg had recently decided the livestock in the surrounding farmlands of the kingdom provided his favored cuisine. His lair was in the nearby White Root Mountains. It was half a day's travel by horseback, but only a quick jaunt by dragon wing.

"One more reason to leave, right?" I said.

"That's for certain," Elrick said. "There's even rumors the king wants to send prisoners to the dragon's lair as some kind of appeasement offering. We have to leave before it's too late."

"Before it's too late for what?" Bree's familiar, warm voice broke through the tavern noise. She stood at the end of our booth in her long brown skirt and off-the-shoulder peasant blouse. Her light copper hair was done up in thin braids that circled her head like a halo, enhancing her angelic appearance. She leaned closer, placing two metal cups of cider in front of us.

"Before we're taken to the dragon Baldramorg as an appeasement offering," Elrick grabbed his cup and took a drink.

Bree rolled her eyes. "Not that again. Stop listening to tavern rumors."

"Have you thought about what we talked about?" Elrick said. "No more delays. Tonight's the night."

Bree glanced back at Stumpy Jake. "I don't know. Uncle Jake would never forgive me for leaving him without help."

"He's the reason we're in this mess," Elrick glared at the squat bartender. "He promised us that castle entertainers live the high life. He made it sound like we'd be swimming in gold coins, surrounded by fair maidens."

Bree put her hands on her hips. "Well, since when has Uncle Jake not juggled the truth? He probably got a finders fee for bringing you two starry-eyed dreamers into that castle."

Elrick pointed at her. "Which is exactly why you shouldn't feel bad about leaving him high and dry."

She studied both of us. "So, you're serious this time? You're really leaving tonight?"

"Yes," I said. "After the feast when everyone is well drunk. You should really come with us. It's not safe around here."

My voice sounded a little too desperate. Bree was merciful and pretended not to notice.

"Well," Bree pursed her lips. "Originally, I did only promise to help through last season. I've put in my time, and then some. And Uncle Jake certainly has made his share of false promises to me. It is tempting."

"Ho there, barmaid." A hulking man with a bushy, black

beard lumbered over to Bree's left side. He held a tankard of ale that was almost empty. He looked her up and down, a creepy smile on his wet lips. "You lonely tonight?"

Bree slid her right hand behind her back. A soft, white glow began to radiate from it. A milky haze spread across her right eye along with an oozing trail of yellow liquid. Several open sores appeared on her neck.

She turned to face the big man, her smile revealing an alarming mosaic of yellowed and missing teeth. "You seem strong. I'll bet you're good at fighting off disease." She coughed into her hand, then placed it on his chest.

He glanced down at her hand, the back of it now covered with green lesions.

The bearded man's eyes went wide as his focus jumped from her face to her hand. He took a quick step back. "Oh. No… I'm sorry. So sorry. I, um, have to… wash up." He turned and rushed through the tavern, wildly brushing off the front of his shirt as he burst out the front door.

Bree smiled and turned back, the illusion of the sores and missing teeth dissolving away.

Elrick and I applauded.

"I like the dripping eye effect," Elrick said. "Is that new?"

"Yes," Bree said. "It really adds, don't you think?"

"Definitely."

Bree sat down on my side of the booth and slid close. A thrill of excitement shot through me. I don't think it would've bothered me even if her eye was dripping.

Magical abilities were something of a mystery. They generally emerged when a child came of age, and could be trained to a greater degree of potency like any other ability. Magic didn't seem to be tied to family lineage, lands, elixirs, or a hundred other variables that scholars had studied and pulled their hair out over. As far as I knew, there was no rhyme or reason as to whom the magic fell upon. It was an innate gifting, or cursing, depending on how you looked at things.

For those with powerful magic that lent itself to warfare, their path was pretty much set. Either join an army or a secret enclave, or hide it at all costs. Luckily for Bree, the illusory forms of magic, at least at the lower levels, were generally looked upon as parlor tricks, and nothing to be feared or exploited. Even so, Bree used her magic sparingly, and the objects of her illusions were often drunken tavern-goers who had a reputation for telling tales.

Thankfully, most people lacked any sort of magical ability. In my experience, those with power at their fingertips tended to use it poorly.

"Well?" Elrick spread out his hands. "Are you in or not?"

Bree paused, glancing around the tavern. "I can't deny I'm tired of this place. I'm tired of Uncle Jake ordering me around. I'm tired of drunken oafs leering at me. I even got propositioned by Sir Archinlanks today. That fool is dangerous."

"Archinlanks?" I stared at her.

She nodded. "He was in here earlier with some of the other knights. Strutting around, bragging about slaying a dozen ogres or some nonsense. Then he grabbed my hand and told me I'd make a great birthday present. I nearly bashed his head with a flagon of ale."

I clenched my jaw. "That filthy dog."

Elrick slammed his fist on the table. "I wish they'd throw him to the dragon. He has five concubines and it's still not enough for that swaggering creep."

"So, what'd you do?" I said.

"Sir Farlsburg came in with news about the kingdom," she said. "Archinlanks got distracted and I slipped away."

"That seals it," I said. "I think it's time we all slipped away. For good."

Bree took a deep breath. "All right. I'm in."

Elrick lifted his cup high. "Hear, hear."

"On one condition," she said. "We head for Calladia."

"What? No." Elrick clunked his cup back on the table. "As soon as father sees me he'll start lecturing me about taking over the farm. He doesn't understand the life of an entertainer."

"Can you blame him?" she said. "You're stuck performing for a horrible king that you can't wait to run away from."

"It's better than being a barmaid," he said.

"All right, All right." I put out my hands like I was calming children. "We don't have to decide right now. But, to be honest, Calladia is a great option. You've always told me stories about growing up there, it sounds really nice."

"It's beautiful," Bree said. "Plus it's only three days' travel."

Bree spoke of Calladia with a twinkle in her eye. I figured traveling with her to a place that brought her such joy would probably bring us closer together.

"Then let's do it," I said. "Let's go to Calladia."

"Oh, sure," Elrick said. "Take her side. Big shock."

"Well, where would you go?" I said.

Elrick frowned. "I don't know. There's always Nilleston."

"That's even farther," Bree said. "And it smells. It's full of pig farms."

"But plenty of bacon," he said.

"Bree!" The gruff voice of Stumpy Jake cut through the air. His beady eyes glared at our table from his perch behind the bar. He motioned Bree over. "Customers are thirsty."

Bree sighed. "Duty calls. Hopefully for the last time."

She scooted out of the booth and headed back to the bar. My heart soared at the thought of Bree leaving the kingdom with us. She'd always been hesitant about the idea before, and I'd had my doubts that she'd ever agree to come. But thankfully, something had changed. Maybe it was the steady stream of unwanted, drunken advances in the tavern, maybe it was the looming threat of the dragon, or maybe, just maybe, she was warming up to me. As long as I was somewhere in the mix, I was happy.

Elrick frowned and mumbled something to himself.

"Oh, stop pouting," I said. "Calladia is a great first destination. I didn't say we'd build a summer home there."

He shook his head. "It's not that."

"All right, what is it?"

"Archinlanks," he said. "What if he comes after my sister again?"

The thought sent a shiver through me. "I don't know. But you heard her. She's clever. She got away."

"I know but... Don't you ever wish you could do something? Like, just pummel one of these big oafs."

"Well, sure, but what are you gonna do? Take on the whole castle guard?"

He stared into his cup. "I know. It's just... Lately, it's really getting to me. I've had these dreams. You'll probably laugh but I've had dreams that I could stand up to them and fight back. Vivid dreams that I actually had the strength to stop them. To protect people." He gave me a nervous glance as though waiting for me to tease him.

"I understand, Elrick." I gave a thoughtful nod. "Believe me, I do."

Elrick was hitting me where it hurt. One of the nice things about being a traveling entertainer was that you only had to take care of yourself. Getting too tied to a place made you care. Caring was dangerous. Especially in a place like Grandelon where King Mulraith ruled with an iron fist. This, of course, left a trail of injustice and oppression. Generally the people that cared and tried to fight back were promptly hurled into a dungeon, never to be heard from again.

When I first started training with the staff, my only thought was to defend myself on the road. As I became more skilled, the thought of striking back against the tyranny I saw around me was tempting. But the harsh truth was, Grandelon was ruled by a powerful sorcerer king and hundreds of soldiers. I was just a simple bard with a quarterstaff.

A smattering of applause went through the tavern as Wyatt finished an upbeat tune on the flute. He caught my eye and waved me over.

I grabbed my lute and slid out of the booth. "All right, I'm going to play a song with Wyatt. At least something good will come out of my lute tonight."

"Good idea," Elrick said. "Bree always gets a bit misty-eyed when you play."

"Okay, now I'm going to hurt you."

"No, really. I've seen her. She practically swoons."

"On your honor?"

"On my honor."

I paused for a moment, weighing the sincerity in his eyes, then weaved my way through the tavern.

Wyatt graciously let me join him on the stage. Of course, this merely consisted of two stools crammed together in a corner, but it was still nice of him to share the musical space.

He was a master at his craft, so there was no need to discuss details beforehand. He merely nodded at me, then launched into a soft melody that rose and fell like an eagle in the breeze. Wyatt had the rare and amazing ability to entice the imagination with his wordless tunes. I was so entranced with his delicate handling of notes, I nearly forgot to play.

I layered in a light plucking pattern to elicit a sense of musical adventure. The addition of the lute seemed to brighten the mood, changing the dreamy tones of the flute into a carefree melody. I closed my eyes and imagined strolling through a sun-drenched forest with Bree at my side.

Those occasions when I was lucky enough to play with an

artist of Wyatt's caliber were high points of my musical journey. The joy of falling in sync with another instrument and getting lost in a melody was a thing of magic. Maybe Wyatt was right and there was something transcendent about what we were doing.

A clattering of chairs and raised voices disturbed my musical reverie. Probably some drunken oaf stumbling his way through the tavern. I shut my eyes tight and tried to focus on the song. A muffled scream finally broke my concentration.

I glanced up to find soldiers dragging Bree from the tavern with Sir Archinlanks following close behind. My fingers fumbled across the strings as I stood to my feet, my heart beating heavily in my chest.

Elrick hurried to the stage, his eyes wide with alarm.

"Archinlanks took Bree!" He pointed to the front door with a jabbing motion. "He's taking her to the castle as his new concubine."

CHAPTER 2

ELRICK AND I gathered our things and left The Slaughtered Boar in a rush. A thin sliver of moon cut through the darkness like the slash of a blade. Our boots beat a quick path down the cobblestones. The squat, wooden houses blurred together in a wash of brown. Candles flickered in a handful of windows as we passed.

The evening streets ushered weary travelers home from a long day of work. We weaved swiftly around a drunken tavern patron as he stumbled down the shadowy lane.

Archinlanks, Bree, and the soldiers were nowhere in sight. My stomach was a storm of anger and anxiety.

"What do we do?" Elrick said.

"I don't know," I said. "But we can't let him take her."

"Well, we can't go up against the whole castle guard either."

The heavy truth of his words hit me like a hammer. Even if we caught up with the soldiers, what could I do? They were heavily-muscled trained killers. They probably dreamed of the day a spindly jester and a lute-wielding bard would challenge them to a fight.

"All right, maybe we can't fight them," I said. "We have to think of something clever."

Elrick stayed quiet for a few moments. "Like what?"

"I don't know. Maybe you can use those acrobatics of yours."

"To do what? Entertain them to death?"

I sighed. "This is terrible. We should've left when we had the chance."

"Who knew this would happen? I thought tonight's revels were our way out of here."

"Wait." My mind lit up. "Maybe it is. There's still a feast tonight. Plenty of drink for all those armor-clad thugs."

"Ah," Elrick grinned. "Right. Our plan could still work."

"Exactly. Let them stuff themselves with food and wine until they pass out like pigs. Then we find Bree and slip through their bloated fingers while they snore the night away."

Elrick rubbed his hands together. "Fantastic. What should we do in the meantime?"

"They want a performance? We'll give them our best. Keep them high on their own arrogance so they drink themselves into a stupor. And when they wake up tomorrow and we've vanished like spirits, they'll wonder how they ever got so spun around that a bard and a jester hung them out to dry."

Elrick laughed. "We'll be legends. Maybe you can write a song about us."

"I might just do that."

When we got back to the castle, we parted ways, each heading to his chamber to prepare for our final performance.

It wasn't long before there was a loud knock at my door and I was ordered to the feast. I left my chamber, making my way to the great hall.

The great hall was the largest area in the castle and held the biggest fireplace I'd ever seen. A vaulted ceiling and a huge black metal chandelier housing a ring of candles made the room feel even more grand. Decorative tapestries in deep purple hung from every wall. It would have been a wonderful place except for all the loud, drunken nobles currently occupying it.

The dinner platters of spit-roasted pig had been picked clean. The heavy aroma of burnt meat still hung in the air. Bits of spiced fruitcake lingered on the long, wooden table that curved in a half-circle away from the king's throne. Since my daily provisions consisted of leftover bread, old vegetables, and gristle, my stomach was not happy to be teased with epicurean delights that I could smell but not touch.

Wine and mead were flowing freely in silver goblets. King Mulraith sat at the apex of the table on his finely carved wooden throne. He was tall and slender with a face like an old reptile. His crimson robe cascaded down his thin frame, the firelight giving it a bloody sheen. Even in the midst of a loud celebration, he wore a grim expression, as though he were ready to incinerate the room with a blast of sorcerous fire.

Unless you were a high level power mage, it was unwise to upset a sorcerer. Their commitment to the corrupting elements of nature eventually transformed their countenance into a skeletal visage, with little of its former humanity left. When someone took such a dark path to gain power, you stayed on their good side.

The queen's chair sat empty beside Mulraith, as it had for the last few years. Rumor had it that she'd flirted with the dashing Sir Vellice, and even encouraged him to kiss her hand in the middle of a great feast for the king. After that night, the queen and Sir Vellice were never seen again. The very next day, a statue of a knight kissing the hand of a queen, bearing an uncanny resemblance to both of them, graced the south end of the great hall near the servants' entrance. No one dared to ask if sorcery was involved, but no one thought it a coincidence either.

The remainder of the places around the curved table were

occupied by knights, and two slave girls who rubbed the broad shoulders of Sir Archinlanks as he guzzled mead.

Everyone was slurring their words and speaking twice as loudly as they needed to. Every few seconds a chorus of laughter burst out for a joke that probably didn't warrant the response.

Elrick paced nearby, shaking his arms out as he loosened up for his performance. His striped dark red and gray jester's outfit provided a nice counter to his tall leather boots. His thoughts on entertainers' outfits were similar to my own. Avoid the bright, flashy colors common in the trade, and opt for deeper, muted tones. It provided an air of mystery. A hint of danger. A question in the mind of the audience that would be answered with the performance. At least, that was the hope.

For my part, I kept my look simple. Charcoal pants with a brown tunic and a dark crimson vest. All of it was swallowed up in an earthen cloak. Many of my contemporaries wore big, poofy hats accented with a garish feather. They claimed it added show-manship to their performance. I found it ridiculous, and since Bree had commented favorably on my flowing chestnut hair on more than one occasion, I stuck with what worked.

I nodded at Elrick and started toward him just as King Mulraith called out.

"Jester!" The king waved Elrick over. "Entertain us like a good little dog. Quickly now."

Elrick rolled his shoulders, then launched into a series of back handsprings landing with a full flip in front of the king.

The surrounding knights gave a lackluster mix of applause. Elrick danced, unfazed by the weak response, spinning by the table's edge, and grabbing candlesticks as he moved. Without losing a beat, he began juggling them, maintaining his nimble footwork all the while. I smiled, admiring his skills.

I knew there wasn't much time before my performance. My

mind worked fast, putting together a string of phrases that would overly inflate Sir Archinlanks latest tale of conquest.

Some nights, the music and lyrics flowed from my brain with ease. Those were the nights I felt confident that all the hours I'd spent practicing the lute and pursuing the life of a bard had been divine destiny. This wasn't one of those nights. My phrasing seemed awkward and amateurish. The chord progression felt uninspired. After what had happened with Bree, I couldn't seem to focus.

An uproar from the table roused me from my musical stumblings.

Elrick no longer juggled. He'd switched to the finale of his performance, a blurry combination of spins and flips. It was a calculated move, since at this point, the knights generally grew bored and tried to pelt him with fruit.

"Dance you little monkey," Sir Glimdrigul hurled an apple. "Dance."

Elrick flipped backwards and the apple whizzed by his head. I tried to refocus my attention on improving my song. There wasn't much time before Elrick was done and I was on the chopping block.

The knights erupted in another drunken howl as Elrick spun away from a volley of lemons. He did a smooth transition into a somersault and ended up beside me.

"Rough night," He whispered in my ear. "Hope you have a good song ready."

"Still working on it." I whispered.

"Work fast. The dogs are rabid." He arched into a series of cartwheels, neatly dodging a crossfire of oranges.

"Bard!" The king yelled out in his raspy voice. "Come. Sing for us!"

A chorus of hurrahs filled the air, followed by the resounding thunder of knights banging on the wooden table.

"Jester, leave us," the king said. "Go back to your hole."

The knights laughed and hurled a fresh volley of fruit at Elrick who nimbly spun and twirled away from every projectile.

Elrick paused next to me, wiping his brow. He glanced at me with raised eyebrows. "Best of luck."

My fingers found the familiar strings of the lute and I took a deep breath, preparing for my first song. I took a step forward just as the large wooden doors at the back of the room burst open with a thunderous echo.

A herald dressed in flowing blue and purple garments strode into the throne room and blew the ascending six note announcement of entry. I'd never been so relieved to have my song interrupted.

Sir Farlsburg marched into the room right after the herald. His dark eyes held a wild gaze, and his lips were pressed into a thin line. I stepped aside as he advanced to the king's table and took a knee.

"Rise and report," the king said.

Sir Farlsburg stood, his helmet tucked neatly under one arm. "The dragon Baldramorg draws closer with each day. Cattle are consumed. Crops are destroyed. The threat will reach the town before long. The dragon may come for the castle itself, majesty."

Angry curses and grumbles spread among the knights.

King Mulraith steepled his fingers before his lips, his eyes staring into the distance. He remained quiet for a moment.

"Majesty, I—" Sir Farlsburg started.

King Mulraith held up a hand, his eyes suddenly focused. "The commoners appeal to their hope in the Eternal One. A hope that hasn't hindered the spread of my power, nor shall it stop the dragon. I shall take matters into my own hands and show them who's really in charge. We shall make an appeasement offering. A steady supply of food. Perhaps we can keep Baldramorg at bay for the time being. If not, we slay him. But that effort will be costly."

Sir Archinlanks slammed his fist on the table with a resounding thud. "Savage creature! I will slay the foul serpent."

"Nay, Archinlanks." The king put out his hand as if to calm a beast. "You've only just returned."

The six foot five monstrosity that was Sir Archinlanks stood up. "When the fight calls, I will answer! I will smite him with my shield." He grabbed an empty platter and flung it at a servant carrying a ceramic pitcher. The platter obliterated the pitcher with a crash and drenched the servant in a wash of red wine. The knights applauded the accuracy of his aim.

"I will smite him with my spear." Sir Archinlanks grabbed a tall candlestick with a ring of raised candles and hurled it at the herald. The candles ignited the herald's bright clothes and he danced around in a wild panic, trying to extinguish them. The knights broke out in laughter as servants nearby doused him with pitchers of water.

"And I will crush him with my fists." He grabbed an orange from a fruit basket, squeezed it until it split apart, then threw it at my face.

Oranges, even partially crushed, aren't as soft as you'd think when they strike you in the eye socket at full speed. A throbbing pain spread through my skull. The strong odor of citrus filled my nostrils while the laughter of drunken nobility filled my ears. I wiped the dripping remains of the orange off with my sleeve, blinking away the stinging residue.

The king regarded Archinlanks with a blank expression. I couldn't tell if he was proud or disgusted by his emotional display.

"A dragon is not an ogre," the king said. "You will temper your rage once you behold a dragon with your own eyes. You shall make the journey to the White Root Mountains tomorrow with an offering for Baldramorg. The dissenters in the dungeon will do nicely. Take a contingent of soldiers and my elite archers. I shall enchant their arrows in case the dragon turns and you need to bring him down."

"Thank you, father." A sly grin broke out on Archinlanks' face as he lounged back into his seat. The two slave girls resumed rubbing his shoulders.

"But take heed, boy." Mulraith fixed Archinlanks with a stern gaze. "Maintain your distance. Send a squire to proclaim the offering. Someone expendable. It will take many lives to turn his will."

Archinlanks gave a quick nod. "Yes, father."

King Mulraith turned back to Sir Farlsburg. "Is that all?"

"One more report, majesty," Sir Farlsburg said. "Our forces grow strong at Witchpaw Canyon. Calladia is poorly defended. A small guard, but mostly farmers and hunters. It should be ours in a fortnight, then we can move on the villagers in the foothills of Kroth and further establish our rule."

Cheers broke out from the knights seated all around.

A hollow sensation formed in the pit of my stomach. They were mounting an attack on the peaceful town of Calladia. This was Elrick and Bree's hometown, and I couldn't imagine how they'd take the news, especially since they still had family living there. I glanced back at Elrick. He stood in the shadows at the back of the room, his hands balled into fists.

The corner of Mulraith's mouth curved upward. "I am most pleased to hear it."

"But the wolves plague us, majesty," Sir Farlsburg continued. "They ambush us in the lanes. They ambush us in the forest. The devils attack us at every turn."

The king flicked his fingers as if shooing a fly. "They are of no consequence. We shall break Calladia and expand our rule. Ready the soldiers."

Sir Farlsburg nodded and marched out of the room.

"Now, bard." King Mulraith waved me forward. "Come. Entertain us. Sing for my son."

I closed my eyes, trying to forget the mounting anxiety of the evening. The best thing I could do was play a song that would inspire these royal pigs to drink themselves into a stupor.

Pushing aside my troubled thoughts, I strolled toward the center of the room. My fingers plucked a sprightly pattern to lighten the mood. The instrumental lead-in was a staple of professional bards. It offered a perfect excuse to warm up the fingers, and gave time for a drunken crowd to calm down and realize a song was coming.

"Rise, Sir Archinlanks," the king said.

Sir Archinlanks rose, crossing his powerful arms over his chest. Even without his suit of armor, he was an intimidating presence. A fresh cut ran across his square chin, and a swollen cheek bone told the tale of his recent battle.

"Sir Archinlanks met over twenty ogres at the Ford of Vendellin." the king said. "An ambush meant to destroy him. Those cowards even stole his sword before he could react. That would have been the end of most warriors, aye?"

"Aye!" The crowd answered.

Hearing the number of ogres escalate from twelve to twenty in the span of a few hours wasn't surprising. It would probably reach triple digits by morning.

"But not Sir Archinlanks," the king continued. "He slew thirty of them and returned without a scratch."

The crowd cheered and raised their glasses.

"Now, bard." The king motioned to me. "You must sing for us a tale of his latest victory. But first, a gift for my son. His latest concubine."

Two guards marched into the great hall, dragging Bree along with them. She wore a delicate white gown with lacy shoulder caps. Roses intertwined into a crown graced her forehead. But instead of royal jewelry, her wrists were shackled in iron.

Bree's dress was soft and regal but her expression was of utter contempt. She glared at Archinlanks, and her jaw was set as the guards dropped her at his side. Bree met my eyes for a quick moment, then looked away as though she wanted to forget we'd almost got away from all of this.

Every muscle in my body tightened. My fingers froze and the music stopped. I wanted to leap over the feasting table and strangle Sir Archinlanks with my lute strings.

"Happy birthday, my son," the king raised his glass and took a drink.

The knights cheered and returned the toast, sending another healthy swallow of wine down their greedy throats. Archinlanks took a long drink, then pulled Bree close, moving his cup to her mouth. She shook her head and looked away. Archinlanks shrugged and took another drink.

"Now then, Bard," King Mulraith said. "A song of praise for my son, the champion. A song to exalt his prowess in battle."

My body trembled with anger. I'd never desired the path of a warrior until that moment. My training with the staff had been for protection against forest bandits and wild animals. But now, witnessing the injustice of a tyrant's power against someone I cared about, I wanted to use every ability I had to stop it. It sickened me that I had to play the fool and sing false praise to this monster of a human being in front of me.

"Bard!" The king narrowed his eyes. "Awake from your stupor. Sing for us."

The glimmer of hope that we could still escape tonight burned like a tiny ember in my heart. Even if it was the smallest campfire the wind was about to extinguish, the memory of Elrick's efforts urged me on. Perhaps it was still possible. I had to at least try.

I began a slow plucking of low notes. Thankfully, I didn't have to put a great deal of musical thought into it. Most of my battle songs followed a similar pattern. The speed of my plucking would increase as the song progressed, I'd sprinkle in a few minor chords to hint at tragedy, then layer in heavier patterns, and crescendo with major chords, declaring victory, my voice rising with the conquest.

I'd tried more complex arrangements but they were generally

met with disapproval. The musical taste of swaggering knights seemed to favor the simple and familiar. And since I was well acquainted with the tortured screams of those who displeased the king, I had strong motivation to comply.

"Brave Sir Archinlanks set forth…"

I sang with my eyes closed to simulate reverence.

"Damsels wept as he rode north."

A light sigh came from the slave girls who waited on Archinlanks. I doubled the rate of my plucking.

"Then suddenly, the ogres came.
Waves of ghoulish, hideous frames.
Erupting from their darkened dens,
their foul intentions known to men.
Most would flee on sight of ogre,
green of skin and manners vulgar."

I attacked the strings with greater intensity.

"But Archinlanks stood firm and fast.
His sword was lost, the die was cast.
He struck with naught but dining tool,
the ogres fell, the ogres knew.
Their time was up, their mortal coil
would shed and sink into the soil."

My voice soared, a gritty edge punching the word soil.

There was a light smattering of applause. I admit it wasn't my best work, but considering the pressure of my current situation,

I'd say it wasn't half bad. After all, I'd found a rhyme for ogre on the spot. That alone deserved credit.

"You didn't include the number of the slain," the king frowned. "When over fifty ogres are dispatched, I want to hear the number."

"I'll remember that, your majesty." I gave a slight nod.

"Sing a song about my birthday present." Archinlanks pulled Bree tight under his arm. "She may resist me now but soon she'll come around. I'll have her bowing to my every wish. Mark my words."

The knights laughed and cheered.

Their merriment at such a horrific scene echoed in my ears, and something inside me snapped. The room blurred into a smear of lights and shadows, as all noise receded into the background.

My focus landed on Bree. Her eyes were tight, and her mouth was locked into a frown of disgust as she pushed away from Archinlanks' thick torso. His drunken laughter was the only clear sound. The black strands of his hair swept across his thick forehead as he pulled Bree close to him once more.

A strange numbness washed over me and I turned toward Archinlanks. Laughter continued to resonate throughout the room as I strode forward, gripping the neck of the lute and lifting it over my head.

Sir Archinlank's eyes went wide as the rounded base of my lute came crashing down upon his blocky head. There was a terrific splintering of wood and a chorus of gasps and curses as he toppled to the floor.

I stood there for a moment, the broken neck of my lute still clutched firmly in my grasp. Footsteps closed in behind me. A sharp pain shot through the back of my skull, and the room spun away as my legs collapsed.

CHAPTER 3

SOMETHING RUMBLED BENEATH me. I cracked my eyes open to catch a glimpse of aspen trees through iron bars. The early morning sun lanced through the slender white trunks and hit my eyes like a dagger. A stabbing pain flared in my head. I shut my eyes tightly, taking a deep breath to steel myself against the sharp sensation.

Nearby, hooves clomped over stone and earth. Muted conversations and the chirping of birds filled the air. I opened my eyes once more to find myself in a small prison wagon. Iron bars surrounded me and afforded a view of a forest at the base of a mountain. A canopy of yellow leaves swayed gently with the breeze.

Over thirty soldiers in chainmail rode horseback alongside the wagon. Archinlanks led the procession with a group of archers, two dozen strong.

The back of my head throbbed from whatever had knocked me out. I had a feeling I was lucky to still be alive.

The horse-drawn wagon jostled over the terrain, and I propped myself up on one elbow. A thrill went through me at the sight of

Bree sleeping at the other end of the prison wagon. Obviously it wasn't the best news that she was stuck in here with me, but it was better than being stuck under the arm of a beast like Archinlanks. She still wore the same white gown, only now it was streaked with dirt, and torn down the side.

"Hey, look who's finally up," A familiar voice said.

I turned to find Elrick sitting beside me, his forehead wrapped in a white cloth with a dark red smear in the middle. His colorful jester's uniform was splattered with dried stains across the front.

"Elrick!" I sat up, a fresh stab of skull pain scolding me for my actions. I paused, waiting for the pain to subside. "What happened?"

He raised his eyebrows. "What happened, indeed? Let me tell you the tale of a castle bard who went insane and smashed his lute over the head of the king's son. Ring any bells?"

I leaned back against the bars. "Right… I'm sorry. I just couldn't take it. I had to do something."

Elrick nodded. "High treason is definitely something."

Bree looked so peaceful sleeping only a few feet away. A sickening feeling churned in my stomach that my actions had put her in prison. "So, why are you and Bree here?"

"I suppose because we're nearly as foolish," Elrick said. "Soldiers were closing in on you and we joined in like two doomed peasants challenging knights to a duel. Talk about a short-lived fight. Honestly, it's a miracle any of us are still breathing."

My eyes drifted to the well-armed soldiers surrounding the wagon. "Where are they taking us?"

"Oh, that's the best part. Do you realize where we are? White Root Mountains, my friend. Because of our treasonous actions, most notably yours, we are granted the privilege of being the first appeasement offering to the dragon Baldramorg."

Anxiety fluttered in my chest. I leaned close to Elrick. "I don't suppose you have any clever ideas of escape."

"Escape? This?" He motioned to the soldiers surrounding us. "Don't jest with a jester."

"Well, I don't want to just give up."

"Then pray for a miracle."

Bree stirred, her eyes blinking open. She caught my eye and sat up, her soft smile breaking the doom of our situation. "I wasn't sure if you'd wake up again after that cudgel."

"Is that what hit me?" I said.

She nodded. "I hear it makes a better weapon than a lute."

"I'll remember that."

A loud clang of metal commanded our attention.

"Quiet, treasonous dogs." A young soldier, his thin facial hair straining to resemble a goatee, held the tip of his spear against the wagon bars. "Or I'll silence you for good."

I'd learned from experience to be wary of the younger soldiers. They were often desperate to prove themselves and establish their authority. When challenged, they could become the cruelest of captors. Since they were taking us to the dragon, Archinlanks would make sure we got there alive, but that wouldn't stop this soldier from making it a painful journey if we weren't careful.

"My apologies." I lowered my head in feigned submission.

"Just watch yourself, bard." The soldier clanged his spear once more against the bars. "I'll take any excuse to rid this world of you and your horrible music."

It was one thing to threaten me, but the musical insult really stung.

"Filkrin!" An older soldier with a salt and pepper beard glared at his subordinate. "Get away from the wagon."

"They were plotting, sir," Filkrin said. "Probably trying to escape."

"They're not going anywhere," the older soldier said. "Now get back and watch the rear flank like I told you."

Filkrin nodded and steered his horse away. The older soldier frowned at his departure like a disappointed parent, and for a brief moment I beheld him with a thankful heart. But when he looked at me, his eyes narrowed and his hand gripped the hilt of his sword. For a frightening second, I thought he was going to trot over and run me through. Instead, he spurred his horse and trotted ahead in the procession. Clearly no one in this company was coming to our rescue.

I made sure no one was close by, then leaned toward Elrick.

"Can you pick the lock of this cage?" I whispered.

He shrugged. "Maybe."

Bree scooted closer and lowered her voice. "I told you to practice more."

"What good would it do?" Elrick said. "I pick the lock, then what? Run from horses? Fight off the king's best soldiers with our bare hands?"

"You never know," I said. "Maybe a bear will attack and scatter the soldiers. Maybe an earthquake will shake the ground and a chasm will open underneath them."

"Or maybe the Eternal One will bring a storm," Elrick spoke theatrically. "And lightning will strike down every soldier but somehow leave us unharmed. That's when we make our move."

I frowned. "Hey, I'm just saying it would be nice to get out of here if there's a chance."

He leaned his head back on the bars and closed his eyes. "Jonas, I think our chances are all used up."

The next few hours were spent mostly in silence. Every so often, when the terrain caused the soldiers to drift away from the wagon, we'd speak in low tones about plans of escape. None of our plans seemed remotely feasible. I finally convinced Elrick to try to pick the lock. He made a few attempts when soldiers weren't paying attention, but to no avail. He blamed a lack of proper tools and trembling hands, caused by our impending meeting with a dragon.

At midday, the soldiers came to a halt. We were on a hill covered with blackened trees. If I hadn't known there was a dragon nearby, I might have thought a forest fire had torn through the area.

Beyond the fire-ravaged timber, the terrain descended at a sharp incline to a bowl-shaped clearing. At the end of the clearing yawned the dark opening of a large cave. Scorched earth marred the opening – a not-so-subtle warning of what lay within.

Archinlanks turned his horse to face the company. "We're here. Ready your weapons." He lifted a water skin to his mouth but only a thin trickle of water came out. He frowned, scanning the soldiers' faces. "Where's Filkrin?"

The young soldier with the thin goatee trotted forward. "Right here, sir."

"We passed a stream a few miles back." Archinlanks tossed the water skin to him. "Fetch me some fresh water."

Filkrin held his own water skin forward. "You can have mine, sir. It's still half full."

Archinlanks glared at him. "If I wanted your filthy water I would've asked for it. Now go fetch me fresh water, boy."

Filkrin nodded and turned his horse around, heading back down the mountainside.

"Archers," Archinlanks said. "Take defensive positions in the woods. If he becomes dangerous, put him down."

The archers readied their longbows and made their way into the scorched trees.

A strange mix of terror and numbness flooded through me. I shared blank looks with Bree and Elrick. They seemed to have the same sense of detached doom. We were about to come face to face with a dragon, and there was nothing we could do about it.

"The rest of you, follow me to the cave," Archinlanks continued. "Let the prison wagon lead the way."

"Wait." A burly soldier next to Archinlanks held out his hand.

"The king said to send a squire to accompany the wagon. We were to keep our distance."

Archinlanks clenched his jaw. "I will decide what happens here, captain. If you have a challenge to my orders, speak now."

The soldier shook his head. "No, my lord."

"Good," Archinlanks said. "Then carry on, men."

With a quick snap of the reins, the wagon jolted forward. We left the cover of the forest and descended into the small valley. Grim-faced, the soldiers watched us as we moved to the front of the group. Some of them sneered and spat at us as the wagon trundled by.

Soon, the creaky jostling of the wagon was the only sound. The concave shape of the clearing amplified every noise. Bree and Elrick shuffled to either side of me until we sat shoulder to shoulder, our eyes fixed on the dark cave ahead.

"I guess your lock-picking days are over," I whispered.

"Not that it matters much," Elrick said.

The soldiers marched in a thick procession behind us. Since the door to the prison wagon was in the back, even if Elrick had picked the lock, this was probably the worst possible situation in which to attempt an escape.

When we were halfway across the clearing, a deep rumble like distant thunder rolled out of the cave. The horses forgot their military training for a moment, stamping and whinnying in protest against our current trajectory. The soldiers used their reins to keep the horses in check, reminding the animals they were in this together, whether they liked it or not.

Streams of smoke licked at the mouth of the cave. The wagon trembled beneath me, moving in time with the muffled thud of something large approaching. The horses took several steps back, straining against the soldiers' desperate efforts. The prison wagon rolled backward and angled sideways, our horse trying to get as far away from the cave as it could.

The massive head of the dragon emerged from a thick cloud of smoke at the cave entrance. His dark green scales gleamed like a thousand polished shields. Eyes like bright emeralds scanned our company, while ribbons of smoke curled upward from his angular nostrils.

The ground shook beneath his dangerous talons as he thundered into the clearing. The sheer size of the creature was beyond belief. His muscle-covered bulk rose higher than the buildings of Grandelon. Most terrifying of all were the rows of sharp, interlocking teeth that wrapped around his reptilian head.

"O, great and mighty Baldramorg." Archinlanks projected his voice like a town crier. "We come with an offering of appeasement, and beseech your good graces."

"Appeasement, you say?" A voice deeper than the earth, with the force of a war trumpet, came from the dragon's mouth. There was something strangely hypnotic about that voice. It was terrifying and beautiful all at once.

"Yes." Archinlanks cried out. "We are from Grandelon Kingdom. We present these prisoners to you as an offering of peace."

A shiver went through me at the announcement. My whole life had led up to this moment where I was nothing more than a quick meal for a dragon.

"In exchange," Archinlanks continued. "We ask that you leave our kingdom alone. There is a town called Blensprill just north of here with twice the sheep that we have and plenty of cattle as well."

"I wish the people of Blensprill could hear him," Elrick whispered. "Maybe they'd come to our aid."

"I'm well aware of Blensprill." A quick blast of smoke came from the dragon's nostrils. "Quite frankly, their sheep leave a bad taste in my mouth. I suppose it's the bitter herbs in their pastures. A terrible shame."

"Well, there's always Nillestown," Archinlanks fumbled. "A little farther west but worth the trip. Pig farms as far as the eye can see."

"No, no, no." The dragon shook his mighty head. "Quit your infernal speech, you wretched human. All of Ashrellan is mine for the taking. I go where I please. And lately, I'm pleased to fly over Grandelon. I find your cattle delicious. Plus, I enjoy the view of a castle in the distance as I watch humans fleeing my shadow."

"We can bring you cattle." Archinlanks sounded desperate now. "And more prisoners. Behold, here are three criminals in this prison wagon as our first of many appeasement offerings."

The dragon moved forward, the earth rumbling beneath us. To my horror, the beast lowered its great head to the wagon. I froze, my breath catching in my chest. Elrick, Bree, and I crammed into the opposite corner of the wagon, as far away from it as possible.

The dragon's bright emerald eye stared at us through the bars. Crimson lines spread across its surface like the withered branches of a winter tree.

A blast of hot air and smoke filled the wagon, and the dragon's head lifted. My body sagged as I finally let go of the breath I'd been holding.

"They look a bit thin for my taste," The dragon said. "But I must say, your soldiers have a little more meat on their bones. Once properly roasted, I bet they could be quite satisfying."

The color drained from the soldiers' faces, a few of their jaws going slack. In better circumstances, this sight may have provided me with a twisted sense of pleasure. But to see these battle-hardened warriors reduced to fear only raised the anxiety in my heart.

"Please, O mighty one." Archinlanks voice trembled. "We'll bring you more prisoners. Big, fat ones."

"Fat ones, eh?" The dragon looked skyward as if considering the offer. "You see, the problem is, I prefer the cows in your kingdom. There's something unique about their flavor. Maybe it's the feed your farmers give them. A hint of rosemary perhaps. Either way, I'm not inclined to cease eating my way through your little kingdom."

"We can bring you animals," Archinlanks pressed on. "The fattest in the land. All we seek is peace."

"Peace, you say?" The dragon looked toward the tree line behind us. "Then why do over twenty of your archers have arrows trained on me at this moment?"

"N-No." Archinlanks stuttered. "They are merely my personal bowmen, oh great one. They travel with me wherever I go. I gave them strict orders not to shoot."

"Hidden archers with bows drawn, ordered not to shoot?" His bright green eyes narrowed. "Why must you humans always come to me with lies? If you're not trying to steal my treasure, you're trying to deceive me. It's quite tiresome. Oh well, let's get this over with."

A fireball blasted from the dragon's mouth, hurtling toward the forest in a bright streak of flame. The line of trees where the archers lay in wait exploded into a raging inferno. A chorus of anguished cries rose up as the trees sent a wall of smoke skyward.

There was no semblance of order after that. Horses reared up with high-pitched whinnies. The soldiers that weren't thrown to the ground galloped their horses away at full speed.

A blast of hot wind tore through the prison bars as the dragon flapped its mighty wings and took to the air. The horse pulling the prison wagon bolted forward. I was thrown against the bars, the fresh injury on my head awakening with another stab of pain.

In his panic, the horse galloped straight for the mouth of the dragon's cave.

"We've got to get out of here!" Bree cried out.

The bowl-shaped clearing that had seemed so quiet only moments before now echoed with screams and the thunder of hooves. But all the sounds were eclipsed by the ear splitting roar of the dragon above. In a great, sweeping dive, the beast descended upon the fleeing soldiers. His dangerous claws swept across the clearing, launching soldiers skyward.

Our horse continued to charge into the dragon's lair. I watched in horror as the shadow of the cave swallowed us up.

The wagon jostled and bounced as we hit uneven ground inside the cave. I grabbed the bars to steady myself.

Elrick shook the door of the cage in desperation. "It won't open. What do we do now?"

As if in answer to his question, the prison wagon pitched forward. The horse let out a frightened whinny, and we tumbled down a steep incline. The wagon fell to its side, then slid down a dark tunnel. Bree screamed as the wagon rolled. My body was thrown helplessly against my friends and the bars of the wagon.

CHAPTER 4

A S THE WAGON continued a precarious roll down the tunnel, a bright gleam caught the corner of my eye. I had about a second to wonder at the sight before we came to a crashing halt. The wood framing of the wagon broke apart and the horse pulled free.

I lay on my back, breathing heavily, trying to calm my racing heart.

Thin shafts of sunlight broke through cracks in the ceiling above, revealing a broad cavern. The floor of the circular space was something out of a dream. Rolling mounds of golden treasure sprinkled with multi-colored gems.

With a wild thrashing against his remaining leather straps, the horse tore away from us and galloped out of the cavern, his terrified whinny echoing against the stone walls.

I met the wide-eyed glances of Bree and Elrick. "Everyone all right?"

Bree nodded.

Elrick rubbed his knee. "I won't know until I stand up. Pretty sure I broke at least one bone."

The sagging frame of the broken wagon leaned against a pile of rocks. I sat up and could barely believe my eyes. Golden coins as plentiful as stones littered the floor, along with all manner of jewelry, goblets, and armaments fit for a king's palace. I picked up a golden coin nearby just to make sure it was real. "Am I the only one seeing this?"

Elrick scooped several coins into his hand, holding them up to his face. "I've never held so much gold in my life."

Bree stumbled to her knees. "I say we grab a handful and go. If that dragon comes back, this will be the last sight we'll ever see."

"A handful? I'm grabbing pocketfuls." Elrick began stuffing coins in his pockets.

I got clear of the wagon and stood on the edge of this sea of gold. The collection of treasures laid out before me was beyond belief. Even Grandelon Castle had nothing to compare with the vast array of priceless objects surrounding us.

Bree and Elrick walked up beside me. No one spoke as we marveled at the shimmering floor of the cavern.

I took a few steps and learned rather quickly that mounds of coins, while beautiful to behold, don't make for a stable walking surface. I stumbled forward, trying to maintain my balance.

Bree followed behind, and Elrick brought up the rear, scooping up gold every few steps. Since we lived our lives struggling for survival, it was hard to blame him. If it wasn't for the sheer terror of imagining the dragon flying back and roasting us for desecrating his golden cache, I could've spent hours admiring something so few had ever seen.

"What's wrong with you?" Bree motioned to Elrick's pockets which had become bulges spilling over with coins. "How about you focus on finding a way out of here?"

"First off." Elrick held up a finger. "I already know there's a way out of here. Do you hear that?"

Bree squinted her eyes. "Hear what?"

"Exactly. The horse found a way out, or you'd still hear him. And second…" Elrick stooped over and grabbed more gold. "…I'll never get a chance like this again. And I know I'll regret it if I don't grab all I can while I'm here."

She shook her head. "My own brother. Consumed with greed. Sad."

"You know what's sad?" Elrick said. "You begging me for money when we get out of here because you didn't grab some yourself."

"Oh, that's mature. Trust me, I won't beg for–" Bree stopped, her eyes fixed on something ahead.

"What?" I looked around, feeling my anxiety rise. "What is it?"

"I don't believe it." She started forward at a brisk pace.

I looked over at Elrick, but he simply shrugged and hurried after her.

By the time I caught up to Bree, she was standing face to face with a silver orb. An intricately carved white circlet rested on the top of the orb. Bree's face was reflected in the orb, with the circlet gracing her forehead in the mirror image.

Bree let out a slow breath, then lifted the circlet from the orb.

"Well, well, look who's suddenly into treasure." Elrick crossed his arms. "Maybe I'm not the greedy one after all."

Her brows knitted. "This isn't about getting rich, this is a true treasure."

"What is it?" I said.

"An illusionist's circlet." Bree studied it, her lips slightly puckered. "At least, I think it is. I saw a master illusionist wearing one just like it in Calladia when I was a child. The visions she was able to create were astonishing. Father said it was the circlet that enhanced her powers."

"Father?" Elrick gave a sour look. "What does father know about magic? All he knows is farming. And lecturing me about not being an entertainer."

"And you probably should have listened." Bree raised her eyebrows. "You'd be safe at home right now instead of almost becoming dragon food."

"Look who's talking," Elrick said.

"That's enough," I said. "We all made questionable choices. Now let's grab some gold and get out of here. Bree? You going to try that on for size?"

Bree smirked and put the circlet on her head. The delicate, intertwining bands of the headpiece gave her an air of royalty. She closed her eyes, and an oval moonstone set in the front of the circlet glowed softly.

The piles of gold ahead shifted as if something were moving underneath. A curving path disturbed the coins on the ground. It headed right for us like an animal burrowing its way through the treasure.

Suddenly the coins burst into the air near our feet and the towering form of a huge, golden serpent loomed above us. His white eyes glowed, and his sharp fangs gleamed as he let out a sharp hiss.

I stumbled backward, tripping over a silver vase. The momentum took me over the top of a mound and I tumbled down a pile of coins. I slid to a stop several feet down, next to a skeleton clad in silver chainmail.

Bree and Elrick rushed to the top of the mound.

"You okay?" Bree called down.

"Yeah," I said. "Just lost my footing."

"I'm sorry," she said. "I didn't know the illusion would be that incredible. This circlet definitely enhances what I can do. The snake looked real, right?"

"Too real," Elrick said. "My heart almost stopped. And look at poor Jonas. What if he'd fallen on a spear?"

"I'm fine." I lay there for a moment, catching my breath.

"Why a snake?" Elrick said. "How about something less terrifying?"

"Oo, What about a phoenix?" Bree said. "They're magnificent."

"Fine, make a phoenix. Just give us a warning first." Elrick looked down at me. "You okay down there?"

"Yeah." I sat up, taking in my surroundings.

The gleam of the chainmail next to me caught my attention. There was no telling how long it had been there, but it looked brand new. A silver that gleamed like nothing I'd ever seen, and there wasn't a mark on it. And yet, the skeleton within it was blackened and shriveled like the unfortunate soul had been roasted by dragon fire.

An irresistible urge moved me to touch the chainmail. I had to know what this fine bit of craftsmanship felt like. At my touch, the mail shone with a radiant glow. Energy surged into my hand, up my arm, and through my entire body.

The cavern melted away. A swirling, silver energy surrounded me like a whirlwind. Bright points of light blinked to life all around me.

I was frozen in place, locked between reality and a strange world of magic. Energy continued to flow through me. The sensation of strength prompted me to action like the sound of a war horn in battle. If I'd had a sword at my side I would've drawn it and shouted a challenge to anyone who stood against me.

In an instant, the silver energy disappeared, and I was back in the dragon's lair, sitting on gold coins next to a blackened skeleton. His chainmail was gone. I flinched at the sight of it now on my arm. It covered my torso and ran all the way down to my waist.

Elrick and Bree rushed to my side.

Bree kneeled down. "What'd you do? Why are you wearing that?"

"I-I don't know," I said.

"Ho there!" A resonant voice said.

I turned, but no one was behind me. "Who said that?"

"'Tis I, Flyngard. A warrior who bows to no one." The voice

was rich and somewhat theatrical, but with a gritty edge that made me wary.

I stood up abruptly, scanning the area. There was no one in sight besides Elrick and Bree.

"Where are you?" I said. "Show yourself, Flyngard."

"Who are you talking to?" Elrick looked over his shoulder.

"Alas, I cannot show myself," Flyngard said. "For I am nowhere. And everywhere. I am the heart of a fighter that lives on. I am cursed, and yet I endure to bring swift and terrible justice upon my captor."

I motioned to Elrick. "Surely you heard that?"

Elrick furrowed his brow. "Heard what?"

I turned to Bree, raising my eyebrows. "You heard him, right?"

"Heard who?" She said.

"That voice," I said. "A strange warrior that calls himself Flyngard."

"Mind thy tongue, knave," Flyngard said. "What you call strange has overthrown champions, driven back armies, established kingdoms, slain the dragon, destroyed–"

"Okay, okay," I said. "I got it. You're a legend and everything. Where are you? Why can't I see you?"

"I walk unseen in a world no eye of nature can behold," Flyngard said.

Elrick put his hand on my shoulder. "Jonas, seriously. Who are you talking to? I'm starting to worry."

"Jonas, is it?" Flyngard said. "My new armor-bearer. We shall do great things together, yes?"

I looked down at the chainmail. "It must be some kind of enchantment. Flyngard, are you bound to the chainmail?"

"Indeed," Flyngard said. "For years I fought valiantly wearing this mail. I slew many foul beasts and enemies of Ashrellan. Until the dark sorcerer Rastvane imprisoned me within the metal. The chains of this mail are the chains that hold me until I vanquish him."

I motioned to the chainmail. "There's a warrior named Flyngard trapped within the mail. Enchanted by some sorcerer named Rastvane."

"Really?" Bree leaned close, examining the mail. "And he's talking to you?"

"Yes."

Elrick studied my eyes. "You know, they did hit your head pretty hard with that cudgel. Maybe this voice–."

"I'm not imagining this." I glared at him. "Trust me, there's a voice. Besides, if there's no enchantment, how did this armor magically appear on me?"

Elrick shared a blank look with Bree.

"Who is this skinny lad, and this fair maiden, who dare to question us?" Flyngard said. "Friends? Foes? Shall we dispatch them?"

"What? No. They're friends. Look, I don't have time for this. Elrick, help me get this off."

Elrick stepped forward, taking hold of the chainmail at my shoulder. I grabbed the end of the mail at my waist and lifted. A shock of energy surged through the metal and radiated outward. Elrick and Bree were thrown to their backs, their bodies sliding across the golden coins.

"Oh." I held up my hands. "Um, sorry about that."

Bree sat up, her eyes narrowed. "What was that?"

"I don't really know," I said.

"I wouldn't try to remove the mail," Flyngard said. "Not until the enchantment bonding is complete. The results could be disastrous. At least for those around you. I'll be fine, of course. Although, I wish you wouldn't. I do miss talking to people. Skeletons don't make for good company."

I sighed. "I can't remove the chainmail yet. Some kind of magical bonding."

"Great." Elrick stumbled to his feet. "He could've mentioned that first."

I felt the smooth metal links of the chainmail, wondering how long I would have to wear it. "I guess I'm keeping this for a while."

"Well, it's armor." Bree shrugged. "At least you're stuck with something that'll help protect you."

"That I will," Flyngard said. "And I shall aid you in battle. What quest are you on, young Jonas? Whom shall we vanquish?"

"No, there's no vanquishing going on," I said. "I've never vanquished, nor do I have plans to vanquish. I just want to get out of here before the dragon gets back."

"Ah, yes, Baldramorg the dragon," Flyngard said. "Gremthorne, my old armor-bearer, was foolish to face him. He paid dearly. As did I. Years trapped in this cave. Lonely years. I nearly fell into despair. I reflected back on my youth when—"

"Listen," I interrupted. "I'm sorry about all that but we're kind of in a hurry."

"Ask him if he knows a way out of here," Elrick said.

"Indeed I do," Flyngard said. "Several ways. Narrow and quite treacherous. Especially without a map. I'd take the north passage if I were you. Easily the safest route. It leads to the mouth of the cave."

"The mouth of the cave?" I said. "That's not safe. Baldramorg is out there laying waste to the soldiers. If we walk out there, we'll be next."

"Perhaps," Flyngard said. "Though, if the slaughter has already commenced, there's a good chance he's distracted with dragon bloodlust. Grasping victims in his claws and flying them high in the air before setting them on fire and hurling them to the earth like a flaming catapult. A grand display to warn others of his might. You know how they are in battle."

"No, I don't," I said. "I've never seen a dragon before today and I never want to see one again."

"Pity," Flyngard said. "They're extraordinary creatures. Either way, the north passage is your best chance of escape."

I sighed. "He says there's a north passage that's the only safe way out. It takes us right back where we came from. He says the dragon is probably distracted. Apparently they hurl their flaming victims to the earth."

"Of course." Elrick nodded. "Typical dragon behavior."

"How would you know?" Bree said.

"I hear things."

Bree shook her head. "Well, I don't know how much we can trust an enchanted soul within chainmail but I guess we don't have any other choice."

"All right." I looked toward the sloping entrance we'd come from. "Let's see if we can find the north passage."

"Wait," Flyngard said. "Gremthorne had a fine sword. His skeleton certainly doesn't need it. You should take it before you leave. No magical properties, but quality craftsmanship."

"I'm not really trained with a sword," I said.

"Oh, well there's plenty of war hammers and clubs in here as well. And over on the east wall is a nice collection of spears and daggers. Take your pick."

"I'm not really trained in those either."

"Great heavens, boy," Flyngard said. "What kind of warrior are you?"

"I'm not a warrior. The only weapon I use is a staff."

"Hm, staff, eh? Well, I suppose that's something. There's a nice Veltian night staff over there by the three golden shields. A night elf ranger snuck in here one night, quiet as a mouse, for a little burglary. Of course, dragons have fantastic hearing and he was promptly ignited. But he left behind a fine staff with a bit of magic in it."

"What's he telling you?" Bree said.

"There's a good staff over there." I pointed to the shields. "Guess it wouldn't hurt to grab a weapon on the way out."

"Okay, hurry," she said.

True to Flyngard's story, in front of the golden shields lay the fallen remains of the night elf. All that was left was tattered and burned leather armor clinging to the withered corpse of the unfortunate thief. A black staff with silvery flecks was still clutched in his shriveled hand.

I knelt down and grabbed the staff. "Sorry, friend. I'll take good care of this." My skin crawled as I slid it free from the skeletal grasp.

The staff was light and cool to the touch. A faint hum of energy emanated from its smooth surface.

"Veltian night staff," Flyngard said. "A deadly weapon in the right hands. Quite difficult to break and not without some unique powers."

"It has powers?" I said.

"Aye. A favorite among night elf rangers. A well-placed strike sends out a burst of energy like a punch from a storm golem."

I gave the staff a few practice swings, wondering if Flyngard actually knew what he was talking about. "Well, it has wonderful balance. I've never felt anything quite like it."

"It's no sword but it'll do in a pinch," Flyngard said.

There was a brown cloak and a rugged-looking leather pack nearby, so I grabbed them as well. If we had to travel, it was always wise to have the proper supplies. King Mulraith would never allow us to set foot in Grandelon again, so it was time to strike out on a new journey and find a better place to live.

As I made my way back, Elrick was in the process of pulling a cloak off a skeleton.

"All right," I said. "Ready?"

Elrick shook out the brown cloak, then wrapped it around himself. "I am now. It's hard to sneak around in a jester's outfit."

"And you think I'm nonchalant in this gown?" Bree motioned to her white dress.

"Well, help yourself." Elrick made a sweeping motion. "Plenty of failed dragon slayers in here. I'm sure they wouldn't mind if you took their clothes.

She frowned. "I don't know. Doesn't seem right."

"It's either that or hike down the mountain in that frilly thing," Elrick said.

Bree furrowed her brow and marched forward. "Fine."

Elrick and I followed behind until Bree located an open wooden chest spilling over with clothes and jewelry. She rifled through the apparel, finally landing on dark brown pants, tall leather boots, a tan tunic and a brown leather vest of armor. She stood up, apparently satisfied with her haul, then reached back for a dark green cloak.

"Give me a minute." She moved behind a mound of coins, her arms filled with clothes.

Elrick pointed at me. "No peeking. I'm watching you."

"Wouldn't think of it," I said. "At least, I wouldn't look. I'm trying my best not to think of it."

He frowned. "Maybe you should turn around."

"It's a mound of coins. I can't see through it."

"Yeah, well, it's my sister and it's weird that you like her."

I put a finger to my lips. "Keep your voice down."

He rolled his eyes. "You don't think she's figured it out by now? The way you stare at her like a lost puppy."

"That's ridiculous."

He arched a brow. "Really? You should see yourself. Lost puppy eyes every time."

I held up my new staff. "You want a taste of this thing? I'm dying to try it out."

"Oh, sure. Challenge me when I'm defenseless."

"Well, what are you waiting for?" I motioned around the room. "Weapons galore."

He crinkled his nose. "I don't know. I have a bad history with swords. Remember my cousin Fornell?"

I nodded. "How's his ear?"

"Most of the hearing is back." Elrick's eyes brightened at something behind me. "Hey, what about that?"

Elrick moved toward a golden statue of a howling wolf. The statue was adorned with an ebony necklace fashioned from a curving row of black claws. He lifted the necklace from the statue and put it around his neck.

He spread out his arms. "What do you think?"

"I thought you wanted a weapon," I said.

He shrugged. "This could do some damage. Plus it makes me look dangerous. Who would dare challenge me while I had this on?"

"Had what on?" Bree came strolling over in her new clothing.

As much as I liked her barmaid outfit, her new look was a close second. The earth tones accented her copper hair and blue eyes. Plus, the form-fitting travel clothes were nothing but complimentary to her athletic frame.

"You look great." The words just slipped out before I could temper my enthusiasm.

She grinned. "Thanks."

"You look like a ranger," Elrick said. "All you need are daggers and a bow."

Bree unsheathed a pair of daggers that were hidden beneath her cloak. "Way ahead of you. Found these while I was changing."

"Nice." Elrick motioned to his claw necklace. "What do you think of this?"

She shook her head. "I don't think so. That's a necklace for some kind of hunter warrior."

He frowned. "Well, you've got your circlet and all your ranger clothes. Jonas has his enchanted chainmail and a staff. What about me? Don't I get anything?"

"How about your pockets spilling over with gold?" Bree said.

"This is an object of value." He pointed to the necklace. "It's different. What if it's magic?"

"What if it's cursed?" She said.

He waved her off. "Jonas, what do you think?"

I shrugged. "Hey, if you like it, keep it."

Elrick grinned, adjusting the necklace. "Excellent. I think I will."

"Great. Can we go now?" Bree raised her eyebrows. "We're really pushing our luck, staying in here for so long."

"Hey, I'm ready." Elrick motioned to me. "Jonas, lead the way."

I traveled as quickly as I dared across the shifting mounds of gold, committing the sight to memory. If I made it out of the dragon's lair alive, I was definitely going to write a song about it.

CHAPTER 5

TRUE TO FLYNGARD'S instruction, a passage opened up at the north end of the cavern. My spirit lifted at the thought of leaving the lair before the dragon returned. I quickened my pace, leading the three of us into the dark entrance.

The passage weaved up a steep incline. At first I had to tread carefully, straining to see in the dim light and feeling my way along the rough walls of the tunnel. But as we advanced, the passage grew brighter, the sunlight at the other end streaming through.

Soon the bright outline of the opening shone before us, promising a chance at freedom. We crept to the opening, not daring to speak. The sounds of chaos and screaming had stopped. An eerie silence filled the air.

Soldiers' bodies lay strewn across the bowl-shaped valley, unmoving. Some were charred and still smoking. The sky was empty. No dragon in sight.

I waited for several moments, my skin tingling with anxiety. A lump formed in my throat at the smell of burnt flesh in the air.

"I think he's gone," Elrick whispered.

Bree put a finger to her lips. "Shh."

We waited in silence for a while longer, not daring to step into the sun.

"You will eventually set foot outside, right?" Flyngard said. "I've never seen such cautious adventurers before."

"Yes, we are cautious," I whispered. "That's why we're not going to end up stuck in a dragon's lair like you."

"That wasn't my fault," he said. "I warned my former armor-bearer, but he wouldn't listen."

"What's he saying?" Bree said.

"Hey, how come you guys get to talk?" Elrick said. "I get shushed, and you guys can just chatter away."

"Because we waited until all was clear," Bree said.

"Oh, sure, like you know."

"Flyngard," I said. "You say you know dragons?"

"A fair bit," he said. "Though I'm no scholar. But I have slain one. A mighty, red-scaled beast. Some said it was merely an adolescent, but on my word, it was full grown. The day I faced him was a bleak winter's morn. The clouds were gray and–"

"No time for tales," I said. "I just need your advice."

"Tales?" He said. "You doubt my veracity?"

I sighed. "Fine. I'm sure it's all true. But right now, we have to move. You can see what lies before us, right?"

"Aye. The enchantment allows me to see through my armor-bearer. Though I can sense a great deal more."

"All right, what do you think?" I said. "The battle appears over. The skies are clear. Is the dragon gone?"

"You never can be certain with dragons. But if I had to chance a guess, I'd say he flew off, fueled by the rage of battle. He's either out for revenge on his attackers, or wearied by the fight and out searching for food. I wouldn't want to be a sheep right about now."

I turned to the others. "Flyngard thinks there's a good chance he flew away. Maybe headed to Grandelon for revenge."

"I hope he takes out King Mulraith," Elrick said. "That would make this all worthwhile."

"Well, let's be quick about this," Bree said. "Step quick and step lightly."

She led the way out of the passage. We all hurried forward on the balls of our feet. When we got halfway across the clearing, we had to pick our way around the fallen soldiers. A few of them lay on their sides, almost as if they were just napping, but the gruesome and unnatural twist of their limbs, or the pool of blood around them, told the awful truth about their fate. Some were completely charred, thin wisps of smoke still rising from their bodies.

A chill went through me at the sight. This was the field of death we'd almost been a part of.

I stopped short at the sight of Sir Archinlanks flat on his back. The color had drained from his face. His vacant eyes stared up at the sky, his lips were slightly parted, as if he were trying to express one final thought.

It didn't seem real that this giant of a man, who only a day earlier had the power over a kingdom, now lay dead on the ground. He'd marched into this valley with the unassailable might of his soldiers and the dead-eyed skill of his archers, only to have it all taken away in an instant.

"You hear that?" Elrick said.

In the distance, the sound of an approaching rider grew louder. I looked around but there was nowhere to hide.

A mounted soldier galloped through the scorched trees into the far side of the valley. It was Filkrin, the young soldier who had left to get water for Archinlanks. He reined his horse in as he took in the smoking aftermath of the battle. His eyes narrowed when he spotted us.

"What have you done!" He glared at me. "You've killed Sir Archinlanks."

"No." I shook my head. "It was the dragon. He did all this."

"You stand over his slain body and deny your hand in his demise?"

"I just found him like this," I said.

"Lies!" He said. "You were no match for Archinlanks. You must've used the dragon attack to sneak up and stab him in the back like the coward you are. Foul traitor!" Filkrin snatched a crossbow from his back, leveled it at me, and fired.

A sharp hiss split the air and something thudded against my chest. The arrow bounced away from me and clattered harmlessly to the ground.

Filkrin stared at me, his eyes wide. "What devilry do you practice? You won't get away with this, vile assassin. Mark my words."

He wheeled the horse around and galloped back into the forest.

Bree moved closer, looking from my chest to the fallen arrow. "Are you okay?"

I felt my chest as if I might discover a gaping wound. My fingers slid across the smooth surface of the cold chainmail, unable to detect a mark. "Yes. I think."

She picked up the arrow, examining the sharp tip. "This is a war arrow. You're lucky it didn't break the mail."

"We showed that young whelp, didn't we?" Flyngard said. "It'll take more than a crossbow to bring us down, eh?"

"This mail can stop war arrows?" I said.

"Aye," he said. "And more. The enchantment encircles you now. But don't press your luck. Just ask the skeleton of my former armor-bearer."

"Come on." Bree pulled me forward. "Before he comes back."

We raced away from the clearing and into the blackened forest. The smoke and ash choked the air, making breathing difficult.

When we hit the downward slope of the mountainside, green bushes and trees began to redeem the scorched earth. A fresh breeze swept up from the foothills, cleansing the smoky air.

Bree stopped and pointed eastward. "We should head east. There's a man named Clive Brandall that runs a farm in the foothills. He used to come into the tavern now and then. Believe me, he's no friend of the king."

"How well do you trust him?" I said.

"Word is he housed spies at his place who were looking to overthrow Grandelon," she said. "He's the only one I can think of that might help us. Unless you know of anyone else."

I shared a blank look with Elrick.

"All right," I said. "Lead the way."

Bree turned away from our previous path, taking us on a switchback trail through thick brush. Elrick followed, and I brought up the rear.

"Ah, life on the road again," Flyngard made a noise like he was taking a deep breath, which was strange since he had no body. "How I've missed it. Sun shining upon the green hills. The sway of the trees in the wind. The sense of adventure with a new quest… By the way, what is our quest?"

"To stay alive," I said.

"What?" Elrick looked back.

"Nothing." I shook my head. "I'm talking to Flyngard."

Elrick furrowed his brow and looked away.

"I'm not crazy," I said.

"It's still weird," he said.

"Staying alive is not a quest," Flyngard said. "No more than eating supper or lying down to sleep. A quest goes beyond the commonplace, sometimes even putting one's life at risk in the very pursuit of it."

"Thank you. Very informative," I said. "Not interested in the slightest."

"Well, perhaps you just haven't experienced the true thrill of a noble quest. Think of the great deeds to be done. Villagers can be saved. Foul creatures destroyed. Sorcerers vanquished."

"You're talking to the wrong guy."

"But today could be a day of deliverance," he said. "We could set our sights on Dragontooth Mountains. I can show you the way of the champion, and we can defeat the evil Sorcerer Rastvane together."

"Dragontooth?" I said. "Are you insane? I'm not going there."

Elrick looked back. "Now the chainmail is telling you where to go?"

I nodded. "He wants to go to the Dragontooth Mountains."

"Is he insane?" Elrick said.

"That's what I said."

"We must go there," Flyngard said. "That's where Rastvane dwells."

"Yeah," I said. "And that's where travelers go to die. I've never heard of anyone making it back alive from that place."

"And yet, I live," Flyngard said.

"Sure," I said. "With your spirit imprisoned in chainmail, forced to serve whoever wears you. You made it back alive all right."

Flyngard didn't speak for a few moments. "You have a dark tongue, Jonas."

The eastern side of the mountain proved difficult to travel. Thick brush and rock outcroppings made it impossible to follow a straight path. Fine gravel covered the ground and sent us to our hands and knees more than once.

I lagged behind Elrick, allowing a healthy distance between us so he wouldn't give me strange looks when I spoke with Flyngard.

Flyngard attempted to bolster my appetite for adventure by recounting his own past victories. He went into great detail about leading the charge against the goblin invasion of Crelstaff Plains. Of course, I'd never heard of Crelstaff Plains, or any goblin invasion that may or may not have taken place, so it was difficult to know how much he was embellishing actual events.

I stayed quiet during his tale-spinning, choosing to save my breath for the difficulties of the road.

Towards the end of the tale, Flyngard claimed seventy two goblins had fallen by his sword. That was my breaking point.

"Seventy two?" I said. "Oh, come on. What's the real number?"

"On my honor," Flyngard said. "Seventy two. I could claim seventy three but an archer shot one of the devils just before my blade found its mark, so I gave him the credit."

"Listen, I've spent the last six months writing songs about knights that exaggerate their battles beyond all sense of reality. I know how these stories grow into tall tales."

"Songs?" Flyngard said. "You are a musician then?"

"Yes. A bard."

"Great heavens above, a bard." Flyngard spoke the words with breathy reverence. "My prayers have been answered. I've always imagined my exploits to be perfect musical fodder for a songwriter. And I've never had a song written about me, can you believe it? I have so many tales of victory. Do you have your lute handy? Perhaps we can compose on the journey."

My heart sank at the mention of my lute. My original Clarg, gone forever. Even though it gave its life for the noble deed of smashing against the head of a monster, I mourned the loss of such a fine instrument. "My lute was destroyed. And I've had my fill of writing battle songs."

"But those are the best kind. What else would you write? Flower-laced melodies about your beloved Bree?"

"What?" My face flushed. "What are you talking about?"

"Please, lad. Don't take me for a fool. Even if young Elrick hadn't made your intentions clear, I can feel the quickening of your heart when you look at her. The tone in your voice when you speak with her. It's quite obvious. Though I must say, her intentions are a bit clouded. Perhaps her eyes are set on another."

"No, they're not."

"Aha, see?" He said. "Your protest reveals your heart. But fear not, young Jonas. I can help you win her over. They say a maiden's heart is most touched by a shared adventure."

"Nice try. I'm not going on a quest."

Flyngard grunted. "Fine. What would you do instead? Hope to win her heart with sap-filled minstrel songs of love?"

"At this point, I wouldn't mind penning a few of those."

"Nay, young one. Save that for the proposal of marriage. For now, I have tales to tell. What should we write about first? My vanquishing of the North Mountain trolls? Or perhaps my ogre encounter at Westfallen Hills. Or maybe–"

"Look, no offense. I don't want to write another battle song."

"But you're a bard. That's what bards do."

"Not this bard. Not anymore."

Flyngard was quiet for several moments. "The sorcerer's sting endures once again. After yearning for my tales to be lifted up in song, at long last I meet a bard, but a bard who has turned his back on his time-honored calling."

"Oh, please."

"A bard who abandons songs of victory for songs of love unrequited."

"Hey, it's not unrequited. At least not yet."

"And what chance will you have, once she learns you turned your back on the brotherhood of bards?"

I laughed. "There is no brotherhood of bards."

"There used to be. In better times."

"Well, I never heard of it, and I never swore any creed. And I'm done writing songs about warriors in battle."

My chainmail felt noticeably colder.

"Alas," Flyngard said. "A curse lies upon my head."

We hiked through the remainder of the afternoon, making our way down the mountainside. Thankfully, Flyngard lapsed into silence, allowing me to concentrate on navigating the difficult terrain.

My aching legs were grateful when the steep incline eased into the rolling terrain of the foothills below. A thickly wooded forest stretched out before us as the sun dipped behind the mountain, casting the valley in a haze of shadows.

A few wild berry bushes grew at the edge of the forest, and we scavenged as much as we could to satisfy our hunger and thirst. The red berries were sweet and refreshing, especially after our difficult descent. For the hundredth time on this journey, I scolded myself for not searching the fallen soldiers for water skins and food rations before our travels began.

"I'm still starving." Elrick plucked another berry and popped it into his mouth. "Why on earth didn't I grab a bow? I saw one in the dragon's lair. I could've hunted fresh game."

"You were too busy filling your pockets," Bree said.

"How far are we from Clive's farm?" I said. "Can we make it there for supper?"

"I'm guessing we're a few hours away," Bree said. "Although, I've only been there once and I was coming from another direction."

"So, what are you saying?" Elrick said. "We're lost? Starving and lost?"

"Oh, quit whining," she said. "I don't hear you coming up with any plans."

Elrick frowned. "Fine. Sorry. I'm just hungry. And thirsty. And tired." He dug his hand in his pocket and pulled out a few coins. "But at least I'm rich."

Bree shook her head.

"Pretty sure a stream cuts through further in," I pointed into the shadows of the thick forest. "I spotted one on the way down."

"I noticed that too," Bree said. "I've been dreaming of reaching it ever since."

I nodded, yearning for a long drink from a cool stream. The berries had offered slight relief, but at the mention of the stream,

I felt thirstier than ever. If my legs hadn't been so weary from the climb, I might have run toward it right then and there.

We ate another handful or two of berries, then headed into the forest.

The dusky light of evening gave way to the black of night, the thick canopy of trees allowing fleeting glimpses of stars to peek through.

While there was certainly a peaceful aspect to the smell of fresh pine and the soft rustling of the wind through the branches overhead, the deep shadows on all sides were a little unnerving. I couldn't help but flinch when rodents scurried through the underbrush at our approach. Worst of all was the occasional guttural groan or twig snap from an unseen creature deep in the shadows of the forest. It gave the imagination far too much to play with.

I'd made the unfortunate decision to lead the way. I turned my head at so many sounds that my neck started to hurt. According to the tavern tales I remembered, the leader of the pack was the one that got taken out first. After about an hour, my hand began to cramp from keeping such a tight grip on the staff.

We reached a place in the forest where the trees grew further apart, allowing the pale light of the full moon to shine through. My spirit lifted with the soft illumination and the thinning of the forest. Fireflies blinked to life, floating in a sea of shadows. There was almost a magical feel about this part of the woods.

Just ahead, I could hear the soft trickling of the stream. Bree gasped and met my eyes. We smiled at the shared realization of fresh water within reach. Without a word, we rushed forward.

It wasn't much more than a shallow ribbon of water that wound a crooked path through the trees. But half a day's travel spent kicking up dust into a dry mouth will turn the smallest stream into the grandest oasis.

I dropped to my knees and plunged my dry face in for a long drink. I couldn't remember ever feeling so refreshed.

Bree knelt by the stream, bringing handfuls of water to her mouth. Her eyes remained closed as though lost in the moment. Elrick took a more dramatic approach, splashing his face with water, drenching his hair and tunic.

"I'd give ten gold pieces for a water skin right now," Elrick said. "I don't want to leave this place."

I drank until my stomach felt bloated, then breathed deeply, enjoying the rich scent of earth and pine.

The moon bathed the area in its pale light, covering the forest in an ethereal glow. I let out a long breath as the soft trickle of the stream washed away the day's worries.

Elrick lay down near the stream, letting out a contented sigh. "Let's rest awhile. It's been a long day."

"No argument here." Bree leaned against the trunk of a tree.

"Really?" Elrick turned his head. "For the first time today you're not going to argue with me?"

She smirked. "I don't have the energy."

"I'd say a rest is long overdue." I lay down on the cool ground near Bree.

It was strange to think that only the previous night, she'd been trapped under the arm of Sir Archinlanks, doomed to be his concubine. I smiled at the knowledge that she was free from him forever, free from the castle, and free from any further entanglements of Grandelon Kingdom. And now, here she was, only a few feet away, and we were traveling side by side. I imagined us reaching a faraway city where we could make a fresh start.

Sleep came so quickly I didn't even realize it until I awoke to the sound of howling.

CHAPTER 6

I SAT UP, BLINKING at the forest around me through bleary eyes. Had the call of a creature awakened me or was it a dream? The shadows of night told me I'd been asleep for a couple of hours. The gleam of moonlight around us suddenly seemed more ghostly than peaceful.

"Did you hear that?" Bree was on her feet, her eyes darting back and forth.

Apparently the howl wasn't a dream.

"Wolf?" I said.

"I think."

"I tried to wake you," Flyngard said. "You're a deep sleeper. Not a good trait for an adventurer. We'll have to work on that. There are wolves nearby. It's a shame you don't have a sword handy."

Bree gasped. "Where's Elrick?"

I looked toward the stream where Elrick had lain. He was nowhere in sight. I jumped to my feet and turned in all directions, scanning the trees. "I don't see him."

Bree knelt down, examining the ground where I'd seen him last. "No sign of a struggle. Maybe he just went to relieve himself."

The howl of a wolf echoed through the forest nearby. My heart leapt and I gripped my staff tightly. Bree stood up, drawing both daggers.

Another howl, this time from the other side of the forest. How many were out there? Adrenaline surged through me. I widened my stance and watched for any sign of movement in the shadows.

"All right, easy now," Flyngard said. "Your heart is racing. Don't pass out on me. That would only seal our fate. I just got out of that lair. I don't want to be stuck in this forest for the next few years."

A pair of yellow eyes shone in the shadows to my left, followed quickly by several others. They advanced through the trees, slow and silent. The creatures seemed to multiply, and soon I counted over a dozen pairs of eyes. My chest tightened with panic. I took a deep breath, steadying myself.

A white glow caught my attention. The stone in Bree's circlet illuminated her face in a soft light making her seem at home in this ghostly forest.

A circle of fire erupted around us, flames stabbing into the branches above. The wolves yelped and retreated from the fire.

I raised my eyebrows at Bree, grateful and impressed by her enhanced abilities. She gave a quick nod back, her face tightened in concentration. As long as the illusion held, perhaps the wolves would flee, and we could escape.

"Excellent," Flyngard said. "Bree is quite skilled. She may just save us all."

A deep, resonant howl came from beyond the fire, sending a chill across my arms. It seemed unnatural, like a cross between a large wolf and a war horn. The wolves stopped their yelping and everything went silent.

My desperate hope was that some unknown beast had emerged and scared the wolves away. As long as this new creature was as fearful of Bree's illusory fire as the wolves were, we had a chance.

"This doesn't bode well for us," Flyngard said. "That was no ordinary wolf, mark my words."

I nudged an elbow into the chainmail, hoping to quiet Flyngard.

Two tall, shadowy forms stepped into the ring of fire, dashing away all my hopes. The figures passed through the flame without flinching, and while their brown, hooded cloaks shrouded their identity, they couldn't hide the broad shoulders and warrior-like physique.

"Fight well, Jonas," Flyngard said. "Every warrior must someday come to an end. At the very least, you can go down swinging, aye?"

My anxiety levels had already reached their peak. At this point, all I could do was watch in stunned silence as the figures walked up to us.

The ring of fire disappeared, and the glow from Bree's circlet died. She tightened her grip on the daggers, her expression was stoic, as though she were resigned to our fate.

The figures removed their hoods, revealing large wolf heads. One was gray, the other was tan, with white around the eyes and muzzle. Their eyes and mannerisms seemed far more human than wolfish. A large pack of around twenty wolves filed in behind them like dutiful soldiers.

"Ah, lycan watchers," Flyngard said. "As noble as they are deadly. As long as you didn't accidentally desecrate their forest, they may have mercy."

"I am Talmotock," the gray wolfish figure spoke with a hint of growl. "One of the lycan watchers of the Northern Forests. You entered our forest without permission, ate of our berries and drank of our stream."

A chorus of howls broke out among the wolves.

"Oh, that's not good," Flyngard said.

"However," Talmotock said. "You have retrieved an ancient

artifact and joined our cause. And since you are no ally of the treacherous King Mulraith and wish to aid in his demise, you are free to travel the forest." He took a step forward and loomed over me. "But tread carefully. Should you attack one of our pack unprovoked, you will experience a vengeance so terrible that you will regret the day you were born into this world."

My body was trembling, so it took a moment to find my voice. "Thank you. I understand."

"Then may your journey be swift and your cause just. Farewell." Talmotock replaced his hood and turned away, heading into the forest.

"Fortunate," Flyngard said. "Most fortunate."

Half of the wolves trailed behind Talmotock. About a dozen wolves stayed behind with the remaining lycan.

The strange creature stood before us, his intense gaze shifting from Bree to me as though trying to decide which of us would taste better. In the dim moonlight, his wolfish eyes held a golden glow.

"Listen," I said. "We had a friend here with us. Have you seen anyone else in the forest?"

The lycan cocked his head as if he were having trouble understanding me.

"Do you understand what I'm saying?" I said. "Can you help me?"

His eyes narrowed and a deep growl resonated from his chest.

"Careful," Flyngard said. "Lycans can be touchy."

I took a step back and held out my hand. "Easy. No harm meant. I was just—"

Broad, paw-like hands emerged from his sleeves, sharp claws extended.

"Jonas?" Bree flashed wide eyes at me.

"No." I put up both hands. "Please. I'm sorry."

The lycan reared back, breaking into a hearty laugh. "You

should have seen yourself just now. Oh man, were you scared. I could've kept going but I was afraid you'd wet yourself."

The voice was familiar. It reminded me of Elrick but deeper, with a harsh edge to it.

He opened the top of his cloak, revealing a necklace fashioned from black claws. "Remember this?"

"Elrick?" Bree's wide-eyed expression was a mix of surprise and horror.

The wolfish Elrick gave a slight bow. "At your service."

"Wonder of wonders," Flyngard said.

"But…" I couldn't find the words. "…How?"

The lycan shrank both in size and stature, the tan, furry head transforming into Elrick's familiar face.

He smiled. "Surprise. I'm sure this is all a bit strange."

"A bit?" Bree said.

"All right. A lot strange. Definitely the strangest night of my life. But I'm telling you, I feel fantastic. I've never felt so strong. Like I can take on the whole castle guard." Elrick flexed his muscles, which looked odd now that he'd returned to his slim form. "Isn't Talmotock incredible? I love the way he talks. It's stately but deadly at the same time."

"Slow down." I said. "What happened?"

"I know, I know." He put out his hands. "Lots to talk about. But I do need to eat soon. I'm starving. Lycans have big appetites." He turned to the wolves. "Who else is hungry?"

A chorus of yapping went through the pack. A thin, brown wolf moved toward me. He whined and licked his chops.

"No, Florfack." Elrick moved in front of me. "Jonas does not look tasty. What did we talk about earlier?"

The brown wolf whined.

"Right," Elrick said. "No humans. We stick to wild game."

A chorus of howls broke out among the pack.

Elrick gave an exasperated grunt. "Fine, you can attack the occasional human but only if they're really, really bad."

The brown wolf panted happily.

"But not for food," Elrick said. "Only for justice."

The wolves yapped and barked.

"All right, yes, go hunt. It's time to eat," Elrick said. "I'll stay here and talk to my friends for a while."

The wolves turned and trotted into the forest.

Elrick smiled and jerked his thumb at them. "Great pack. A little wild, but good hearts."

"You can understand them?" Bree said.

"Yes." Elrick grinned. "My world just got a whole lot bigger."

I shook my head. "Am I still dreaming?"

"Let's just say you both owe me because I saved all our lives." Elrick pointed to his claw necklace. "And it's all because I wore this necklace. Even though some people tried to discourage me." He arched a brow at Bree.

"Well, how should I know what it was?" Bree said. "And I still say it looks ridiculous on you."

"It looks fierce on me." He adjusted the necklace. "And it is an object of great worth, just like I thought."

"You thought it was magic," Bree said.

"Whatever," he said. "This necklace has history. It was owned by the great lycan warrior Smitepaw. Legend has it, he turned the tide of battle in the great ogre uprising at Oxburrow Hills."

"Where?" I said.

"I don't know," Elrick shook his head. "Talmotock told me a bit of lycan history while you were asleep. I forgot some of the details. Anyway, he was so grateful I'd recovered the necklace, he invited me to join the brotherhood of lycans. Incredible, right?"

"I don't understand," I said. "You became a lycan willingly?"

"Of course. Why wouldn't I?"

"Well, they're creatures of the night. Cursed forever."

Elrick chuckled and patted my shoulder. "Oh, Jonas. Sweet, innocent Jonas. You read too many children's fables. Lycans are noble fighters. They balance the scales of justice."

"The boy speaks truth," Flyngard said.

"Even now, they're trying to stop Mulraith," Elrick said. "They've been thinning the army massing at Witchpaw Canyon."

I remembered Sir Farlsburg's report of wolf attacks against the king's forces. "Sir Farlsburg did mention that."

"Exactly. They've been the guardians of the forests and the surrounding provinces for ages. Talmotock recounted some of their glorious battles to me while you slept. Frankly, I'm honored that he invited me into the pack. He said I had the heart of a wolf. Do you believe that? They must've sensed something in me. Wolves are good judges of character, you know."

I rubbed my temple. I felt like I was struggling to wake up from a dream. "This is all very strange."

"Agreed," Elrick said. "But hey, don't feel bad they didn't ask either of you to join. I can put in a good word if you want."

"No," I said quickly. "That's all right."

Bree held up her hand. "Yes, please don't ask."

Elrick shrugged. "Suit yourselves. You're missing out though."

"I agree with Elrick," Flyngard said. "It's quite an opportunity. Your companion is now a dangerous ally."

Bree put her hand on Elrick's shoulder. "Are you sure you're all right with all this?"

He gave a serious nod. "More than all right. I've felt powerless for long enough. The next time some creep like Archinlanks messes with you or anyone else I care about, they're going to regret it."

She gave him a warm smile. "This is pretty crazy, you know?"

"Yes, but in the best way." Elrick tilted his head, listening. "Ah. The hunt is successful. Who's hungry?"

CHAPTER 7

THE WOLVES RETURNED with a half-eaten deer carcass. They seemed to have no trouble diving in and eating their meat raw. Even Elrick transformed back into his lycan form to join them in their carnivorous feast. It was slightly disturbing to watch, but I was so hungry I found myself a little jealous.

As starved as we were, Bree and I insisted on starting a fire and cooking our portion. The wolves seemed confused by our need to cook the meat, gathering around Elrick and yapping as though asking questions about a strange human ritual.

There were several moments of what sounded like wolf heckling, as I grew the flame and skewered pieces of meat to cook over the fire. Luckily, I couldn't understand them, and Elrick refused to translate. He just chuckled every so often at their yapping.

After our long trek with little more than berries to eat, the deer tasted like fine cuisine. The rich, savory meat was the best thing I'd eaten in a long while. Elrick ventured into the wood while we ate, returning after a time with a few large leaves, stuffed and tightly wrapped.

He held up the bulging leaves. "Berries and some root vegetables for the journey."

"Nice," Bree said. "Good thinking."

A white wolf strolled up to Elrick with a water skin in his mouth. He dropped it at Elrick's feet and backed away.

"Aw, thank you, Snowfoot," Elrick said. "Very thoughtful."

Snowfoot panted happily.

"Wait, where did you find this?" Elrick said.

Snowfoot whined and looked away.

"How do you know he was bad?" Elrick said.

Snowfoot growled.

Elrick put his hands on his hips. "A mean look on his face? That's the best you've got?"

Snowfoot barked.

"A tax collector for the king, you say?" Elrick tilted his head back and forth. "Well, that's something."

Snowfoot barked once more and scampered into the forest.

Elrick retrieved the water skin, shaking his head. "These young wolves today. What can you do?"

I closed my eyes as I started in on the last few pieces of juicy meat, savoring the taste and feeling my strength return.

"The wolves know of a farm less than an hour from here in the foothills," Elrick said. "It's the only one nearby so I'm guessing it's your friend Clive's place."

"Great," Bree said. "Can they take us there?"

Elrick nodded. "Food and lodging for the rest of the night in a warm farmhouse beats the cold ground of the forest."

"Agreed," I said.

Elrick motioned to a gray-and-black-streaked wolf. "Bawbrey will lead us through the woods."

Bawbrey licked his chops.

"But he wants the rest of your deer for his trouble," Elrick said.

I looked down at the two remnants of cooked venison on my skewer. "I thought wolves liked their meat raw?"

"They do," he said. "But Bawbrey was mesmerized by the smell of your cooking. He's curious."

I sighed. "Fine." I flicked the last couple of bites to the wolf.

Bawbrey scarfed down the meat, barely chewing it in the process.

I stood and brushed off my pants. "All right, I'm ready."

Bree took her last bite of venison and spoke with a full mouth. "Me too."

Bawbrey led the way through the forest, stopping every so often to cock his head toward sounds in the underbrush. At one point he bolted into the nearby trees and returned a moment later with a mouse tail hanging from his mouth. He crunched away and resumed his place at the front of our group as if nothing unusual had taken place.

Fireflies filled the area once more, their lights floating through the trees, mirroring the stars above.

Flyngard let out a long yawn.

"Are you… yawning?" I said.

"Indeed," Flyngard said. "I had a most restful nap."

"You still take naps?" I said.

"Aye," Flyngard said. "My spirit wearies and must be refreshed."

Bree drew closer and pointed to my chainmail. "Are you talking to him again?"

I nodded.

"Did you say he takes naps?" Bree said.

"Apparently so," I said.

"Don't speak of me as some strange creature," Flyngard said. "If it weren't for my clinging to the things that made me human, I might have lost myself long ago. Enchantment or no, I'm still Flyngard the warrior, and I shall return."

"Sorry," I said. "No offense meant. It must be very difficult for you."

"Indeed," he said. "Only the bold survive such an ethereal existence."

"What's he saying?" Bree said.

"He says it's hard to live in his enchanted state," I said.

Bree's brow furrowed. "I can't imagine. How long has he been imprisoned?"

"Uh," I said. "I'm not sure."

"You haven't asked the poor man?" She said.

I gave an apologetic shrug. "I've had a lot going on."

She frowned and motioned to the chainmail. "Ask him."

"Um, Flyngard?" I said.

"I'm here," he said. "And yes, the maiden has a kind heart to ask. The first person, in truth, to inquire of my struggle in many long years."

"Oh." A guilty feeling swirled in my chest for not even considering how he had handled such a long and strange imprisonment.

"What?" Bree said.

"He said no one's asked him about his life in a while."

Bree narrowed her eyes in a scolding manner.

I cleared my throat. "So, Flyngard, how long have you been enchanted?"

"Difficult to say," he said. "When I was first imprisoned in the chainmail, Sorcerer Rastvane gave it to his champion Gholderkrul. A rather vile troll prone to torturing his victims. Rastvane's twisted intent was to force me to witness Gholderkrul's gruesome attacks on the very people I would've fought to protect."

"That's terrible," I said.

"What?" Bree said.

I held up a hand. "Almost done."

"But the Eternal One spared me," Flyngard continued. "The very first battle Gholderkrul took part in, a fracture opened in the ground and he fell headlong to his death on a field of stalagmites. Even my enchanted armor couldn't protect him from that demise. Several years went by before I was found again. It was a very difficult time all alone in that cavern. I barely kept my sanity. Thankfully, Gremthorne, my last armor-bearer, found the remains of Gholderkrul and rescued me."

"That was fortunate," I said.

"Aye. Although, my journey with Gremthorne was short-lived. My enchanted protection went straight to his head. He thought he could steal from a dragon's lair and emerge unscathed. I warned him there were limits to my protection. Of course, you know how that turned out."

"So, how long were you in the dragon's lair?" I said.

"That's where I lost track of time," he said. "If I had to guess, I'd say it was three years. All in all, I'd say it's been around five years, give or take a year."

"Wow."

Bree grunted. "Would you tell me what he's saying already?"

"Sorry," I said. "He was stuck in a cave for about two years on a decaying troll."

Bree's nose crinkled. "Maybe I don't want to know the story."

"Then he was stuck in the dragon's lair for another three. He thinks it's been around five years."

"Five years? That's awful." Bree stayed quiet for a moment, her eyes tearing up. "Is there any way to break the enchantment?"

I shrugged. "I think Sorcerer Rastvane has to be defeated."

"Aye," Flyngard said. "And defeat him I shall."

Bree leaned closer. "Flyngard, you're a welcome companion on our journey. If we can help, we'll do what we can."

"Give her my kind thanks, Jonas. I can see why you're taken with her."

"He thanks you for your kindness," I said.

She brushed away a tear, then turned her head and hurried forward.

"Flyngard, for what it's worth," I said. "I'm sorry."

"Thank you, Jonas," he said. "I feel I should apologize to you as well."

"What for?" I said.

"I misjudged you upon our first meeting. With your constant worry and utter lack of weaponry skills, I feared I might be stuck on the back of a coward."

"Thanks a lot."

"Ah, but I was wrong, you see. When you and your brave companions proved your mettle by raiding a dragon's lair with little concern for his fiery retribution, I have to say, I was impressed."

"Yes, well, we had the soldiers to distract him while we slipped away. All's well that ends well, I suppose."

"Aye, for now," Flyngard said. "But when the dragon picks up your scent and tracks you down, that's truly where your bravery will shine. Most adventurers would be quaking in their boots right about now."

"Wait." I paused. "Did you say, tracking us down?"

"Indeed. He is a dragon, after all."

I froze. "Hold on. What are you saying? He can pick up a scent? Like some hound with a fox?"

Flyngard chuckled. "Well, of course. Surely you know the dangers of raiding a dragon's lair."

CHAPTER 8

BREE AND ELRICK doubled back, noticing my delay. "What is it?" Bree said.

My wild eyes darted from Elrick to Bree. "Flyngard said the dragon can pick up our scent like some hunting dog. And he'll track us down for stealing from his lair."

Elrick's eyes went wide. He dug into his pocket and pulled out a handful of gold coins. "Is it the gold? What if I leave the coins behind? I'll drop them in the forest."

"That may help, but it's not that simple," Flyngard said. "Dragons know when things are missing from their lair. They're quite jealous of their possessions. Once he discovers some of his treasures are gone, he'll pick up your scent and track you down."

I shared a wide-eyed look with Elrick. "He said it won't work. He'll still come after us."

Elrick buried his face in his hand. "Why? Why did I have to be so greedy?"

A chill ran across my skin. "Flyngard, why didn't you say something before?"

"I assumed you knew," Flyngard said. "Why do you think so few dare to steal from a dragon?"

"Is there anything we can do to throw him off our scent?" Bree said.

"Oh, the usual things," Flyngard said. "Cross waterways. Go underground. Get sprayed by skunks. Things of that nature."

I repeated Flyngard's instructions.

"What if we gave our stuff to someone else?" Elrick said. "I could put my cloak on somebody, give them the dragon's gold, then run away."

"Risky and utterly devious," Flyngard said. "That's no solution for a noble warrior."

Bree hit Elrick on the shoulder. "What's wrong with you?"

"Ask Bawbrey to find us a strong scent to cover us," I said. "Some plant or something."

Elrick knelt down to Bawbrey and spoke with him. The wolf barked and jogged forward. After a few minutes, he brought us to a tall plant with mottled purple and black leaves. A smell somewhere between decay and manure wafted over. I could tell right away this was a bad idea.

"This is what we have to smell like to stay alive?" Bree said.

Bawbrey looked up at the plant and barked.

Elrick frowned. "Bawbrey said it will give us an oozing rash as well."

"I think I'd rather get eaten," I said.

"Can't we squeeze juice over us or something pleasant?" Bree said.

Elrick looked down at Bawbrey. "Anything less vile around here? Nice flowers? Fruit? Anything?"

Bawbrey barked.

"There's some wildflowers and elderberries nearby," Elrick said.

"What do you think, Flyngard?" I said. "Will wildflowers and elderberries do the trick?"

"Hard to say for sure," he said. "The more you cover your scent the better."

I motioned ahead. "Lead on."

Bawbrey trotted ahead and we picked up our pace dramatically. I was thankful for the cover of night and the thick boughs overhead shrouding our group from the dragon's keen eyes.

Thankfully, we made it to the field of wildflowers unscathed. The three of us knelt down and rubbed flowers and elderberries over our skin and clothing.

Somehow, Bree still managed to look attractive. The stains and smears of berries and flowers on her face were like the warrior camouflage of some forest ranger. Elrick and I, on the other hand, looked like children that hadn't bathed since playing in the fields all day.

I stood up, putting a handful of flowers in my pocket in case I needed another dose later on. "Well, hopefully that's enough."

"Yes, let's go," Bree brushed off her pants. "Probably best not to stay in one place for too long."

Bawbrey continued his trek through the trees, the three of us following close behind. A short while later, we reached a series of low hills surrounded by pines. The path wound between the hills and ended at a small farmhouse and a barn, nestled at the edge of a forest.

A wooden fence surrounded about an acre of farmland. Chickens clucked in a henhouse, and the distinct sound of a horse snorting echoed from the barn.

"There it is," Bree said. "That's Clive's farm."

Bawbrey looked up at Elrick, whining.

"No." Elrick shook his head. "No chickens. This is why farmers don't trust you."

Bawbrey growled.

"No, they're not keeping all the chickens for themselves," Elrick said. "Listen, they leave all the forest rodents for you, you leave their chickens alone. That's the deal."

Bawbrey growled again.

"Well, I'm sorry you don't like it. That's life." Elrick knelt down and scratched Bawbrey's cheek. Bawbrey leaned into the scratch, closing his eyes. "All right, Bawbrey. Now, off with you. Thank you for bringing us here. And make sure to tell Talmotock how much I appreciate everything. I hope we meet again soon."

Bawbrey nuzzled Elrick's cheek, then turned and scampered back into the forest.

Elrick stood and grinned. "What a scamp. I'm gonna miss that guy."

The mournful bark of a hound dog came from the farmhouse.

"This farmer knows you, right?" I said.

"Yes," Bree said. "I mean, I'm pretty sure he'll remember me."

"Pretty sure?" Elrick said.

"Oh, quit worrying." Bree marched forward, leading the way to the farm.

The rust-brown hound dog trotted out to meet us when we reached the wooden gate of the property. As we walked along the fence line, the dog alternated between barking and a happy sort of panting. It seemed he didn't know whether to greet us or attack us.

When we reached the main house, a bearded man in a gray tunic and pants emerged, lamp in one hand, pitchfork in the other.

"Ho there!" The man spoke in a rough voice. "What do you want?"

"Greetings, Clive," Bree said. "It's Bree from The Slaughtered Boar tavern. I met you a while back."

"Ah, yes." Clive's voice softened as he headed closer. "What brings you here in the middle of the night?"

"King Mulraith threw us in a prison wagon and tried to offer us to the dragon Baldramorg. I escaped with the help of my friends here."

"The king." The farmer grimaced and spat. "Come in. Come in."

Clive unlatched the gate and calmed his hound dog as we entered. "Down Jasper. Easy. Let's go inside. You folks hungry?"

"Starving," Elrick said.

Bree introduced us as Clive led the way to the front door.

He furrowed his brow as he looked us over. "How long exactly have you been in the forest?"

Bree motioned to her face. "Wildflowers and elderberries. There's a chance a dragon is after our scent and we had to mask it."

"You stole from his lair?" He said.

Elrick shrugged. "We didn't know he'd come after us."

Clive shook his head. "Well, I have some fresh garlic. A fairly potent deterrent for their heightened sense of smell. It should help, at least temporarily."

"Thank you," I said.

The sturdy wooden beams of the house looked as though they'd outlasted several generations of farmers. The furnishings were simple and handmade, the smoothed armrests of the wooden chairs showcasing many years of use.

A little girl around five years old stood near the dinner table, rubbing a tired eye and holding a tattered doll under her arm. Her curly brown hair was pulled back in a ponytail.

"Who are these people, papa?" She said.

"Friends," Clive said.

"Why do they look so funny?" She said.

"They've been in the forest a while." Clive motioned to the girl. "This is my daughter Caroline."

"Hi, Caroline." Bree smiled and waved at her.

Caroline waved her dolly's arm at Bree.

"Now go back to bed, Caroline," Clive said.

"But Emma wants to meet the forest people." Caroline held out her doll, dropping it in the process.

The hound dog trotted over and sniffed at the doll.

"No, Jasper." Caroline retrieved the doll. "My dolly."

"All right, Caroline. But only for a little while, and then off to bed." Clive motioned to the dining table. "Rest. I'll get you some food."

"Thank you," Elrick said.

As I headed to the table, I spotted a lute leaning in the corner of the room. "Ah. A fellow lute player, I see."

Clive glanced back with a grin. "You play?"

"I'm the castle bard. At least, I was."

He stopped and turned. "Really? You must be quite skilled."

I shrugged. "Better than some but by no means a master."

He motioned to the lute. "You must play us a tune while I prepare food."

Caroline clapped. "Yay, music."

"Oh, I don't know," I said. "It's so late."

"Never too late for the lute." He motioned to the instrument again. "Please."

As tired as I was, the thought of playing a lute again gave me a burst of energy. "If you insist."

I retrieved the instrument and admired it for a moment. The blonde finish shone like honey in the lamplight. It was an eleven-string lute, similar to my own, but slightly larger and of a higher quality. "Is this an original Clarg?"

"It is indeed." Clive called back as he sliced food on a cutting board.

"It's beautiful. I used to have one, though not this nice."

"What happened to it?" Clive said.

"Um, I kind of smashed it over the head of the king's son."

Clive stopped cutting and looked up. "You jest?"

I shook my head. "Why do you think he wanted to feed me to a dragon?"

"Well done." Clive smiled. "After that story I can't wait to hear you play."

I threw the strap on my shoulder and plucked a few notes to get a feel for the instrument. The sound was more resonant and purer than what my old lute had produced.

"Hey," Elrick stifled a laugh. "Why don't you compose a tune about Sir Archinlanks latest battle."

I smirked. "Now that would be a dark tune... and I'm awfully tempted."

"Squirrel parade." Caroline jumped up and down. "Play squirrel parade."

"Um," I searched my mind for any song with squirrels and came up empty. "Afraid I don't know that one."

"That's because I wrote it." Clive walked to the table carrying a board loaded with sliced meat and cheese, and a bowl filled with wild blackberries. "Caroline, only daddy knows that one."

She hung her head. "Aw."

"Wait," I played an ascending series of notes. "I have one for you."

I began plucking an upbeat tune called The Ogre Rolled into the Bog. It was a snappy little song that usually got kids dancing. For the majority of the tune, the lyrics weren't much more than a repetitious story of a little boy outsmarting an ogre who proceeded to roll down a large hill.

Caroline smiled and swayed with the music, a sight that made all my hours of lute practice worthwhile.

I took a step closer to her and leaned over as I played the last line.

And down, down, down he goes,
Flailing his hands and flailing his toes,
Down he rolls into the bog,
Sinking like a smelly hog.

I repeated the final note with a dramatic flourish.

Caroline laughed and clapped. "Yay. Again. Again."

"Now, now, Caroline." Clive motioned her to the table. "Our guests need to eat. Thank you, Jonas. Your playing is excellent."

"Thanks." I propped the instrument carefully on a chair. "Your lute sounds incredible. It practically plays itself."

As much as I enjoyed playing, my body cried out for food. Those few pieces of deer meat in the forest were but a distant memory for my stomach.

Luckily, Clive offered a generous spread of culinary delights. We ate our fill, and he even gave us some supplies for the road, along with several cloves of garlic. He recommended rubbing the cloves on our skin every so often to offend the searching nostrils of the dragon. I couldn't imagine the smell would draw Bree any closer, but it was better than being incinerated.

We told Clive all about the latest news of the kingdom, our short captivity and trip to the dragon, and our narrow escape.

Clive and Caroline sat across from us at the table. Caroline seemed bored with our news, preferring to stack slices of cheese until they toppled over.

After we finished our tale, Clive studied us for a moment.

"This doesn't bode well for our kingdom," he said. "If Mulraith has lost his son and his army is already moving on Calladia, grief will drive him to lash out in dangerous ways. No one who is a threat to the king is safe." He turned to Caroline. "Pack your things. We will go on a long journey in the morning."

She blinked up at him. "Why?"

"We must travel to a better place."

"I like it here," she said.

He patted her on the head. "I know. We shall return. For now, gather your things."

Caroline frowned. "Okay." She slid off the table and shuffled toward her room.

Clive studied us for a moment. "With the death of his son and the soldiers at his command, Mulraith will surely declare a state of emergency in the kingdom. He will use this as an excuse to further his goals and crush any hint of dissent. There's nothing worse than a tyrant with emergency powers at his fingertips. I wager you're headed to Calladia to warn the people and join their cause."

"Aha," Flyngard said. "A noble quest."

I glanced at the others. "Well, no. I mean, I doubt our aid would amount to much. Besides, wouldn't they be aware of the king's forces? Don't they have scouts in the area?"

"Perhaps," Clive said. "But Calladia is mostly farmers and tradesmen. It might very well be that they're unaware of what's coming. If that's the case, I shudder to think of what will happen. There's a good chance you could change all that."

"Oh, I don't know." I motioned to the others. "It's not like we're warriors."

"Speak for yourself," Flyngard said.

"I bet I could do some damage now." Elrick spoke with a mouth full of cheese.

"Clive is right." Bree stared at him, her countenance set like a statue. "I have family there. We have to go."

"Hear, hear," Flyngard said. "Listen to the maiden of your unrequited love, Jonas. She has a brave heart."

I nudged the chainmail with my elbow to silence him. "I don't think we should get involved."

"I'd imagine you're already involved," Clive motioned to me. "You said that soldier accused you of killing Archinlanks, then rode back to the castle with the news."

A sinking feeling settled in my chest. "Yes, but Archinlanks and his soldiers were killed by the dragon."

"Ah, but you said the only soldier who reported back to the king was the one who didn't see the dragon attack. I'm sure he realized the dragon was involved, but he only witnessed the aftermath. You said he saw you standing over the dead body of Archinlanks and accused you of being his assassin. And that is the report he took back to the castle."

A numbness washed over me. If smashing my lute over Archinlanks head wasn't enough to mark me as the king's enemy, this would certainly put the last nail in the coffin. If the soldiers ever caught up to me, a life's sentence in the dungeon would be the best I could hope for.

"Hold on," Elrick said. "If word goes out that Jonas is some kind of assassin who killed the king's son, he'll be the most wanted man in Grandelon. And you're saying we should go to Calladia? The same place where all the soldiers who want Jonas dead are going?"

Clive nodded. "It could be difficult."

"We can take it," Flyngard said.

"Difficult?" Elrick laughed. "It's suicide. Jonas, tell him."

I gave an apologetic shrug. "It does seem a wild risk."

"But what a heroic endeavor," Flyngard said. "If you survive, maybe bards will write songs about you for a change."

For a brief moment, the thought of another bard writing about me was tempting. Still, it wasn't worth dying for.

"We have to try." Bree clenched her jaw. "But we need to travel in the shadows. Soldiers will scout the main roads."

"You can use the caves in Chellusk Mountains," Clive said. "I have a map."

"No thanks," Elrick said. "I've heard about those caves."

"Don't believe every tavern tale. The caves are the fastest route." Clive got up and went to the corner of the room. He lifted up a floorboard and retrieved something underneath.

Elrick leaned toward me and lowered his voice. "We're not going through the caves, right?"

I shook my head.

Clive returned to the table, placing a white stone and a yellowed scroll before us. He spread out the scroll, revealing a series of crooked paths that resembled the branches of a large tree. "There." He pointed to a winding red path that went from one end of the map to the other. "That's the safe cavern passage through the mountains. The main roads used by the soldiers have to go around the mountains. This will cut right through, saving you over a day's journey. If they're on horseback and you're on foot, you'll need the advantage."

"You've been through these caves?" Bree said.

"Well, no," he said. "I'm a farmer, not an explorer. I got this map from one of the spies who came through here."

"I heard there's cave grabbers in there," Elrick said. "And mammoth spiders."

"I've heard about those caves too," I said. "The stories weren't pretty. They said two trackers went in there armed to the teeth, and were devoured by poisonous slime worms."

"Yes. The trackers and the slime worms." Elrick pointed at me. "Wyatt has a flute song about it. After they set foot in those caves, they never returned."

"If both trackers died," Clive said. "How did anyone ever hear about it?"

Elrick and I looked at each other in silence.

Bree chuckled. "You two are listening to tavern tales? You should know better."

"Sounds like great adventure awaits in those caves, aye?" Flyngard said. "I haven't slain a mammoth spider in ages. Horrible creatures. Faster than you'd think. I wouldn't mind getting another crack at one."

Clive rolled up the scroll and gave it to me. "You may have the scroll. I penned a copy. And you'll need this." He handed me the white stone. "It's a lightstone. Just shake it when you're ready to use it and it should provide enough light for travel."

"A lightstone? Really?" I took the stone and turned it over in my hand. I'd never actually seen one before. They weren't exactly rare, but at around the same cost as a shield, they were beyond my coin pouch. "Can I try it?"

He shook his head. "I wouldn't waste its light. It stays lit for several hours. Longer if it's kept warm in your hand."

"Thank you," Bree said. "This is a generous gift."

He grinned. "I saved it for just such a time. And now, it's late. You should get some rest. I have a hidden room under the barn where you can sleep. You'll find a door underneath the wagon."

"Hidden room?" Bree said. "Do soldiers often come here?"

"Sometimes. They suspect me of harboring spies, but they haven't found anything yet. Although, after what's happened, I expect the king will send soldiers out soon. We should all leave at daybreak."

"Thank you, Clive," Bree said. "For everything."

He smiled. "You're welcome. Sleep well. May the Eternal One see us through these times."

We gathered our things and went to the barn. Sure enough, there was a hidden opening in the floor that led to a shallow space below. It was small and smelled of animals and old hay, but I was free of the castle and Bree was at my side, so I had no room for complaints.

The ceiling of the hidden room was low and we had to duck to move about. A thick layer of hay covered the ground, and there were a few rough blankets piled in the corner. We spread out the blankets and tried to flatten the lumps out of the hay as best we could.

I was so grateful to lie down I wanted to cry. With all the stressful events I'd been through, not to mention the lack of sleep, I couldn't wait to drift off for a while.

A strange blend of berries and garlic scent mixed with a dwindling floral aroma. It wasn't terrible but it wasn't entirely pleasant either.

I turned to Bree. "You comfortable?"

She shifted her shoulder and crinkled her nose. "Not really. This hay isn't as soft as it looks. It comes through the blanket like thorns."

"I think there was an extra blanket over there," I said.

"Already got it." She pulled it up over her body. "Elrick said he didn't need it with his fur. You didn't want it did you?"

"No, go ahead."

I heard a muted growl on my other side. I turned to find Elrick in lycan form, already fast asleep.

"Well, he's already out," I said.

Bree yawned. "I don't blame him. I could use some sleep."

"Definitely." I shifted a bit to get comfortable. "It's funny, even though it's not the best situation, I'm glad we finally got out of the kingdom."

"Not the best situation?" She arched an eyebrow. "You mean rising to the top of King Mulraith's list of enemies and being hunted down by a dragon? That situation?"

"All right. It's pretty bad. It's not all my fault though."

"I'm teasing." She winked. "I'll take this over being a concubine for Archinlanks any day."

I nodded in full agreement.

"You know," she said. "I never did get to thank you."

"For what?"

"Trying to stop him. Even though you practically signed your own death sentence, seeing the look on Archinlanks face when you smashed that lute over his head was priceless."

I smirked. "I didn't really think it through, did I?"

She chuckled. "No, you didn't."

I held her gaze. "I just couldn't let him do that to you. When I saw him grab you like that. Like you were his property. I don't know, maybe it was foolhardy, but I had to do something."

Bree reached out and squeezed my hand. "Foolhardy isn't always a bad thing. Thank you, Jonas."

"You're welcome."

She kept her hand on mine and closed her eyes, a soft smile on her face. "Goodnight, Jonas."

"Goodnight Bree."

The sight of her so close filled me with warmth. I watched her for a while, then shut my eyes. In my relaxed state, sleep came within seconds.

* * *

A soft breeze stirred Bree's copper hair as we strolled together through a grassy field. The sun shone brightly overhead in a cloudless sky. She stopped and grabbed me around the waist, her blue eyes staring into mine. A smile spread over her full lips as she pulled me closer.

"Jonas," Flyngard said. "Can you hear me?"

"Go away," I said.

"Jonas!" Flyngard sounded urgent.

"Not now." I wrapped my arms tight around Bree. "I'm busy."

"Jonas! Wake up!"

My eyes snapped open. I was curled up on the hay in the hidden room under Farmer Clive's barn.

"Soldiers are outside," Flyngard said. "You need to wake the others."

CHAPTER 9

I SAT UP QUICKLY. "Soldiers? You're sure?"

"Yes," Flyngard said. "Hurry."

I shook Bree and Elrick awake and whispered the news. We gathered our things and I led the way up the ladder, out of the hidden room.

Unfortunately, the hinge on the hidden door made a terrible squeak when I opened it. Would my life come to an end all because of a rusty hinge? Thankfully there were no soldiers waiting in the barn when I stuck my head out.

"Ready yourself," Flyngard said. "They're right outside."

I nodded. "I'm ready."

"No," Flyngard said. "Prepare your mind."

"What?" I said.

"You talking to me?" Elrick said from the ladder below.

"No," I whispered. "Flyngard."

"The proper mindset will aid you in battle," Flyngard said. "Lest you falter or shy away when you should charge."

"Don't worry." I scrambled up the ladder and into the barn. "My mind is fine."

"Now, yes. But once the enemy attacks, you might fold," Flyngard said. "You should recite the warrior's chant. Say it with me. Heart of fire. Mind of steel. Will of iron."

"What?" I frowned. "I'm not saying that."

"Don't just say it," he said. "Believe it."

The main barn door burst open and two guards stood there with crossbows. I froze at the sight. Bree and Elrick were still climbing up from the hidden room below. I was the only target for both soldiers.

Two sharp snapping sounds were followed by two hard thuds striking my chest. I watched in amazement as the arrows bounced harmlessly to the ground.

My chainmail radiated with warmth. I looked up at the guards. They shared wide-eyed looks with each other.

"Charge them!" Flyngard said. "Now! Before it's too late."

Fear drove me forward. I sprinted through the barn, led by a desperate impulse to stop them. The soldiers fumbled with their crossbows, readying another volley of arrows. My staff was in my hand before I even realized I'd grabbed it. A strange blend of instinct, adrenaline, and the strong desire to protect my friends urged me to strike.

A broad sweep of my staff struck perfectly across the soldiers' faces. White energy crackled across their jawlines. With stifled groans, the two men slumped to the ground.

A rush of tan fur swept up beside me like a wind. Elrick stood there in lycan form, breathing heavily, his fierce golden eyes sweeping over the soldiers.

He looked over, his narrowed eyes sending a chill through me. "That was amazing. How did you do that?"

I glanced down at the fallen guards, feeling just as surprised. "I-I'm not sure. But there's definitely magic in this staff."

"Look sharp," Flyngard said. "More soldiers. Dead ahead."

Three more soldiers emerged from the darkness, their swords drawn.

They skidded to a stop a few feet from us, their eyes wide at the sight of my lycan companion. A deep growl resonated from Elrick's chest. One of the soldiers backed away.

The lead soldier scowled at him. "Coward! Get back here. You've killed wolves before. Strike him down!"

The soldier shouted a battle cry and charged forward. Elrick leapt high in the air, his agile body performing a twisting arc over the man. He grabbed the soldier's head on the way down and flung him into the darkness like a sack of potatoes.

The lead soldier rushed toward me in my distracted state. A warm current radiated from my chainmail. He thrust his sword at my chest. I pivoted and spun my staff, as if on impulse, and parried his strike. Without missing a beat, I swept the staff upward, the end of it smashing into his nose. A burst of white energy exploded from the staff on impact. The guard cried out, clutching his bloodied face as he stumbled backward.

"That was glorious!" Flyngard said. "Do you see what you've been missing? Who shall be our next victim?"

I staggered sideways, adrenaline rushing through me. I felt light headed with the sudden clash of battle.

Elrick dashed forward, grasping the remaining soldier in the back. The man's eyes went wide, and he cried out as his sword dropped to the ground. Elrick spun him round, then hurled him into the other guard. There was a crunching sound and they both collapsed.

"Did you see that?" Elrick's mouth was drawn back in a wolf-ish smile revealing dangerous rows of sharp teeth. If he hadn't been my best friend, I would've been frightened for my life. "My acrobatics aren't just for show anymore. This is incredible. I've never felt so alive."

I heard another snap, and Elrick howled in pain. He stumbled, clutching his arm. An arrow was lodged deep in his shoulder. Two more soldiers with crossbows crouched about ten yards away in the bushes.

"Elrick!" I yelled.

"Fiends!" Flyngard said. "They'll pay for that."

Bree rushed up to us, her circlet glowing white. The two soldiers in the bushes screamed and batted at their arms and chest. They were covered in tarantulas.

I gritted my teeth and rushed them, taking advantage of Bree's spider illusion. One of them looked up as I approached, just in time to watch the end of my staff close in on his face. He fell back with a muffled groan.

The other guard went for his sword. I brought the staff down on his wrist. There was a cracking sound and he dropped the sword with a yelp. I swung the staff straight up to his cheekbone. A blast of white energy wrapped around his head. He shuddered for a moment, then slumped to the ground.

"We're working together now, aye!" Flyngard said. "Do you feel the fellowship of our battle? Your staff skills and my fighting intuition? It is glorious, is it not?"

I nodded, breathing in quick gasps. I couldn't deny there was something unique about what I'd just experienced. My technique was more accurate and powerful than anything I'd ever executed. There was an intuition, an instinct about attacks and movements that flowed through me, filling me with confidence and deadly purpose.

The scream of a little girl rang out. Thirty yards away, half a dozen soldiers were hauling Clive and his daughter Caroline out of their farmhouse.

Elrick growled and started forward, then stumbled to his knee, whining and clutching his wounded shoulder. He'd pulled the arrow out, and a thin stream of blood ran down his fur.

Bree's eyes locked onto mine. Her face was tight in

concentration, her hands glowing white. "We can't let them take her."

I nodded. There was no other choice. I couldn't leave Clive and his daughter to their captors. There was no telling what they would do to them. Resolve swelled within me to stop this evil from happening. Without another thought, I sprinted forward, the warm energy of the staff flowing along the palm of my hand. My body felt alive with electricity.

"Strike them down, Jonas," Flyngard said. "Let us speak the warrior's chant together. Heart of fire. Mind of steel. Will of iron."

"Not now, Flyngard," I said.

Fiery hail fell around the soldiers as I closed the gap to ten yards. They cried out and shielded themselves from Bree's attack. I knew there were only precious moments before they realized it was all an illusion.

I spun my staff into the head of the closest soldier, his eyes still fixed on the flaming rocks above. There was a crack, and he went down. The sound brought the next soldier around, and he drew his sword in a blur.

There was a flash of silver as he swept the blade toward my chest. Everything seemed to slow. Instinct and action blended into a seamless union. I arched back, sliding under the slashing blade. I rolled to my knees and shoved the end of the staff into his gut. He gasped and doubled over. I spun the staff into his temple and he crumpled.

I sprang to my feet as three guards charged me, swords drawn. An arrow struck one in the chest and he fell backward. I glanced back to see Bree leveling a crossbow in my direction.

The remaining two guards lunged toward me with their blades drawn. Once more, my actions were instinctual, smooth. Almost as if I knew what was coming and had a move ready in response. I spun to the left and swung my arm wide, letting the momentum take my staff right into the back of both of their heads. There was a crackling sound, and a swirl of white energy wrapped around their heads like a halo. They convulsed for a moment, then fell face first on the ground.

The last remaining guard stood several feet away, clutching his sword. He locked eyes with me. "Come on, then. I'm not afraid of you, staff wielder. Come taste my steel."

I spied a palm sized rock on the ground and an idea hit me. It was a long shot, but my confidence was surging. I nudged the end of my staff under the rock and flung it upward, toward the soldier. The stone sped straight and true, striking him right between the eyes. He blinked and swayed for a moment, then fell flat on his back.

"Good show!" Flyngard said. "Excellent work, Jonas. Most invigorating."

My chest heaved as I struggled to catch my breath. I could hardly believe the sight around me. Six guards lay on the ground at my feet. How could I have achieved such a victory?

Caroline clutched Clive's leg, her breath coming out in choked sobs. He knelt down and comforted her.

Bree came jogging up, holding a newly acquired crossbow. "Are you okay?"

I nodded, still catching my breath.

Her eyes glanced over me. "There's not a scratch on you. How did you do that?"

"I'm not entirely sure."

Clive walked over and wrapped his arms around me. "Thank you, my son."

Caroline hugged my leg. "Thank you. You saved my daddy."

Elrick walked over to us, clutching his shoulder. "Aw, I missed all the fun."

Caroline screamed and hid behind me.

"It's okay," I said. "He's a friend."

"You're friends with monsters?" She said.

"Sorry." Elrick shrank back to his human form. "Forgot what I looked like."

Bree went to Elrick's side, pressing a cloth to his fresh wound.

"You're a lycan watchman?" Clive shook his head. "I thought they'd left these parts."

"Well, I'm sort of a new recruit," Elrick said. "Can't speak for the others. Some are in the forest near Calladia. They're making life difficult for the king's gathering forces."

Clive nodded. "That's good to hear. From what you've told me, every ally is needed." He turned to me. "A skilled warrior like you would be quite an asset over there."

"Me?" I shook my head. "I'm no warrior."

Clive looked at the fallen soldiers around me. "I would beg to differ."

"As would I," Flyngard said. "Our unity in combat is undeniable. Far better than any I have experienced. Think of the victories we could achieve in battle. Does not your spirit soar within you at the thought?"

Frankly, the thought was terrifying. "Um, not really."

"Pardon?" Clive said.

"Oh, nothing," I said.

Elrick drew in a sharp breath as Bree adjusted the cloth on his shoulder.

Clive headed into his house. "I can help with that." He returned with a small satchel and tended to Elrick's wound. As he finished with the bandage, Elrick's head snapped up. His eyes were fixed on the road that led to the farmhouse.

"Someone's coming." Elrick focused on the road. "A lone rider on horseback."

I strained to hear but the only sounds were the light rustling of the leaves in the wind, and a scattering of birds chirping the first song of morning.

"More soldiers?" Caroline hid behind her father.

"I don't think so," Elrick said.

The faint sound of galloping hooves thumped in the distance. Seconds later a lone rider emerged on the road, heading toward us at great speed.

"It's Peter," Clive said. "It's okay. He's my brother."

"Uncle Peter." Caroline perked up.

Peter galloped over, reining in his horse as he reached us. He had long brown hair and a heavy beard. His wide eyes scanned the fallen soldiers around us. "Great heavens, what happened?"

"They came to arrest us." Clive patted my back. "But this brave warrior and his companions saved us."

Peter nodded at me. "Thank you, friends. Times like this are meant for people like you."

I nodded back, feeling woefully undeserving of his praise.

"The kingdom is broken," Peter said. "Mulraith is enraged with the news of his son. What was bad has become worse. Dark times are ahead. Anyone considered a threat to the kingdom is being imprisoned or killed."

Clive shook his head. "Eternal One, help us."

"Indeed," Peter said. "Troops are heading east for Calladia. The roads are treacherous. And they search for an assassin. A bard named Jonas. The only safe passage is west to Eldravelle. We must leave now."

Clive patted my shoulder. "As I predicted, Jonas. You have been marked. They will hold you responsible for the death of Archinlanks."

"This is the bard assassin?" Peter fixed his eyes on me. "Now I understand why these soldiers lie before you."

I shook my head. "I'm no assassin. I'm just a bard."

"No need for secrecy here." Peter dismounted. "You're among friends. Clive, we should ready the wagon."

Clive knelt down to Caroline. "Gather your things. And

some food. We must leave." He leaned close and whispered something in her ear.

Caroline nodded and hurried inside the house.

Peter motioned to us. "And what of the assassin and his companions?"

Clive studied our faces. "They must decide their own path. Many thanks to you, my friends. You saved us. I am forever in your debt. The Eternal One be with you."

Clive led Peter toward the barn, leaving the three of us alone.

"To the caves!" Flyngard said. "What a glorious quest. We shall slay mammoth spiders and cave grabbers, and all manner of creatures that come against us. And then to battle at Calladia, aye?"

"Quiet," I said.

"I didn't say anything," Elrick said.

"No, not you. Flyngard wants to go fight the world."

Bree slung the crossbow across her back and tightened the strap. "Well, I'm taking whatever arrows and weapons I can find on these soldiers. I'm not going empty-handed this time."

Elrick nodded. "Good idea."

"I suppose we could go west with Clive," I shrugged. "Offer protection for their journey."

Bree stared at me. "Is that what you want to do?"

I shook my head. "I don't know. My head is spinning. I was dead asleep a few minutes ago and now I'm wanted by the king's army as some kind of bard assassin."

She gave a slight smile. "Obviously, our big plans of leaving the kingdom could have gone better."

"Obviously," Elrick said.

"The way I look at it, we have three choices," she said. "Go west to Eldravelle. Definitely the safest option. Go east to Calladia where the roads are crawling with soldiers and we'll probably get killed before we ever make it there. Or, we go–"

"Don't say it," Elrick pointed at her. "Don't say north to the Chellusk Mountains. I don't want to go into those caves."

Bree rolled her eyes. "Or, we go north to Chellusk Mountains. Head through the caves, and get to Calladia before the soldiers, giving us time to warn everyone that war is coming."

"Or, option four." Elrick held up four fingers. "We go deep into the forest. Sneak through the trees. Maybe we'll find my old wolf pack. It'll take longer but—"

"By then it'll be too late," Bree said. "We'll get there in time to see the aftermath of a massacre. What's with you? What happened to all your lycan bravery?"

"Bravery out in the open land is one thing. I know what I'm getting into. Caves filled with darkness and creatures unknown are another."

I let out a long breath. "So, the caves take us there faster. What happens when we arrive at Calladia?"

"Assuming we don't die in the caves?" Elrick said.

"Then we warn the people," Bree said. "Give them time to prepare for battle."

"Even if they prepare, they're outnumbered," I said. "They can't stand against the king's army. So, if we can't really change the outcome, why take the risk?"

"You can't predict the difference we could make." She searched my eyes. "Jonas, I have family there."

I stayed quiet for a moment, unsure of what to say. "Bree, I want to help. There's nothing I'd rather do than stop the king and his army. But I'm just one man. I'm a bard. I play music."

"Jonas, your music is a great gift. But so is what you've accomplished here. At your feet lie half a dozen soldiers trained in combat. I've never seen anyone fight like you did today. Not to mention Elrick. Think of the damage he could do as a lycan."

"True. Did you see what I did to those soldiers?" Elrick

adjusted the bandage on his shoulder. "And once I heal up, I'll be ready for more."

"Bree speaks truth," Flyngard said. "We are a force to be reckoned with."

"If you go with me to Calladia," Bree said. "Who knows? Maybe we can turn the tide of battle."

"Hear, hear!" Flyngard said. "I like her spirit."

There was a tug of war going on in my head. I couldn't deny that protecting Clive and his daughter against the soldiers had given me an amazing sense of fulfillment. My involvement had actually changed their destiny and saved them from the dungeon, or worse. That accomplishment was beyond anything I'd experienced in the last several years. The thought that I could do that for more people stirred a powerful longing deep inside me. The main problem, of course, was the risk. Heading through the caves and into battle was inviting grave injury and quite possibly the end of my life.

Bree's deep blue eyes held me in their gaze, waiting for an answer. What choice did I have? From what I could tell, she was set on the journey, and I couldn't let her go alone. It was dangerous enough with three of us watching out for each other.

An odd sense of peace came over me as I resolved to go with her. I decided that no matter what else happened, at least I would be at her side, doing everything I could to protect her and anyone else I was able to help.

I took a deep breath. "All right. We go north to the caves."

Elrick sighed. "I knew it."

"I'm not too thrilled about the idea myself," I said. "But I can't see another way."

Bree leaned in and kissed my cheek. "Thank you, Jonas. This could be the beginning of a far better future."

Caroline emerged from the house carrying her father's lute.

She walked over and handed it to me. "My daddy said to give this to you. He said a bard needs a lute."

I held the lute delicately as if it were made of glass. "His Clarg? I can't accept this."

"When people say that, daddy always says they have to." She turned to Elrick. "Can you turn into a monster again?"

Elrick grinned and grew into the hairier, wolfish version of himself. He raised his paws. "Boo."

Caroline flinched, then chuckled. "You're scary."

"Aw, you hurt my feelings." Elrick sniffed and pretended to wipe away a tear.

"You're a silly monster. Well, bye." She scampered back inside.

Bree smiled at me. "No matter what else happens, we saved that precious little girl. Maybe we can save more like her."

"I hope so," I said.

We gathered what we could from the fallen soldiers. Those that were still alive, we left gagged and bound to nearby trees.

We took three of the soldiers' horses, bade farewell to Clive, Caroline, and Peter, and galloped north for the Chellusk Mountains.

CHAPTER 10

THE ROAD NORTH meandered through pine-covered foothills. Purple flowering vines wound up the trees, filling the air with their sweet scent. The cold morning air combined with the deep shadows of the trees made for a chilly ride.

I gripped the reins in one hand and held my cloak tightly with the other, trying to keep from shivering. Bree had thought ahead and secured an extra cloak for herself from the soldiers. She rode casually through the trees, looking relaxed as if she were as warm as toast. Of course, she had suggested we should all grab extra cloaks for the journey. An hour of trembling had me wishing I'd listened to her. Elrick claimed he had no need. He'd remained in his lycan form all morning to ward off the chill.

Clive had cleaned and dressed Elrick's shoulder before we left the farm. After a few hours of riding in the morning sun, Elrick ditched the wound dressing, proudly displaying his nearly-healed shoulder.

By mid-morning, we reached the base of the mountain. Elrick's sharp eyes spotted a cave, and we rode toward it.

The slate-gray tips of the Chellusk Mountains pierced the sky, and a hawk glided on the wind currents overhead. Sparse clusters of shrubs with twisted roots clung to the mountainside.

The mouth of the cave looked like a hungry stone giant waiting for us to offer ourselves up as his morning snack. My horse reared his head back and snorted as if to say, 'There's no way I'm going in there.'

Since the cave entrance was around ten feet high and there was no telling how narrow the caverns would become as we continued on, it was time to say goodbye to the horses. Although I preferred riding to walking, I couldn't stomach the thought of abandoning my horse deep within the cave labyrinth. My head still swam with tales of the creeping horrors lurking inside.

Elrick shook his head and whined. "These caves aren't the only option, you know. It's still not too late to change our minds."

"Yes it is." Bree dismounted and started removing supplies from her horse's saddlebags.

"Agreed," Flyngard said. "Our path is set. It would be foolish to entertain doubt at this point."

I gave Elrick an apologetic shrug and dismounted.

"Somethings not right," Flyngard said. "I sense a sinister presence."

"Great, thanks," I said. "I'm already nervous about the caves."

"No. Not the caves," he said. "Something else. Get your things. Hurry."

I grabbed my supplies from the back of the horse and hoisted them over my shoulder. As I turned back to the cave, a large shadow darkened the sky overhead. A chill crept through my bones. My head snapped up to see the huge bulk of the dragon Baldramorg. He glided through the air, his serpentine body weaving below the clouds like some great, green snake crawling over a field of cotton.

My horse reared up with a high-pitched whinny.

"To the cave!" Flyngard said. "Now!"

An ear-piercing screech thundered down from above as the dragon plunged downward.

"Run!" Bree sprinted toward the cave.

Without a word, Elrick and I ran after her. Elrick grabbed Bree and carried her forward with such speed that I felt like I was merely walking. They disappeared into the darkness of the cave mouth.

Another great screech from the dragon sent a thrill of horror through me. Its dark shadow spread ever larger on the ground around me.

"Faster!" Flyngard said. "Faster!"

As the shadow of the dragon grew, I realized I'd never make it to the cave in time. I dared not look at the descending monstrosity above, or I might collapse from terror. Instead, I pressed forward, bracing for the flames that would soon consume me.

A rush of tan fur emerged from the cave and my body was swept up into Elrick's large furry arms.

"Hang on," he said.

With a terrific surge of speed, Elrick bolted into the cave. The darkness swallowed us up, and I could hear the rapid patter of his paw-like feet echoing through the tunnel.

The ground thundered beneath us. Elrick faltered for a moment, then regained his footing and sprinted forward. I glanced back to see the mammoth head of the dragon poised at the cave entrance. Thankfully, he was much too large to fit inside. His glowing emerald eyes locked on us as he took a deep breath.

"Uh oh," I said. "Flyngard? How strong is that enchanted protection of yours?"

"With dragon fire at our heels?" Flyngard said. "I can't promise anything. I'll do my best to shield the both of you."

There was a blast behind us, and the cave lit up as if the sun had burst through the stone walls. Bright orange streams of fire surged behind us. Waves of heat washed over me like a heavy blanket.

"Hurry!" I cried.

Elrick leaned forward, breathing hard, his wolfish legs pumping with inhuman speed. A blast of heat tore into us, and suddenly we were engulfed in flames.

There was a terrible moment when the heat became unbearable, and it felt like I was going to burst. A second later, Elrick ducked into a narrow side-passage and the cool darkness of the inner chamber washed over us like a mountain breeze. Elrick continued forward for about twenty feet, his pace slowing, until we found Bree waiting in the shadows.

Elrick fell to his knees, dropping me unceremoniously on the cavern floor.

"Elrick!" Bree rushed over and knelt beside him.

The dragon fire behind us died away, and the utter darkness of the cave swallowed us up.

I rolled to my knees and retrieved the lightstone from my pocket. I shook it, and a soft glow radiated from the center, spreading outward until it shone white. The stone's illumination was as bright as a torch, but instead of a warm orange light, a white glow fell about the area. My friends looked like ghosts trapped in a dark void.

"Curse that dragon fire," Flyngard said. "Almost took out my armor-bearer for the second time. You must thank Elrick for me. His speed is impressive. Although, without the aid of my enchanted protection, I doubt either of you would have made it."

Elrick was on his hands and knees, breathing heavily. Thin lines of smoke rose up from his back.

"You all right?" Bree patted his shoulder, then drew her hand back and blew on it.

Elrick sniffed. "Does anyone else smell burnt hair?"

Bree looked at his smoking back, then frowned. "Um, maybe a little."

I stood and walked behind him, holding up the lightstone.

The fur on his upper back was burnt. "You may have gotten a bit singed."

"Terrific," he said.

"Here, this should help." I took off my cloak and used it to pat down his back. "You know, what you did was incredible. You saved us all."

"Yes," Bree put a tentative hand on his shoulder. "Thank you, Elrick."

His wolfish lips drew back, revealing sharp teeth. "I was pretty incredible, wasn't I?"

Bree smirked. "Don't let it go to your head."

Flyngard cleared his throat.

"Oh," I said. "I should mention, Flyngard protected us with his enchantment as well."

"Please thank him for us," Bree said.

"He can hear you," I said.

Bree leaned forward, cupping a hand over her mouth. "Thank you, Flyngard."

"He's not hard of hearing," I said.

She shrugged and leaned back against the stone wall. "I need to rest a minute."

"You and me both," Elrick said.

We sat for a while, refreshing ourselves with a little water and dried meat Clive had packed for us.

A deathly silence hung in the cave. Every sound we made echoed off the stone walls, heralding our presence. It felt like we were disturbing some ancient crypt.

"I think my eyes have adjusted." Elrick's eyes glowed yellow as he scanned our surroundings. "Cover that stone for a second."

I cupped my hands over the lightstone, allowing the natural darkness of the cave to blanket us once more. The spaces between my fingers lit up as the light tried to escape, causing my hands to glow like they were filled with magic, but otherwise the cave was dark.

"It's actually not that bad," Elrick said. "I can't believe how well I can see in here. I think I could find my way around even without that stone."

I uncovered the stone. "Great. You'll be the first to see the cave beasts when they come for us."

"Don't put that thought in my head," he said.

"All right," I took out the map and unrolled it. "Let's check this before we get lost."

Bree and Elrick huddled around me as I opened the map. Bree grabbed one side of the map so I could hold the stone above us. The red line started from where we entered and appeared to be the only path through the mountain. Several caverns branched off in either direction, while the red line continued straight for a long way. Halfway through the caverns, the path became far more erratic. The map would definitely save us from going the wrong way once we reached that point.

"Let's double back to the main path," I said. "Then it looks like it's straight ahead for a long time."

"Yes, if we can trust this map," Elrick said.

I rolled up the scroll and tucked it deep into my pocket.

Bree raised an eyebrow at me. "Well? You ready?"

"I suppose." I took a deep breath and led the group forward.

We made our way back to the main cavern and headed deeper into the mountain. The lightstone's radiance brushed over the gray walls around us, briefly revealing the coarse features of the stone before darkness slid back over it.

We walked in silence for several minutes. I half expected an immediate attack from something large and hungry. But everything was quiet except our own footfalls echoing through the cavern.

"I hear bats," Elrick whispered. "There's bats in here."

"It's a cave," I said. "What'd you expect?"

"They're flying vermin," he said. "Disease carriers. They travel in swarms. How'd you like a swarm of disease-filled fangs sinking into your skin?"

"You know, I figured you'd be braver as a lycan."

"Lycans are forest creatures. We don't like enclosed spaces."

"How do you know? Did you ask around?"

"It's instinctual."

"Would you keep it down?" Bree whispered. "If there are creatures in here, I don't want to announce our presence."

"I thought you said those were all tavern tales," Elrick said.

"Most likely, yes," she said. "But I don't want to take any chances."

We kept on the path for the next hour in relative silence. Even Flyngard was quiet. Either he'd fallen into his strange enchanted sleep or he was bored since there was no one around to fight.

At first, the only evidence that anything was alive and moving in the stifling quiet of the caves was the sound our boots made on the cavern floor. Gradually, as caverns branched off from our main path, other sounds came to us from deep within. There was a high-pitched screeching which I assumed to be bats. Elrick was quick to confirm this with enhanced hearing.

Equally annoying was the squeal of rats. Their eyes glowed red when the lightstone hit them, and they scurried away as if they'd forgotten how bright the world could be. These were the better sounds. Sounds we could connect to creatures we understood. But as we delved deeper into the mountain, the noises became far stranger.

As we continued on, an inhuman roar came from deep within the caves. The sound was somewhere between a bear and thunder, and just powerful enough to make your legs go weak and set your imagination on edge. Everyone froze and fell silent. We just looked at each other with wide eyes, then started forward again without a word. What was there to say? Whatever the thing was would surely destroy us if we had the misfortune of taking a wrong turn. Just when my heart had slowed down to a normal rhythm again, I heard something scratching against stone up ahead.

I lifted the lightstone higher, hoping to see farther down the cavern. "What is that?"

"Something with claws," Elrick said.

"Yeah, but how big are those claws?" Bree said.

The scratching grew in intensity as if something were trying to burrow into the walls.

I stopped. "Hold tight. No need to disturb… whatever it is."

We waited in silence and the scratching stopped. I turned to Elrick, hoping for some wild canine intuition. He narrowed his eyes as he scanned the dark cavern ahead, then shrugged his hairy shoulders.

I frowned and took a few steps forward. The scratching started up once more. My feet froze in place, panic starting to kick in.

"The best thing to do is charge ahead," Flyngard said. "Go in with a war cry and your weapon at the ready. Otherwise, fear will make things worse."

"Oh, sure," I said. "And run right into the fangs of some cave spider."

"See?" Flyngard said. "Fear has you picturing creatures in every cave."

"Did you say spiders?" Elrick's voice faltered.

"I was talking to Flyngard."

"Quiet." Bree readied her crossbow. "Weapons ready."

Elrick and I nodded and followed her lead. With my free hand, I grabbed the staff and stole forward.

The scratching sound faded away as if the creature had rushed down another passage. We continued on for a few moments in silence, listening for any signs of danger.

The passage ahead was strewn with rubble. Sections of the

wall were gouged and pitted as if gem miners had dug out a cache. I held the lightstone close to the wall, examining what looked like deep claw marks. I leaned forward and ran my hand along one of the marks, feeling the cool, rough stone against my fingertips.

There was a grating sound and suddenly the wall fell away. I pitched forward with a gasp, and rolled into a narrow passage, disturbing a layer of dust. There was a loud thud and the ground trembled. I coughed as the dust swirled around my head.

CHAPTER 11

"JONAS!" BREE'S VOICE sounded muffled.

I caught my breath and raised the lightstone. The wall had closed behind me. I was in a dark, narrow passage.

"On your feet," Flyngard said. "It might be a trap."

My heart quickened. I leapt to my feet and spun around. I clutched my staff and prepared for an attack.

"Jonas!" Elrick called.

"I'm here," I said.

"Where?" Bree said.

I paused. "I'm not really sure."

"The wall closed behind you," Elrick said. "How'd you open it?"

"I don't know." I continued to watch both sides of the dark passage, waiting for something creepy to leap from the shadows. "I was just feeling some claw marks, and it opened."

"What's over there?"

"A narrow passage."

"How far does it go?"

"Hard to say."

"Jonas," Bree said. "Look for a lever or anything that doesn't look natural. Maybe we can open the wall back up."

"All right."

"I'm not sensing anything in here," Flyngard said. "Perhaps it's a secret passage, not a trap."

"Let's hope so." I secured the staff on my back and, using the lightstone as a guide, felt all around the wall for any hidden levers.

"I'm doing my best to look over here." Bree's muffled voice called out. "But it's pretty dark without your lightstone."

"Sorry." A twinge of guilt went through me. I'd left my friends in darkness. "Elrick, can you see okay?"

"Don't worry," Elrick said. "With my new vision it's actually not too bad."

"Speak for yourself," Bree said.

I continued to search the wall, casting frequent glances around me.

When I couldn't find anything obvious right away, I gathered some rubble on the ground and made a mark where I'd fallen in. Better to have a starting place and work my way outward.

My temporary anxiety dwindled away, gradually replaced by frustration as time wore on and I still couldn't find anything. I decided to be more systematic about my search, starting from the top of the wall, feeling every inch of it. I searched the wall from top to bottom, covering several yards in either direction. Nothing felt remotely like a lever, just the irregular, rough surface of a stone wall. It was bad enough being stuck in these dark caves, but it was far worse being separated from my friends.

"Jonas?" Bree called. "You still okay in there?"

"Yeah." I sighed and leaned against the far wall, taking a moment to rest and drink some water.

"We can't find anything," Elrick said.

I paused. "Me neither."

There was a long period of silence. None of us wanted to admit I was trapped in here, and if I was, there were no good solutions.

Finally, Elrick spoke up. "Maybe the passages meet up ahead."

He was grasping at straws and we all knew it. Still, there wasn't much else to be done.

"Yeah," I said. "Mark the place with rocks. We can always trace our way back if we have to."

"Bree already did that," he said. "Let's go forward twenty paces and make contact."

"All right." I gave one last desperate glance at the wall, then sighed and walked twenty paces. "Elrick? Bree?"

"Yes. We hear you." Elrick sounded a bit more muffled. "Twenty more?"

"Okay." I advanced another twenty paces and stopped. "Can you still hear me?"

"Yes." Elrick's voice sounded far away. "Bree says she can barely hear you but it's still pretty clear to me. Twenty more?"

"All right." I headed forward once again.

The narrow passage banked away from the main path. My heart sank. The slim hope that the passages would meet ahead was melting away.

"Elrick?" I called out. "Can you hear me?"

There was an indiscernible muffled voice. I put my ear to the wall and could barely make out Elrick's response. My shoulders sagged. There wasn't much else I could do but continue forward and hope for the best. I shouted for them to continue on, hoping Elrick could hear me, then adjusted my pack and started walking.

The stale air in the passage was laced with a hint of decay. The only sounds were the soft padding of my boots on the dusty ground. I traveled in silence for a long while, but the constant quiet started to get to me.

"Flyngard?" My voice gave a slight echo in the passage.

"Aye," Flyngard said.

"Um, how are you?"

"As good as a warrior trapped in chainmail can be, I suppose."

"Right. I'm sorry about that. I wish I could do something for you."

"You can."

"Oh?"

"Indeed. You can write a song about my tales of valor."

I sighed. "I told you. I'm not writing any more battle songs. At least not for a while."

"But you have a lute now. There's no more excuses. Don't turn your back on the brotherhood of bards."

"Not that again."

"Well, as a bard I should think you'd want camaraderie. Once I saw four bards playing a song together on their lutes, each with unique but complimentary parts. You've never heard such beautiful music."

"Let me guess, it was a battle song."

"Naturally."

"Well, I must admit, that does sound nice. I used to play with a flute player named Wyatt but he never claimed to be a bard. Truth be told, I've only met one other bard in my travels."

"I see," Flyngard said. "And did he scold you for not joining the brotherhood?"

"Never mentioned it. He was a lute maker named Jarret. He ran a shop in Harklenest in the south. I still remember when he came through my town in Callenshore and played in the main square. I was only fourteen at the time, but I'd never heard such amazing sounds. It was like a light from heaven showing me that much larger things were out there, beyond my little fishing village. So, I gathered my belongings and joined him as an apprentice. I worked at his shop for room and board and learned to play."

"It appears we are not so different after all, young Jonas. I left home when I was but a lad. You have an adventurer's heart like mine. Were your parents sad over your departure?"

"I was already on my own by then. They died when I was thirteen. They were part of the guard during a battle that nearly destroyed our town."

"My apologies, son. A rough turn at such a young age. What did you do?"

"Well, there wasn't much left for me other than joining the local fisherman or training with the town guard. Frankly, I couldn't take the smell of fish anymore, and I had no interest in the dangers of the guard. But everything changed when that bard came through town. When he filled the air with the music of his lute, those sounds were a thing of magic. Joining him and leaving town was like finding buried treasure."

"I understand. More than you know. The wanderlust runs deep in my veins as well. And I do love the sound of the lute."

"Yes. Unfortunately not everyone appreciates music. Earning a living as a traveling musician was a lot harder than I expected."

"Well, my cousin Guntram was a leech collector. Count your blessings."

I chuckled. "Yeah, I suppose there are worse things. I guess I imagined the life of a bard to be more carefree. When I left the lute shop four years ago, my head was full of dreams. I played in town squares, celebrations, any place that would have me. Barely earned enough to eat. After two years of disappointment, even fishing started to sound like a good alternative. Then I ran into Elrick. He was performing as a jester in the town square at Corglian Village. We found a great camaraderie as traveling musicians. We joined forces and found that his acrobatics set to my lute playing earned more than we'd ever made on our own. It was still a meager living, but better than before. Of course, when we heard that the castle at Grandelon needed entertainment for the king and his court, we thought it was the opportunity we'd been waiting for. Little did we know."

"A painful lesson learned is a lesson not easily forgotten. And you survived, that's the important thing."

"Yes. And I met Bree in the process. In a way, it makes it all worthwhile."

"Aye. I suppose you'll be composing songs about her from now on."

"Precisely."

"So much for my songs of valor."

There was a faint scratching sound behind me. I spun around, holding the lightstone forward.

"Flyngard?" I whispered. "Did you hear that?"

"Aye," he said. "We're not alone in here."

My chest tightened with anxiety. I lifted the lightstone higher, hoping to see further down the passage.

"Best to keep moving," Flyngard said. "Always move away from the sounds of the unknown."

"I won't argue with that."

I turned back around, and the lightstone revealed a creature waiting in the darkness. A human-like figure with glowing yellow eyes and a featureless face.

Six long, segmented arms spread out from its body like a spider about to envelop its prey.

CHAPTER 12

I FROZE AT THE sight of the spider-like creature. A whip-like tail twitched behind it, a sharp spine marking the tip. Pale gray arms reached for me, the elongated fingers ending in wicked claws.

"Attack!" Flyngard cried.

A moment of shock at the sight of this gruesome creature proved my undoing. Spindly limbs surrounded me before I could reach my staff. Clawed hands grasped my arms, digging in with painful strength.

There was piercing pain at my neck and all my muscles seized. I dropped the lightstone, the white glow disturbing the dusty ground with a soft thump. Flyngard said something but every sound was muted and distant. My vision blurred and a heavy fatigue washed over me.

There was a quick sensation of movement as my body heaved forward. I was vaguely aware of being carried down the cavern and through the narrow tunnel. My body was numb and every-thing was dark.

A calm feeling of detachment washed over me like I was

slipping into a dream. Somewhere, far away, Flyngard was scream-ing at me to wake up.

*   *   *

My eyes blinked open to darkness. A throbbing sensation pulsed at my temples.

"Move slowly," Flyngard said. "Best to let them think you're dying."

I tried to lift my head, but a painful shock flared down my spine and I decided not to move for a while.

"That's the poison trying to take you out," Flyngard said. "Without me, you'd be cold as a winter's night right about now."

"Poison?" My voice came out in a hiss. My mouth was unbear-ably dry. I couldn't swallow. I needed water.

"Yes," Flyngard said. "The cave grabbers have you. Don't be alarmed. There's only three nearby. Dozens more within range but if we're quiet, we won't have to face them all."

My heart dropped. "Three?"

"Yes. Three or four," Flyngard said. "Maybe five. Hard to know for sure. Best to move quietly or they'll rush over and sting you again. My armor is strong but I can't stop everything."

A flash of panic went through me. I looked around, straining to take in my surroundings. A thin shaft of light broke through the ceiling of a large chamber, providing sparse illumination. A series of shallow ledges were hollowed out in the walls of the chamber. Upon closer inspection, I realized I was on one of those ledges, and other shadowy forms lay motionless on ledges nearby.

I rolled to my side, my skin radiating with pain. I winced, trying not to groan. "Why does it hurt everywhere?"

"Cave grabber poison. Very deadly. I protected you from most of it, but these creatures have a bit of magic in them. I could feel my enchantment wavering a little during the attack."

My mind flashed back to dropping the lightstone in the

narrow passage. I searched my pockets and felt the area around me in vain. I'd lost it in the caves.

I eased off the ledge, a prickling sensation spreading up my legs as I got to my feet. My head swam, and I had to hold the wall to steady myself.

"Get down and hold still," Flyngard said. "Movement up ahead."

I crouched low and held my breath. Another cave grabber crawled into the far end of the cave from a narrow tunnel about twenty yards away. The insect-like movements of the strange creature sent a shiver through me. Its yellow eyes were like dim lamps lighting the cave just ahead of it. It crawled up to two other cave grabbers, then all three disappeared through another tunnel.

"There's a stroke of luck," Flyngard said. "The fewer eyes on us the better."

I reached behind me, relieved to find the comforting shape of my staff still strapped to my back. My only thought was getting out of this place as fast as possible. There were at least a dozen dark tunnels leading out of the cave.

"Which way is out?" I said.

"Difficult to say," Flyngard said.

"You didn't notice when they dragged me in here?"

"I got a little turned around. But they definitely brought us higher up into the mountain. The tunnels they dragged us through all led upward."

I sighed. "Fantastic."

The remaining creature made moist, clicking noises at the far end of the cave. It was huddled up against one of the ledges in the wall. My skin crawled at the thought that he might be devouring some other victim like me, poisoned and dragged to this hideous lair. Resolve welled up in me to find an exit, any exit, and go as fast and as far away from this place as I could manage.

I crept forward to the nearest tunnel, keeping my head low.

The narrow passage was too small to walk through. I'd have to crawl my way to freedom.

I looked into the murky blackness of the tunnel. "Well, here goes."

"Wait," Flyngard said. "Put your head in and listen for movement first. You don't want to come face to face with one of those things in there."

I nodded and crawled slowly into the tunnel. I stopped and listened intently, wishing I had Elrick's ears. "I don't hear anything."

"All right then. Onward."

I took a deep breath and crawled forward. The tunnel led downward, deeper into the mountain. The slope was gradual, and I hoped it wouldn't change dramatically and send me into an uncontrolled roll.

The stone was rough to the touch. The surface felt scarred and pitted. Could those creatures have burrowed these tunnels out of solid rock? The thought made me dread another encounter.

"So," I whispered. "What happens if I do run into another one? How do I fight it? Do they have any vulnerable spots?"

"I'm unfamiliar with these creatures. I'd stick with tried and true methods. Go for the eyes."

"I thought you said you'd slain creatures far and wide."

"I have. But mostly on land. In the light of the sun or by the glow of the moon. Where I can see as well as the beast attacking me. These cave creatures can see in the darkness, while we're blind. We're at a great disadvantage."

"And you didn't think this was important to mention before we entered the caves?"

"I was excited for the challenge. Besides, as your fair Bree said, it's the only path to get us there in time. Not to mention good cover from the dragon."

"Well, now I don't know where I am or where my friends are."

The thought of my friends still walking free provided some

comfort. At least they weren't trapped in my situation. As I crept forward, I wondered if I would ever see them again.

I continued on, my progress painfully slow. "I imagine my knees will be a bloody mess after this."

"Doubtful," Flyngard said. "My armor will protect you."

"The chainmail doesn't reach my knees."

"No matter. The enchantment surrounds you."

"Really?"

"Indeed. Just as it shielded you and Elrick from the dragon fire. Your supplies are protected as well."

The thought of being surrounded by magical protection was bewildering. A thought hit me and I reached back. I felt the shell-like curve of the lute still nestled in my pack. Normally I'd credit a wild swing of fortune that it hadn't been smashed. But now I marveled that I was covered by a supernatural enchantment. Although, as I'd just experienced, I wasn't invulnerable. Besides these horrible cave grabbers, there were plenty of things out there that could end my life.

The tunnel suddenly crumbled beneath my hand and I lurched forward. I grabbed a solid portion of the floor to keep from tumbling over. Cold wind washed over me from below.

"What did you do?" Flyngard said.

"Nothing," I hissed. "The tunnel collapsed."

"What's down there? I can't sense anything."

"Darkness," I said. "It's all darkness. Everywhere. I hate these caves."

Faint scratching came from deeper in the tunnel ahead.

My heart pounded in my chest. "Oh no."

"There's one ahead of us," Flyngard said. "Turn back."

"Back to their lair? Where all the corpses lay waiting to get eaten?"

"At least you can stand and fight. You have little chance in this tunnel."

I clenched my teeth. Every decision was horrible. "Fine."

I crept back, away from the collapsed portion of the tunnel, and caught my breath. The narrow width of the tunnel made changing directions difficult and awkward.

The moment I started back up, a scratching sound came from above. I swallowed hard. Another creature was at the other end of the tunnel.

"Do you hear that?" I hissed.

"Aye. Take heart, young Jonas. It's not the first time I've been surrounded. You must fight like a cornered beast. Like a madman. Who knows? You may still live to tell the tale."

I retrieved my staff, the end of it scraping against the stone in the cramped space. I gripped it in both hands and leaned back. My head hit the top of the tunnel and I hissed.

"There's no room to fight in here," I said. "What am I supposed to do?"

"Go for the eyes."

The scratching from above increased in volume. The creature was close. How did it travel so fast in this narrow tunnel? I took several deep breaths, trying to steady myself. I made some practice lunges with the staff. My movements were clumsy and weak. My confidence drained away.

A soft glow came from the tunnel above, moving toward me.

"He's close," Flyngard said. "Get ready."

"I can't do this." My palms were slick with sweat. "It's too cramped in here to fight."

"Confidence, Jonas!" Flyngard's tone took on a gruff edge. "Remember the warrior's chant. Heart of fire. Mind of steel. Will of iron."

The two dim lights of the cave grabber's eyes emerged from the tunnel ahead. He was closing at an alarming rate.

My body shook. "I-I don't know."

"Say it, Jonas!" Flyngard shouted. "Heart of fire. Mind of steel. Will of iron."

"H-Heart of fire," I stuttered.

"Say it! Believe it!"

I gripped the staff. "Heart of fire. Mind of steel. Will of iron."

"Yes! Now strike him down! Slay the beast!"

The dim eyes of the creature were just ahead. Two clawed hands reached for me. I pulled back and drove the staff forward with all my might. The end of the staff exploded with white energy and I felt the pressure of the impact as it penetrated his skull. There was a horrible screeching cry and the cave grabber thrashed violently against the stone walls. A trembling sensation went through the tunnel. The creature gave a hissing sound, then rolled onto its back.

Everything went still. The cave grabber lay there, his segmented limbs still twitching.

"Well done, lad," Flyngard said. "Well done."

I breathed a heavy sigh of relief. I'd actually defeated the gruesome creature. A glimmer of hope rose within me. Maybe I could escape these caves after all.

There was a loud crack, and the floor of the tunnel gave way. A rush of cold wind washed over me as I fell headlong into the darkness below.

CHAPTER 13

THERE WERE FEW things I'd experienced in life that matched the sheer terror of free falling into a dark pit. My limbs flailed, desperate for any handhold to break my rapid descent. All I could think about was a field of stalagmites waiting to greet me.

A dim light shone below. My body rushed toward it. It looked like thin roots covering a light from a deeper chamber. I curled up and braced for the impact.

Thin strands of what felt like sticky cloth wrapped around me, slowing my descent. I broke through the strands and careened helplessly into a wide, open chamber.

Several cracks in the walls allowed sunlight to lance inward, and as I continued my free fall, my eyes began to adjust to the dim light. A network of thin webbing spread across the entire space. There were multiple levels of webs, like a series of irregular blankets spread out to receive me.

The chamber was alive with movement. Dozens, perhaps hundreds, of hairy spiders crawled along the walls and webs in every direction. The spiders were the size of wolves, with a tight grouping of six luminous red eyes that pierced the darkness.

"Mammoth spiders," Flyngard spoke breathlessly. "There's so many. We must be in the nest."

It was like hearing my death sentence. I wanted to yell at him to be quiet but I was too terrified to speak. All I could do was fall helplessly into a new nightmare.

Several layers of webbing tore as I fell through them. They slowed my fall but weren't strong enough to stop me completely.

I could tell that my disruption of the nest was not a welcome one. The spiders grew more agitated by the second. They scurried along the webbing at a frightening pace, an endless swarm of eight-legged monstrosities streaming inward. Luckily, I was falling too fast for them to catch me.

Near the base of the chamber were several layers of webbing that finally stopped my descent. My body came to a stop a few feet off the ground. I lightly bounced on this thick layer, my body partially wrapped in the sticky substance.

"That was fortunate," Flyngard said. "We should move quickly though. They look angry. And hungry."

I struggled to free myself from the webbing, but it held fast. "I'm stuck."

"Hold on. I'll see what I can do."

A building warmth emanated from the chainmail and the webbing began to loosen.

A surge of mammoth spiders poured down from several layers of webbing above me. The sound of their advance was like a rushing stream coming ever closer. Panic spread through me. My breath came in short gasps. They would reach me in seconds.

The webbing around me gave way and I tore my arm free. I struck at my remaining bonds with the staff. Bright currents of white energy shot through the thin lines of webbing. The energy traveled upwards, causing the spiders above to tremble in place.

My body dropped to the floor and I sprang to my feet. A large mound of bones covered the floor a few feet away. It was a mass graveyard for a wide variety of creatures. I winced at the sight of human remains mixed in with the rest.

I shot a desperate glance around me, looking for an escape. "Flyngard. How do I get out of here."

"I sense wind," he said. "There. By the old robe."

Near the base of the hideous pile of bones was a narrow chute covered in dried blood. The chute disappeared into the wall, the entrance half covered by a tattered old robe that lay crumpled on the ground.

There was no time to think about the years of unsavory fluids that had traveled down that chute. At the moment, it was my only escape.

The spiders recovered and continued their advance. Dozens of the hideous things glided down on strands of silk directly overhead.

I sprinted toward the chute, several spiders dropping to the ground just behind me.

I reached the opening as a huge mammoth spider descended on a web right in front of me. Six glowing red eyes stared straight into mine.

A primal scream escaped my lips, and I lashed out with my staff. In a blast of white energy, the spider split in two. A spray of dark liquid hit my face.

"Go!" Flyngard shouted. "Now!"

Without even a glance back at the crawling nightmare behind me, I scrambled into the chute on hands and knees, moving the tattered old robe and stuffing it into the opening behind me. I prayed it would block the spiders long enough for me to get away.

The chute was a narrow tunnel set on a steep, downward angle. The concave base was cold and slick. I crawled my way forward but my hand slipped and I hit the floor face first. My body began to slide, and since there was nothing to grab onto, I plunged into the darkness ahead. I slid on my belly through the narrow tunnel, gaining speed. The smell was an unbearable mix of rot and waste. I suppressed the urge to vomit, holding my breath instead.

My heart beat faster as the chute went on a steeper pitch downward and my slide became precarious. At this speed, there was no way to stop. I only hoped the chute ended in something soft.

A faint light shone ahead. The chute was coming to an end. My muscles tensed, and I covered my head.

The angle of the chute curved into a gradual slope that spat me out into a dimly lit cavernous space with a high ceiling. I rolled onto the dirt floor, colliding with a pile of bones. Several rats scurried away at my sudden arrival.

I lay there for a moment, half covered in bones, trying to collect myself after the horrible events I'd just experienced. I had no frame of reference to compare what I'd just been through with anything else in my life. It was like having the worst tavern tales come to life all around me.

Rats squeaked nearby, probably wondering if I was close enough to death to provide their next meal. Countless bugs crawled among the bones and decay around me.

I breathed a sigh of relief that I was still alive, and immediately regretted it. The stench of rotting carcass filled the air. I staggered to my feet, only to double over and throw up.

"I'm guessing it doesn't smell very pleasant in here," Flyngard said.

"I can't breathe." I coughed. "I have to get out of here."

I stumbled across the terrain of death lined with bones and filth, eager for a breath of normal air. The cavernous room was lit with the soft glow of rocks embedded in the walls. They were rough lightstones, scattered sporadically along the walls and ceiling.

The vaulted space seemed large enough to hold a castle. I

quickly moved past the remains of unfortunate travelers the caves had consumed through the years, heading further into the expansive chamber.

Soon I was able to take deeper breaths, grateful that the stench grew less pervasive the further I traveled into the cave. I retrieved the water skin from my pack and took a long drink.

"Such a large cave," Flyngard said. "I wonder if it's a natural occurrence or if some giant creature dug it out for their den. It's large enough for a dragon."

A shiver went through me. "Oh, thanks for that thought."

"I'm merely pointing out possibilities."

Toward the far end of the space, the lightstones in the walls gave off a subtle illumination. Thankfully, there were no giant shapes in sight that could pass for a sleeping dragon. The only landmarks were three huge boulders by the far wall. The sight of a high, arched doorway between the boulders sent a thrill through me.

"A way out." I jogged toward the doorway, eager to get as far away from bones and spiders as I could.

"Or is it a way in," Flyngard said.

"What?"

"Well, you assume it's a door leading out of the mountain. What if it just leads further in? Do you even know which direction you're headed?"

"No idea. But if those spiders come flooding down that chute after me, I don't want to be in here."

As I drew closer, I could tell the doorway was closed by a gray door made of rough stone. There were no knobs or handles that I could see. Maybe it wasn't a door at all but a sealing off from the only way out.

There was a deep grating sound like stone sliding against stone. The floor trembled and one of the three large boulders near the door moved. The boulder seemed to be splitting apart. I stopped, bewildered at the sight.

The other two boulders trembled and followed the same strange movement.

The shape of the first boulder shifted and slowly took the form of something I recognized. A man. A rough, misshapen statue come to life. My eyes didn't want to accept the sight before me. I blinked several times, hoping the whole, terrible vision would go away.

The rock giant turned, his blocky head angling down toward me. His limbs and features were jagged and coarse. It was like the early stage of a sculptor's work before his chisel really got down to the task. Glowing red bands of energy encircled his neck and wrists like mystical jewelry.

The giant leaned forward until his head was only a few feet above me. A shiver went through me at the immensity of the creature. Its head was the size of a small cottage. I trembled as I met his gaze. His deep eye sockets housed dark purple stones with speckles of white that resembled a night sky.

"Run, Jonas!" Flyngard shouted. "Run for your life!"

I couldn't move. All I could do was stare helplessly into those giant, starry eyes.

CHAPTER 14

THERE WAS A sharp pinch at my back and a heavy pressure on my shoulders. I grunted as the air left my body and I was lifted upward. My clothes tightened against my chest and my limbs flailed helplessly. The stone giant held me pinched between his rough fingers as he stood to his full height. He had to be almost as tall as the castle walls back in Grandelon.

"You were a good soul, Jonas," Flyngard said. "It was a pleasure knowing you."

"What is it?" A deep, booming voice spoke from above. It had an inhuman quality, like heavy stone sliding over earth.

"A man, I think." The giant that held me spoke. His resonant voice made my teeth tremble.

The three stone giants leaned closer, their monstrous heads looming over me.

"It's a horse." The third giant spoke with a voice a bit higher and more gravelly than the others.

"Horse? Guntrick you mud head, this is a man." The giant lifted his hand higher as if to showcase me to the others.

Guntrick squinted and shook his head. "Nah, that's a horse."

"Brindel," the first giant said. "Tell him it's a man."

Brindel grunted and sat down, making the ground tremble. "I don't care what it is. Throw it back to the spiders. I was taking a nap."

"You're always taking a nap."

"I'm meant to be still. That's my nature. And, in case you forgot, Migmulk, it's your nature as well."

"One part of my nature." Migmulk lifted one of his fingers, the size of a tree trunk. "I'm still a defender at heart."

Brindel let out a laugh that resembled a small earthquake. "Ancient history. Sit down and accept your fate."

"As long as we're up, I'm hungry." Guntrick leaned closer to me. "Should we cook him or just eat raw today?"

"Just throw him in your mouth and go back to sleep already," Brindel said.

To my horror, Guntrick opened his mouth and moved toward me. I closed my eyes and tightened into a ball.

Suddenly, I was yanked through the air, my body swinging with the momentum.

"No." Migmulk wagged his finger. "I want to talk to him first. It's been so long. I want to hear about what's happening in the world."

"This cave is your world," Brindel curled up against the wall, reverting back to his boulder shape. "Accept it."

Migmulk opened his other hand and dropped me onto it. He held me at eye level.

"Tell me little one," he said. "Who are you?"

For a moment, I couldn't talk. I tried but only groaned and started coughing. So much adrenaline and panic had surged through me over the last hour, I couldn't think straight.

"See?" Guntrick said. "It can't talk. It's a horse. Shake it. Maybe it will whinny."

"Speak up," Flyngard said. "Quick."

"I'm Jonas." I blurted out before he could shake me to death. "I'm just a bard. Please let me go."

"A bard?" Migmulk's rocky brow rose with a grating sound. "You mean, you make music?"

I nodded.

Migmulk leaned closer, narrowing his eyes. "What kind of music?"

"I play the lute." I retrieved the lute from my pack and held it forward.

Migmulk let out a long breath which knocked me over. "Music… Great mountains, I haven't heard music for so many long years."

"What about my rock smashing?" Guntrick said. "You said I had natural rhythm."

"Oh, you do, Guntrick, you do." Migmulk nodded. "But your singing is… well…"

Guntrick folded his arms. "Well, no one else will sing. It's better than the constant clatter of bones down the spider chute."

"Would you two shut up," Brindel said. "I'm trying to sleep."

I stood back up and readied my lute. "Would you like me to play a song for you?"

Migmulk gasped. "Really?"

"Sure. If you promise not to eat me."

Migmulk's mouth contorted into a crooked smile. "Deal."

"Aw." Guntrick frowned. "But I'm hungry."

Migmulk waved him off. "Can you play something slow? I like slow songs. Something about the hills and the trees. Or maybe the mountains."

Guntrick tore two rocks off the wall, sending a shower of fragments over Brindel.

"Hey." Brindel glared at him.

"Sorry." Guntrick held up the rocks. "I can join in with rhythm."

Migmulk shook his head. "Not yet. Let's hear his song first."

An old nature song called Wind Path came to mind. I thought it would be fitting. I closed my eyes to keep my mind off the fact that I was standing on a giant hand lifted dangerously high in the air. Hopefully he didn't forget about me and start clapping to the music. I started in on a slow plucking pattern, pleasantly surprised at the natural acoustics in the cave.

"Whoa, whoa." Migmulk held up his other hand. "What's the hurry little bard man?"

I stopped playing. "What do you mean?"

"You're playing so fast. I told you, I like slow songs."

"Me too," Guntrick said. "Stop rushing it."

Since Wind Path was one of the slower songs in my repertoire, I decided to play it again at half speed. I began a much slower progression of notes.

"Nope. Nope." Migmulk shook his head. "Better, but still much too fast."

"Maybe he's scared of us," Guntrick said. "His fingers are probably trembling with fear."

"Is that it?" Migmulk said. "Are you frightened little bard?"

"No." Actually, I was terrified. "Let me try again."

If they wanted slow, I could easily deliver. I plucked the first note and let it ring out. It echoed through the empty room and I waited until all traces of it had faded into silence. Migmulk closed his eyes and breathed deeply. I plucked the next note and let it resonate through the chamber. Migmulk kept his eyes closed, his crooked smile broadening.

I continued through many more notes, singing a few, select lyrics, holding each word as long as my breath would allow. By the time I was halfway through the song, I could've played the whole piece at normal tempo about twenty times over. I decided that would be a great place to stop, so I plucked several strings at once for a grand finish and took a bow.

Migmulk kept his eyes closed for so long, I began to wonder if he'd fallen back to sleep.

He finally opened his eyes and nodded. "Music… How I've missed it."

"Me too," Guntrick said. "Play another."

The ground shook as Brindel stood to his feet. Water fell from his deep eye sockets and flowed through the cracks in his rocky face like mountain streams. "I'd forgotten how beautiful it could be."

"Nicely done," Flyngard said. "Play more. They won't kill you if they like your music."

"This is a glorious day," Migmulk said. "Don't worry little bard. You can stay with us. We'll keep you safe from the spiders and I won't let Guntrick eat you or step on you like our last friend."

"Hey, that was an accident." Guntrick motioned to a crushed skeleton on the ground next to a makeshift shelter. "I liked little Curat. He was good-natured for a goblin."

A chill went through me at the sight of the crushed goblin. As relieved as I was that my music had turned my situation from afternoon snack to musical pet, things were still going horribly wrong. I had to talk fast before they turned me into their song bird, forced to play the slowest songs in history, only to end up trampled under their monstrous feet.

"Um," I stammered. "Listen, there's far more music beyond this mountain. Better music. Imagine a town square filled with musicians. Harps, flutes, booming drums and crashing cymbals. Not to mention choirs of singers, their voices soaring in three part harmonies. My music pales in comparison to sounds like that."

Migmulk frowned, his head bowing low. Brindel sat back down with a thunderous impact. My musical sales pitch wasn't going well.

"If only." Migmulk sighed. "We once walked the world outside as you do, little bard. But now… now we live here."

Guntrick let out a heavy sigh. "Forever. Forever in this cave."

"Why don't you leave?" I said.

Migmulk chuckled. "Perhaps one day we shall walk freely through Ashrellan once more. For now, this is our home. But, all things considered, it's not so bad."

"Speak for yourself," Brindel said.

Migmulk waved him off. "It could be worse. I mean, there's plenty of cave creatures for food. We get to smash spiders when they get too close. And this cave is big enough for us to move around in."

"Yeah," Guntrick said. "And I've invented one hundred and twenty four games using old bones. I can teach them to you."

"And half of them aren't bad," Migmulk said. "Maybe you can sing for us while we play."

I swallowed hard. My nightmare of being kept as some kind of musical pet was starting to materialize.

"Oh, I can't stay," I said. "My friends need me. The whole town of Calladia is counting on me. I have to warn them. They're about to be overrun by soldiers."

"Another battle, another war." Migmulk shook his head. "Always another war. Even if you could help, they'll just end up fighting again. Besides, you're a bard. What can you do to stop a war?"

"Tell them you're a great warrior," Flyngard said. "With me at your side, it's not really a deception."

I cleared my throat to delay my response. How could I possibly convince them I was any kind of warrior? I decided to walk the tightrope between truth and extreme exaggeration. "I'm part of a fighting team. Yes, I'm a bard but I'm also a warrior powered by strong magic. I fight with a mighty lycan and a great illusionist. Together we have conquered enemies and delivered the oppressed. If I don't rejoin my companions, our fighting strength will be broken and the battle will be lost."

"Well said," Flyngard said. "If I could, I would clap right now."

Migmulk shared a stoic glance with Guntrick. Perhaps I had broken through. Suddenly, they burst out laughing.

"Wondrous words, little bard," Migmulk said. "I love a good tale."

"Me too," Guntrick said. "Tell another one. Put it to song."

"No, really," I pleaded. "If I don't go, King Mulraith will use his army to lay waste to all of Calladia.

"Mulraith?" The rocks on Migmulk's face crowded in tightly around his eyes. "He is the foul sorcerer that bound us to this cave with a curse."

"And his master," Guntrick said. "The dark sorcerer Rastvane. They put us here. Oh, how I wish I had smashed them when I had the chance."

"Rastvane!" Flyngard cried. "Enemy of all living things! Cursed be his name!"

My mind spun. "Mulraith put you in here?"

"Indeed," Migmulk said. "Forty years ago during the great battle of Iron Hawk Kingdom. We were defenders of Iron Hawk, the stronghold in the Gray River Mountain. We fought against the sorcerer Rastvane, but were defeated. No castle could imprison us, so he cursed us to live out our days in the bottom of this mountain. He forged our bonds with the help of his apprentice Mulraith."

"Great devilry," Flyngard exclaimed. "Rastvane infected another with his vile sorcery."

I paused. "So, Mulraith was Rastvane's apprentice?"

"Yes." Migmulk said. "What do you know of him?"

"He's a tyrant. All of Grandelon is under his oppressive rule. And now he seeks to conquer Calladia and expand his power."

A dark rumble emanated from Migmulk's chest. "Yes. He is a serpent of deception and dark magic. I would stop him if I had the chance. He cursed us with the help of his master Rastvane. We awoke in this cave with these bonds." Migmulk motioned to the red energy encircling his wrist. "Whenever we tried to leave, the bonds caused terrible pain and we fell asleep for many days. After awhile we stopped trying."

Even though my chest still felt light with fear of these giants, it was hard not to feel sorry for them. I couldn't imagine a lifetime stuck in this cave.

"I'm sorry." I said. "I wish there was something I could do."

"Maybe we can," Flyngard said.

"What?" I mumbled, under my breath.

"Well," Flyngard said. "Rastvane and Mulraith used their sorcery to place the curse on them. The same sorcery that enchanted the chainmail you wear. Similar threads of magic can often be undone when pitted against each other. Perhaps it will work in like manner to loose their bonds."

"Perhaps?" I whispered. "Or perhaps it will kill me. I don't know how any of this works."

"What's that?" Migmulk leaned closer. "Did you say something little bard?"

"Oh." I shrugged. "I was just talking to myself."

The rocks crowded together around Migmulk's eyes. "Been down in these caves a while, have you?"

"No, it's not that." I shook my head.

"Tell him about your enchantment," Flyngard said. "If you break their bonds, maybe he'll let you go free."

Once again, I had no good options. Either stay trapped with the giants as their musical pet, or risk the searing pain of tampering with a sorcerer's curse that would most likely end in death. After all, if it knocked stone giants out for days when they tried to beat it, what would it do to me? Still, if there was a chance to see Bree again, it was worth the risk.

"I think I can help you," I said.

"Yes," Migmulk said. "Another song will help pass the time."

"No, I mean I can help break your curse. I have an enchantment that could free you."

Migmulk looked at Guntrick and chuckled. "He's telling more stories. Isn't he delightful?"

Guntrick nodded. "But he has to sing it this time. All right little bard? Sing your tale."

"It's not a tale," I said. "I think I can free you. But if I do, you have to let me go. You have to help me get out of these caves."

Migmulk smirked. "You actually think you can free us?"

"Yes," I tried to sound confident. "I have an enchantment that can break those bonds and free you. But you must let me go in return."

"So you're a bard, a warrior, and a wizard?" Migmulk said. "Is that what you're telling us?"

"Well," I said. "Why don't I just show you. Bring your other wrist close to me. I need to be close to the magic."

"He's quite the entertainer, isn't he?" Guntrick said.

Migmulk shrugged and placed his other wrist beside the open hand I was standing on. The red energy surrounding his wrist was like a wall, surging and glowing with untold strength.

"What now?" I whispered.

"Difficult to say," Flyngard said. "Maybe touch it?"

I gritted my teeth. "I thought you knew how to break the curse."

"I said perhaps. As in, perhaps we can undo it. I didn't say I was certain, and I never said I knew how."

"Great. Thanks for the help."

"He's talking to himself again," Guntrick said.

"It's the caves." Migmulk nodded. "It does that to people."

My path was set and I was out of ideas. I figured I might as well play my part confidently. With any luck, I wouldn't die a painful death.

"All right." I took a deep breath. "And now, I will break the curse."

"Carry on, little bard."

I squared my shoulders and strode forward until I was face to face with the glowing red magic. It was so bright I could barely keep my eyes open. The energy pulsed outward, sending waves of heat over my skin.

"Nice knowing you, Flyngard," I whispered.

"And you as well, Jonas. We had a good run."

I closed my eyes and walked directly into the red energy. There was a bright flash of light and a tremendous sensation of power poured through me. My skin burned like I'd been hurled into a furnace. There was something like an explosion, and I was vaguely aware of being thrown backward as my mind slipped from consciousness.

CHAPTER 15

MY EYES BLINKED open. A small shelter came into focus. I was lying on my back, and my skin tingled all over. I turned onto my side to discover the crushed skeleton of a goblin next to me. I screamed and leapt to my feet.

"Easy," Flyngard said. "It's just a skeleton."

"A crushed skeleton," I said. "Not something I want to wake up next to."

"He's awake." A booming voice said.

Migmulk's colossal head leaned over from above. It was like watching a mountain about to fall on me.

"Feeling better?" Migmulk said.

"I'm fine." I didn't want to mention my tingling skin and the headache throbbing at my temples. Better to keep the illusion of strength if it would help me escape.

"Look, little bard." Migmulk kneeled and laid his massive wrists on the ground at either side of me like the walls of a house. "They're gone. The bonds are gone! You did it. I'm free!"

I was speechless. It actually worked. And I was still alive. "They're gone." I said breathlessly.

"Don't act surprised," Flyngard said. "You're supposed to be some kind of enchanted warrior, remember?"

"I mean, of course they're gone." I straightened and cleared my throat. "Didn't I tell you I could remove them?"

"Indeed you did," Migmulk smiled. "I just... I dared not believe it was possible. I am in your debt."

"Yes, well, just show me the right path out of these mountains and we'll call it even."

The ground shook as Guntrick and Brindel knelt on the floor next to Migmulk.

"What about me?" Guntrick displayed the glowing red bonds on his wrist.

"And me?" Brindel said.

I sighed. I wasn't looking forward to another burning punch in the face from those red bracelets of death. My headache was already pretty bad. I couldn't imagine a threefold increase.

"Okay," I swallowed hard. "Who's next?"

Another two wallops of the red energy was enough to last me a lifetime. When I awoke from the third experience which freed Brindel, I went right back to sleep for three hours straight. At least, that was Flyngard's best guess. Tracking time in dark caves was a tricky endeavor.

My head felt like it was full of syrup. I tried to sit up, but the room wouldn't stop spinning. So, I lay back down and slept for another hour.

When I finally awoke again, I felt much better. I still had the lingering headache but most of the pain had passed.

"How do you feel?" Flyngard said.

"Well, I'm alive," I said. "My body feels like I was thrown against a stone wall, but I'm still breathing."

"And that is all a warrior can hope for."

"Look," Migmulk said. "The bard wizard is awake."

The ground shook as all three rock giants knelt down, their huge heads looming over me.

"We are free, little bard," Migmulk said. "You've done it!"

"Thank you!" Brindel said. "I thought this day would never come."

"Let's celebrate," Guntrick said. "We can put the bard wizard on our shoulders and dance around. Or we can throw him in the air. Won't that be fun, little man?"

I put my hands up. "No! Please! I'd love to stay but I must leave. War is on the horizon. I need to get to Calladia before it's too late."

"Ah, yes," Migmulk said. "The warrior wizard bard is needed. I understand, little one. I doubted your importance to the cause but now I see what you are capable of. Go, with our blessings. May you strike down Mulraith with your powerful magic."

Migmulk pounded on the wall nearby and the stone doorway opened, revealing a long tunnel that led upward. "This passage will see you safely to the forest. Beyond are the Foothills of Kroth that lead to Calladia."

"Ah, Kroth!" Flyngard said. "Great heavens, my childhood home at long last. I miss it so."

"Thank you," I gave a courteous bow to the giants. "Enjoy your freedom. I wish you the best."

"Thank you, little bard. Here is a gift to light your way." The giant opened his hand. A rough lightstone the size of my fist lay on his stone palm.

I took it and gave a slight bow. "Thank you." I smiled and strode toward the doorway, my steps feeling lighter than they had in days. When I reached the entrance, I noticed that the size of the passage would only accommodate someone about my size.

I turned back to the giants. "Wait. How will you leave this place?"

Migmulk grinned. "We travel through stone and earth. We have no need of tunnels."

At that moment, I was incredibly glad to be on their side. "Well, good luck on your journey."

"And you on yours."

The three giants turned toward me and bowed. The odd sight filled me with a sense of wonder. The width and breadth of creation was a testament to the power and beauty wielded by the Eternal One. At times like this I marveled that I was a part of it all.

I waved to the giants and headed down the passage.

The tunnel was a perfectly-hewn path leading steadily upward. This was no natural occurrence, but an ancient passage forged in another time. Perhaps there had been a race of cave dwellers with some grand castle under the mountain that had long since crumbled. One thing I was certain of, if I were a king, I'd never build a castle next door to a hive of giant spiders.

"I must say," Flyngard said. "Your exploits in those caves were a worthy adventure."

I laughed. "By worthy do you mean I almost died about ten times?"

"That is only one part. The greater parts are courage and determination. Not to mention having a keen mind against adversaries, and choosing a clever path. Perhaps you can compose a tune about it."

"Seems a little prideful."

"In that case, I have many adventures of my own. After you write your love ballad to Bree, you would do well to compose a song about my exploits."

"Is that so?"

"Aye. What kind of tale serves the playing of the lute? Ascending the cliffs of Karcargaron? Crushing the mind control nomads of Drahkk? Taming a mountain serpent? Slaying the–"

"Hold on. There's mind control nomads in our land?"

"Not anymore."

I shook my head. "I can't imagine a life like yours. How are you still alive?"

"By the grace of the Eternal One. And I must give credit to my fighting companions. For many years I was part of the Circle of Five."

"What's that?"

"You've never heard of us?"

"No. Sorry."

"Pity. Our deeds were legendary. We were five brave adventurers, several from my home town of Kroth. I was their captain. We had many notable adventures together. But we also saw calamity. Toros, the axe-wielder, lost an arm and nearly died. Cravatak was blinded by the serpent king. Fetriss disappeared after the explosion in the faerie wood. And Grunsel, alas, Grunsel just lost heart after awhile. I suppose he sought the quiet life."

"Sounds like it didn't end well."

"Oh, I wouldn't say that. We had many days of victory and success. We stamped out great villainy and saved countless innocents. What more can you hope for?"

I nodded.

"And now I fight with you," he said. "And we've already overcome much. Tell me, are you feeling your full strength again?"

My headache was ebbing, but there was still an uncomfortable pressure at my temples, and my skin felt like I had a bad sunburn. But I imagined someone like Flyngard didn't want to hear petty complaints.

"Nearly," I said. "I'm not perfect but I'm getting there."

"As am I," Flyngard said. "I've been through a gauntlet of my own. But we live to tell the tale. That is what matters."

"Wait. My contact with the magic affected you too? Can you feel pain?"

"Oh, not in the way you do. It's more like being thrown deep into a dark forest and having to find your way back home. Except the forest is made of angry ghosts and your only weapon is an iron will. It's a bit hard to explain."

"That sounds awful."

"Perhaps at first. You get used to it. It's just another challenge to overcome. A chance to grow stronger. Not many warriors can say they've done battle against both a physical and a magical realm and triumphed, now can they?"

"I should think not." I paused. "How do you keep going?"

"Because there is no other way."

"Well, perhaps not. I don't know, if I was trapped in chainmail, struggling in some strange magical realm, I think I'd be tempted to give up."

"Ah, that is not the warrior's code. Heart of fire, Mind of steel—"

"Yes, yes, I know the chant. I'm just saying, there comes a point, at least for me, where it's just too much. Don't you ever feel that way?"

"Aye, but that is where death lives. When I die, I want to leave this world with fire in my heart and a sword in my hand. I want to grab the villain by the throat and drag him with me as I fall into the pit. To me, any other way would make life a path of despair."

"I suppose… Maybe I'm just not a warrior at heart."

"Then the real question for you, young Jonas, is where does your heart lie? Where do you imagine your heart to be at peace?"

I thought for several moments. "Well, honestly I wouldn't mind just living in some cottage on a hill, surrounded by pines, with Bree at my side… That probably sounds pretty dull to you."

"Not at all. The quiet life is the restful dream many warriors seek when war has passed. Putting down roots, raising a family. A noble pursuit. But there's a time for all things. And now is not the time of rest. We are in precarious days. And if we do not use our abilities and act to stop the tide of evil, there will be no quiet life for us or those we care about."

"Yes, I suppose you're right."

I continued forward on the smooth upward passage for about an hour. Flyngard recounted several tales of valor that he and his Circle of Five warriors had experienced. I had to admit, many of the stories would have made great songs. To pass the time, I took mental notes of the tales and toyed with rhyming phrases.

The passage ahead darkened, looking like a dead end. The sight worried me. What if the tunnel had collapsed? After all, when was the last time it had been used?

"Flyngard," I said. "We may have a problem."

"Aye," he said. "I sense it."

As I drew close, the lightstone revealed what I had feared. The passage ended in a wall of stone.

CHAPTER 16

THE ABRUPT ENDING of the passage didn't seem natural. There wasn't a mound of rubble as if the ceiling had collapsed, or signs of erosion from ages past. The blockage was a smooth wall fashioned to look just like the rest of the tunnel.

"Jonas," Flyngard said. "This is not a dead end but a door. I believe a forest lies just beyond."

My heart leapt at his words. I felt all around the stone, hoping to find a lever of some kind. I adjusted my footing and felt something click under my heel. There was a grating sound and the door began to move.

The dusky, pastel tones of twilight shone through as the stone door slid open. The edge of a lush forest grew thick around the doorway. Fresh, cool air poured into the passage bringing with it the scent of pine. The treetops were framed with a muddy orange glow, as the last moments of sunlight slipped away.

I breathed deeply, a thrill of excitement washing over me. "We made it… I've never been so happy to see the sky. Or breathe fresh air."

"This is a glorious moment," Flyngard said. "Store it in your memories. Think back on it when times are difficult."

The doorway was perched on a narrow ledge about forty feet above the forest floor. The rocky ledge sloped at a sharp incline into the forest. Trees grew along the mountain on either side of me. I stepped onto the ledge and the stone door slid closed behind me. The edges of the door blended so well with the rock around it, I doubted I could ever spot it from a distance.

I scanned the mountainside for any sign of life. "I wonder if Bree and Elrick made it out."

"Either way, you owe it to them to press on," Flyngard said. "The goal was not to reunite, but to warn Calladia of the upcoming battle. With any luck, they're already on their way."

"I hope so." I put the lightstone in my pocket and picked my way down the ledge.

It was steep going, and the earth was loose. I nearly lost my footing several times before making it to the forest floor.

When I finally landed on solid ground, I had to sit for a while and rest. I was in a small clearing in a thickly wooded area that surrounded the mountainside. The dwindling light of dusk was muted even further by the canopy of branches overhead. I leaned against a tree and breathed deeply.

Since I needed to rest anyway, I retrieved my lute and started plucking out some of the initial ideas I'd had for my love ballad. The resonant tones of the strings drifted into the forest like some strange bird from another land.

"What am I listening to?" Flyngard said.

"It's my love song for Bree." I said.

"Nay. There is no love in that song."

"Well, I've only plucked a few chords."

"Yes, but you plucked with a reckless hand. You have to gently coax the notes of a love song."

"Oh? So you're a musician now?"

"I certainly know a love song when I hear one."

"Well, my love for Bree is deep and enduring. The song needs a strong hand."

"I beg to differ. Love is delicate and must be handled with care. You must present your words as a gift to your fair maiden. Poetry softly spoken tells her you are gentle and kind. A strong strum is a wild horse that can't be trusted to carry one safely on a journey. Especially the difficult journey of love."

I frowned. "Are you saying I don't know how to love or I don't know how to write a song?"

"At the moment, I fear both are deficient."

"Well, maybe you don't know what you're talking about. I'm the bard after all. You're a warrior. So why don't you stick to fighting, and I'll handle the song writing, deal?"

"I'm merely trying to help. Perhaps it's lacking words. Have you poetry to accompany the tune?"

"Yes. Sort of. I'm still working on that."

"Well, out with it then. Let's hear your song of the heart."

"No. It's not ready."

"Come now. You may confide in me. I'm something of a poet myself, you know. At least I was in my youth. I can help you compose. And if your lyrics are dreadful, it's not like I could tell anyone about it."

"All right, fine. Here goes." I cleared my throat. "Her eyes sparkle like sapphire gems in the night, her hair shines like a—"

"Stop. This just won't do."

"Hey, I barely started."

"There's simply no mood," he said. "You must establish a mood. A story. Something to give it breath before you launch right into her eyes and hair and the like."

"You know what? Forget it. I'm sorry I even told you."

"Oh, don't be so tender. I can help. Tell me, where did you first meet her?"

"At The Slaughtered Boar."

"Doesn't really lend itself to a love ballad."

"Well, that's where I met her."

"And what was it like when you first met?"

A memory of Bree in the warm firelight of the tavern filled my mind. "She took my breath away. I could barely speak. And she was so kind to everyone in the tavern. Even the drunken fools. And she had this strength about her, like something of magic. Like she was gliding through the place and nothing could touch her."

"Ah. Now that's poetry. Add a bit of rhyme and you're on your way."

"You think?"

"Of course. That's how I wrote about Serenia. The fair maiden in Kroth I am betrothed to."

"Wait. You're betrothed?"

"Aye. She has the face of an angel and the fighting spirit of a badger. The thought of seeing her again is what stokes the fire within me to carry on. Even through years of hanging on the back of a rotting troll, or stuck in a dragon's lair on the burnt corpse of my last armor-bearer. When I see Serenia again, it will all be worthwhile."

I couldn't imagine getting to the point where I was betrothed to Bree only to end up imprisoned for years in chainmail, unable to see her or even let her know I was all right. My eyes teared up at the thought.

"She must be quite a woman," I said.

"That she is, lad."

"Did she know you left to fight sorcerer Rastvane?"

"Aye. The morning I set off for Dragontooth Mountains is the last time I saw her face."

I paused. "Flyngard, it's been a long time. Don't you think she may have… I mean, chances are–"

"I know what you're thinking, young squire," Flyngard said.

"Perhaps my Serenia has taken me for dead. Perhaps she's moved on to another suitor."

"Well, five years is a long time."

"Aye, Jonas," he said. "But my Serenia waits for me. Our love is stronger than dragon scales. It would take more than a sorcerer's spell to break it."

I nodded. "I hope one day I can reach that point with Bree."

"Indeed. The kind of love deserving of poetry."

"I wouldn't imagine you a poet."

"Fighting is not my whole life. Perhaps I didn't have the skill to put voice or lute to my prose, but I wrote straight from my heart."

"Well, in that case, let's hear some."

"Oh, you wouldn't care for my poems. They're rough words from the tongue of a fighter."

"Hey, I told you my lyrics. It's your turn."

Flyngard was quiet for a moment. "Well, all right. I did write one poem I was rather fond of. Although, I crafted the words on the last journey before my enchantment, so I never got to tell her."

"That's terrible."

"Isn't it though? Anyway, it goes like this… I've seen the gold mantle of sunrise on the mount, the great oaks of Havenshore with green as deep as time, the endless blue of the Trenarrian sea, but none, my love, none compares with one glance from you. One touch of your hand. One word from your lips. There is no palace so grand, no journey so glorious, no victory so sweet as my love for you. You, my love, are the greatest adventure."

I let out a long breath. "Great heavens, Flyngard. That was… surprising."

"Don't tease me, knave. These are heartfelt words."

"No, on my honor. That was beautiful."

"Oh. Well, many thanks. It's a touch flowery, I admit."

"And you told me not to write a love ballad? Who are you trying to fool?"

"I don't speak these words to just anyone. It's not the common tongue of a warrior."

"Well, that's one poem I wouldn't mind putting some music to."

"You jest."

"No, really. I think it would flow well with the song I'm working on."

"Well then, by all means, compose away."

I played the lute a while longer, weaving the words of Flyngard's poem with the notes of my song. By the time my legs were rested, I was quite pleased with it. Even though I'd spent little time composing the tune, I could tell it had something special. Sometimes the songs that came easily were the ones that endured.

I played it through again, this time softer, and sang the words of Flyngard's poem as I remembered it. He corrected me here and there until I had it right.

"Well?" I said. "What do you think?"

"I must admit," Flyngard said. "It's quite a moving little tune. At least, for a love ballad. Does this mean we can work on songs of battle now?"

"Perhaps."

The last remnants of sunlight gave way to night. A soft breeze flowed around me, filled with the scent of wildflowers. I took a deep breath and felt my body relax. The chatter of birds and the occasional rustling of squirrels nearby were a welcome break from the muffled silence of the caves. I leaned against the tree trunk and closed my eyes, basking in the rich sounds of life all around me.

* * *

The screech of a bird roused me from sleep. The forest was a good deal darker than when I had closed my eyes.

"Flyngard?" I said.

"Aye." Flyngard yawned. "How long have we been asleep?"

"I was about to ask you the same question."

"Judging from the depth of night in the forest, I'd say a couple hours."

"I didn't mean to fall asleep," I said. "You should've woken me up."

"I figured you needed the rest after our harrowing journey through the caves. As did I. Once you fell asleep, I thought my spirit could use a rest as well."

A dark gray murkiness lay heavily among the thick woods ahead. The sounds of life were far less pleasant than before. The bright chirping of birds and curious squirrels were now replaced by howling in the distance and the ominous hooting of owls.

I staggered to my feet, collecting my things. "That forest certainly doesn't look inviting."

"It looks okay to me," Flyngard said.

"Yes, I'm sure it's easier to be brave when you can't bleed."

"Mind thy tongue, knave," Flyngard said. "When I could take breath into my lungs I would march willingly through any forest or against any foe. I left more than my share of blood on the battlefield."

"Okay, fine, you're very brave," I said. "Forgive me if I don't get a thrill out of dangerous situations."

"Very well," Flyngard said. "Your cowardice is forgiven."

I sighed. "Maybe you should take another nap."

I marched forward, trying not to think about all the creatures that could leap out at me from the shadows.

There were no paths to be found through the forest, and travel soon became difficult. The thick tree roots and the lack of light made it easy to take a tumble face first onto the ground. I retrieved the lightstone from my pocket once again, grateful for the parting gift from the giants.

I lifted the stone high, unable to see a clear way out of the forest. The trees spread out endlessly in all directions.

"Um, Flyngard?" I said. "I don't really know which way to go."

"A warrior learns to sense his way," Flyngard said. "The instinct of a survivor."

"Thank you. Not at all helpful right now."

"Fine. Do you see any paths?"

"No."

"What about a river? Or even a stream?"

"Neither."

"Then seek guidance from the Eternal One and keep walking."

"Right." I headed forward, sending a silent prayer for help to the heavens.

After a few hours of traveling through the dark forest, I hadn't found any paths or streams or discovered a sense for which direction to go in. The luminous glow from the lightstone made me feel exposed, like I was announcing my approach to any beast of the forest looking for a late night snack.

"Flyngard," I said. "This isn't going well."

"Really? No creatures of the night have attacked and we're making good progress through the forest. Seems like it's going pretty well to me."

"Yes, nothing's attacked me yet. But I've got a nagging feeling something's watching me. And for all I know, I'm walking deeper into the forest."

"You're being paranoid. Do you know how many forests I've traveled through at night?"

"Let me guess. Five hundred? And they were all filled with trolls and you slew a thousand of them with your eyes closed, right?"

"Are you suggesting I exaggerate my exploits?"

"Don't you? Every knight I ever knew did."

"Most certainly not. A noble warrior weighs his words carefully."

I let out an exasperated sigh. "Well, I'm not used to all this. I'm lost, it's dark, and who knows what creatures lie in wait for me."

"I suppose you wish you were in your cottage on the forest hill with Bree."

"Yes, a far better alternative."

"One day, Jonas. Use that thought as your guiding star. Something to make the quest worth completing. Then perhaps you will enter the quiet life you dream of."

I nodded. "I might just do that. After all your adventures, that probably sounds dull to you. Maybe the quiet life was never in your thoughts."

"That's where you're mistaken. I fight for all good people, yes, but I fight most for Serenia, my betrothed. And one day, when I break this enchantment, I shall return to her and we shall live the quiet life together. Perhaps I will build my cottage on the hill next to yours, aye?"

I chuckled. "That would be something. I imagine if you were my neighbor, I would never have to fear being overrun by enemies. You'd slay them all before I had a chance to put my pants on."

"Indeed."

A twig snapped nearby and I froze. I lifted the lightstone in the direction of the sound. All I could see was darkness between the shadowy trees. I quietly retrieved my staff and waited several long moments but there were no further sounds.

I took a few steps back, carefully watching the spot where the sound had come from.

"Don't walk backwards," Flyngard said. "Bad things happen."

"I'm not taking my eyes off that spot," I whispered. "The moment I do, something will leap out and attack."

My eyes focused on the spot ahead, waiting for any sign of movement. I continued to back away, trying to gain some distance from whatever was stalking me.

There was a loud snap, and the ground rose up on every side. A spray of dirt hit me and I was lifted several feet into the air. A thick net closed on me like the jaws of a beast.

My limbs were held fast within the netting. I struggled for freedom but for all my effort, I remained suspended above the ground like a helpless animal waiting for the hunter.

"I told you," Flyngard said. "Never walk backwards."

Four hooded figures gathered below, daggers with curved blades gripped tightly in their hands.

CHAPTER 17

WITHOUT A WORD, the hooded figures secured the net I was trapped in, and then dropped it to the ground in a rush. I struggled against the ropes but I could barely move. Panic rose in my chest.

"Can you reach your dagger?" Flyngard said.

"I don't have a dagger," I whispered.

"Who goes on a journey without a dagger?" He said.

"Bree had two. Plus, Elrick has claws. I figured that was enough."

"Well, you figured wrong, didn't you?"

"Yes, thank you," I hissed. "Very helpful, once again."

"Quiet." A gruff voice from one of the hooded figures called out, followed by a swift boot to my side.

They dragged the net for several feet before loading me onto a wooden cart. I studied my captors to get a better handle on my horrible situation. The four men were dressed in rugged, dark clothes, with fine, curved daggers strapped at their sides. Two of them had well-crafted bows and quivers filled with arrows. These weren't common bandits, they were obviously part of some larger, better financed outfit.

"Challenge them to a fight," Flyngard said. "Better to face them now. Who knows where they're taking you."

"Who are you?" I tried to sound challenging even though I was a helpless butterfly in a net. "Let me out and face me, you cowards!"

"I said quiet!" The same gruff voice responded.

The shadow of a club swept by overhead and slammed into my shoulder. It stung. I imagined that without my chainmail it would've hurt far worse.

The wooden cart jolted forward and rumbled along the forest floor.

"At least they didn't kill you," Flyngard said. "That's a positive sign."

"Yes," I whispered. "What a stroke of luck. I wonder what other good fortune awaits."

"Hey, don't take it out on me. I told you not to walk backwards."

I clenched my teeth and fought against the netting. Whatever it was made of was incredibly strong. I doubted I could break free without a sharp steel blade. As much as I hated to admit it, Flyngard was right. I should've brought a dagger.

It was a long and bumpy ride, as the cart jostled over the uneven ground, and by the time we arrived at a large clearing I was certain that a nice bruise was blossoming on my shoulder.

I peered through the netting to find a boar roasting over a healthy fire. My mouth watered as the savory smell wafted toward me.

Over twenty men reclined around the fire. All of them looked similar in dress and armament to the four who had captured me. Some drank from wooden cups, others talked loudly with broad gestures like they'd already had a fair share of ale.

The cart stopped, and I was dumped unceremoniously onto the ground. The net was loosened, and I struggled to get free. I threw off the remaining bonds and staggered to my feet.

A large man with a braided black beard sat on a broad stump nearby. He watched me with a smirk on his face like some king of the forest on his throne. His head was clean-shaven and covered in red markings that resembled daggers. Patches of leather armor hung on his powerful frame. Two bowmen flanked him, arrows readied and trained on me.

"What is this?" The large man spoke with a deep, resonant voice.

"A lone traveler, Sir Graelcin," my hooded captor replied. "Trapped him by the Farolin Stream."

"Stream?" Flyngard said. "Didn't I tell you to look for streams to help find your way?"

"Well, I didn't see any," I whispered.

"What'd he say?" Sir Graelcin said.

"He whispers to himself a lot," the hooded man said. "He may be mad."

"I see." Sir Graelcin stood and straightened his armor.

He strode toward me, his two bowmen following along, their arrows still trained on me. He was a good head and shoulders taller than me and twice as wide.

"We can take him," Flyngard said.

Sir Graelcin loomed over me, his dark eyes locked with mine. "Tell me, traveler. Are you crazy?"

"No," I said.

"Then why do you talk to yourself? And more importantly, why do you travel in my woods without permission?"

"Tell him you travel where you please," Flyngard said. "And if he has any further questions, the end of your staff has all the answers."

I gritted my teeth wishing I could drown Flyngard's voice out.

"I didn't know this was your forest. As for talking to myself, I just traveled through the caves under the Chellusk Mountains. I had to keep myself company."

Sir Graelcin smirked. "The caves of Chellusk Mountains, eh? That's obviously a lie. No one sets foot in those caves."

I didn't remember any mention of a Sir Graelcin from King Mulraith's court. Chances were he was a knight from another kingdom or a knight that went rogue from the king's castle years ago. Either way, there was a good chance he was no friend to Mulraith and I prayed that could work in my favor.

"Trust me," I said. "I would've avoided those caves if I could have. But it was the only way to reach Calladia before King Mulraith's soldiers. They're planning on attacking soon and I journey to warn the people."

Sir Graelcin chuckled. "Ah, an idealist. So, what's your big plan? Warn a handful of farmers to grab their pitchforks and hold off an army?"

A few men nearby laughed.

"Yes." I held his gaze. "And I'll fight with them."

I wasn't sure where my sudden sense of bravado came from. It could be that my instincts told me it was the only language this seasoned fighter would respond to. Either that or I'd been spending too much time with Flyngard.

He shook his head. "A fool's errand. And a soon-to-be-dead fool."

"Why don't you join me?" My reckless speech continued. Maybe the caves *had* driven me a bit mad. "You and your men could really make a difference."

Sir Graelcin laughed. "You hear that, men? Our deaths can really make a difference."

A roar of laughter rang through the clearing.

"Listen, boy." Sir Graelcin put a meaty hand on my shoulder. "I'm no fan of Mulraith, but we have no allegiance to Calladia.

And we're certainly not going to die for it. This forest is our home, and you've trespassed. Which brings us to a more important question. What will you pay for your transgression?"

"Tell him you'll pay a generous amount of bruises to his face," Flyngard said.

I gritted my teeth. "I don't have much. But I can offer you this." I held forth the lightstone.

"Hm." Sir Graelcin took the stone from my hand and examined it. "Lightstone. Not bad. What else?"

I shrugged. "That's about the only thing of value I carry."

His eyes went to my pack. "What's that in your bag? An instrument of some kind?"

A nervous shiver went down my back. I couldn't imagine some forest bandit taking my prized lute. "It's a lute. I'm a bard."

"I thought you said you were a fighter? Going to Calladia to fight with the people."

"I-I'm both," I stammered. "I used to play for the king as his bard. Now I fight against him."

"The king's bard you say." Sir Graelcin's brow lifted. He glanced at the bowmen beside him. "That's odd because we just got word the king's son Archinlanks was assassinated. And by no less than the king's bard."

I shook my head. "He was killed by a dragon and they blamed it on me."

"Oh. A dragon, huh?" Sir Graelcin smiled. "You bards sure can spin a good tale. Tell me, what's your name?"

"Jonas."

"Jonas the bard assassin." He turned to his bowmen. "Yes, that's the one they're looking for, isn't it? The one for whom they're offering a rather large reward?"

The bowmen nodded, narrowing their eyes.

I swallowed hard. I had to switch topics fast. "Listen, if Calladia is taken over by Mulraith's army, they'll attack the surrounding lands too. You think this forest will be safe? What good is a reward if the king's army starts hunting you down?"

Sir Graelcin drew his sword in a flash. The gleam of the long blade shone in the firelight.

"I've met three assassins in my life," he said. "They were some of the deadliest fighters I've ever come across. Like you, they were unassuming in stature, but they were highly trained in combat. Quick. Agile. Deadly." He lifted my chin with the edge of his blade. "Perhaps we should test your skills. See if you really are the bard assassin they're looking for."

"Now you're talking," Flyngard said.

Anxiety swirled in my gut. The last thing I wanted to do was go toe to toe with this giant of a man.

I put up my hands. "I don't want to fight. Just let me go. I'll never travel your forest again."

"Tell you what," Sir Graelcin removed his blade from my chin and let it rest on his shoulder. "You beat me, you keep your lute, and perhaps I'll let you go. But if I win, I get the lute and whatever else you've got in that bag and I turn you in for the reward."

"That deal sounds a little unbalanced."

He grinned. "Well, the one who holds the cards decides the game. What say you, bard assassin?"

"Don't worry," Flyngard said. "I've got your back."

I was out of ideas. Surrounded by hooded forest thugs and stuck in a standoff with their renegade knight. All I could do was pray that Flyngard's enchanted assistance would be enough to keep me alive.

"All right." I drew my staff and took a deep breath. "I accept."

CHAPTER 18

THANKFULLY, SIR GRAELCIN waved off his anxious bowmen and took a few steps back from me. He rolled his shoulders and shook his head as if trying to wake himself up. He pointed his sword at me. "Ready, bard?"

I gave my staff a spin, and took what I hoped was a dangerous looking stance. My goal was to prevent him from charging in like a bull. If I could intimidate him, even a little, maybe his attacks would be more tentative.

"Ready," I said.

Sir Graelcin narrowed his eyes. He gave a guttural cry and charged me, his blade held high. Apparently, I didn't intimidate him in the least. My body felt light with fear.

His sword swept in a downward arc toward my torso. Once again I felt a strange blending of instinct and action. An impulse that harnessed my own skills and executed them with perfect timing and movement. I rolled to the side, sweeping my staff just above the ground. The end of the staff struck his ankle, sending crackling lines of white energy up his leg. He cried out and stumbled face first to the ground.

The merriment in the camp died down. The forest bandits stared at their fallen leader, as if in shock.

Sir Graelcin leapt to his feet, slightly favoring one leg. An angry sneer covered his dirt-smeared face. "A night staff, eh? You didn't say anything about magical weapons."

I rolled back to my feet, my movements effortless. "You didn't ask."

"That's it." He strode toward me, his eyes locked with mine. "No more games."

He lunged forward, the point of his sword driving toward my chest. I spun to the side, striking his knuckles with the staff. White energy covered his sword hand. He grimaced and let go. In a flash, he took the sword up with his other hand and shoved the hilt in my face. The cold steel slammed against my jaw and I reeled backward.

My body hit the ground, knocking the air from my lungs. I gasped, my eyes closing tightly from the pain radiating through my face.

"Jonas!" Flyngard yelled. "Roll!"

I opened my eyes to find Sir Graelcin standing over me, his sword lifted high, ready to drive the blade through my stomach. I turned away at the last moment, feeling the blade glance off the back of my chainmail. Instinct kicked in and I turned back, swinging the staff in a quick arc. The end of it smacked him in the cheekbone, his face lighting up with white energy.

He stumbled backward, clutching his face, leaving his sword stuck in the ground. I leapt to my feet and charged him. I drove the staff into his stomach, looking for retribution after almost getting disemboweled.

Sir Graelcin doubled over with a grunt. I brought the staff down on the back of his head and his body crumpled to the ground.

He lay there a moment, groaning and clutching his stomach. My chest heaved as I tried to catch my breath.

"Nicely done," Flyngard said. "The bigger they are, the harder they fall, eh?"

In a blur of movement, Sir Graelcin threw a handful of dust into my eyes. I winced and stepped backward. I gripped my staff, a surge of panic flooding through me.

"Flyngard," I whispered. "I can't see."

Something meaty and powerful slammed against my jaw. Pain exploded across my skull and I twisted to the side. A series of heavy blows pummeled my torso and I fell to the ground.

"Steady," Flyngard said. "Grip your staff. On my mark, strike upward. Feel my lead."

I lay still, clutching the staff and trying to blink away the painful grit in my eyes. The chainmail warmed with energy and I felt an impulse to attack.

"Now!" Flyngard said.

I swept the staff upward and felt it connect with something solid. Sir Graelcin grunted. I could hear him stumble nearby. Another instinct to strike flowed through me. This time, I simply went with it. I rolled to my feet and made a series of horizontal strikes, moving forward with each one. Each strike connected, causing Sir Graelcin to groan in pain before finally collapsing to the ground.

Everything went silent. The only sound was the crackle of the campfire. I continued to blink, the dust finally clearing from my vision.

Sir Graelcin lay on the ground, wincing. Bright red welts covered his face, and a stream of blood dripped from his mouth onto his beard. One of the bowmen knelt down beside him and put a hand on his shoulder.

"You all right, sir?" The bowman glared at me. "Should we dispatch this dog?"

"I'm fine." Sir Graelcin batted the hand away and sat up with a groan. He swayed, then put his hand on the ground and steadied himself. "Leave him be. He's proven himself. Even if he did cheat with magical weaponry."

The bowman helped Sir Graelcin to his feet. He grimaced and held the side of his face, then stood up straight and fixed his eyes on me. Frankly, his ability to stand after such a beating terrified me. It was one thing to survive a fight with enchanted armor, it was another to have such extraordinary natural fortitude.

"Your skills are impressive." Sir Graelcin rubbed his jaw. "I will spare your life. But you are in my debt for trespassing. You can work with my crew to repay it."

"Thank you," I said. "I appreciate the offer but I have to get to Calladia. I must leave now."

"Forget Calladia," he said. "It's a lost cause. If war is coming, we must strengthen our position in the forest. We could use a fighter like you."

"And Calladia could use you and your men," I said. "And perhaps others will join us."

"Others?" Sir Graelcin chuckled. "There are no armies to be found in this land. Even the warriors of Kroth have laid down their arms. Who could you possibly convince to join your hopeless fight?"

"Those who aren't afraid of the king's armies," I said.

He smirked. "You think you can goad me into battle like some prideful squire? I've had my fill of noble causes. We all have." He made a sweeping motion to the men surrounding us. "You won't find help here, boy. There's no one left to fight."

"I'll find others." My desperate situation was closing in on me. I refused to believe there was no help to be found. I couldn't imagine the destruction Mulraith would command if left unchallenged. A desperate resolve rose within me. "There have to be others willing to stand with me."

Sir Graelcin shook his head. "Perhaps you are mad after all.

Perhaps you can convince an army of madmen to fight with you. Or, who knows? Perhaps the forest creatures will rise to your aid."

A swell of laughter went through the men around him.

Suddenly a chorus of howls rose up all around the clearing. The men drew their swords and turned toward the forest beyond. Several bowmen nocked their arrows and scanned the surrounding woods.

One of them cried out as his bow burst into white flame. He dropped it to the ground and stepped back.

"There's magic afoot," Sir Graelcin said.

One by one, every bow burst into flame and the archers dropped their weapons, backing away from the magical fire.

An imposing, hooded figure with glowing white eyes walked into the far end of the clearing. White flames licked across his cloak as if he'd been set ablaze, and yet he appeared unfazed. The figure was flanked by over a dozen wolves with similar glowing eyes.

The men nearby backed away, their knuckles whitening as they gripped the hilts of their swords.

"Surrender the bard to me," The hooded figure spoke with a low, gritty voice.

CHAPTER 19

"WHO ARE YOU?" Sir Graelcin called out, struggling to keep his voice steady.

The hooded figure raised his arm and a stream of white fire shot into the air. A gasp went up among the men in the clearing.

"I am Fangforth," the figure said. "Lycan mystic of the Dragontooth Mountains."

I suppressed a grin at the realization that it was Elrick. Bree must've been using every ounce of her illusion skills to pull off this visual feat. I had to admit, it was an impressive display. My spirit soared at the thought that they were here. Alive and free from the Chellusk Mountain caves.

"The bard is wanted by the ten mystics of Dragontooth," Elrick continued in a dramatic voice. "They travel to Calladia to call enchanted fire down upon the king's armies. They seek council with Jonas, the mighty bard assassin. Either he comes with me, or the ten mystics will come here looking for him. But they will not be pleased if he is delayed."

Sir Graelcin, flinched, a trace of doubt animating his features. "I've never heard of these ten mystics."

"They do not wish to be known," Elrick said. "Most who cross their path don't live to tell the tale."

Sir Graelcin gave a nervous clearing of his throat. "We have no quarrel with these mystics. The bard was just leaving. Please, take him with my blessing."

Elrick gave a slow nod.

Sir Graelcin shot a serious look at me and made a quick gesture toward Elrick. "Bard, go with the mystic."

I patted my pockets. "Hm, I can't seem to find my lightstone. I wonder where I left it."

Sir Graelcin fumbled for the lightstone in his pocket and tossed it to me. "Here. Leave. Quickly."

I smiled and headed toward Elrick.

Elrick led me from the clearing with a dramatic sweep of his hand. We left the warm light of the bonfire and walked into the dark covering of the trees, the large pack of wolves at our heels.

Once we were out of earshot, Elrick leaned toward me.

"Jonas, it's all right," he whispered. "It's me, Elrick. You can stop shivering."

"I'm not shivering. I know it's you. I recognized your voice."

"Hey, it's okay to admit you were scared. My lycan form can be intimidating. I'm not judging. A simple thank you will suffice."

"Yes, thank you, but I wasn't scared. Where's Bree?"

Bree slid out from behind a tree just ahead causing me to flinch.

"Careful." Elrick held a hand toward Bree. "Jonas still has the shivers. Poor guy had a big scare back there."

I glared at Elrick, then strode forward and grabbed Bree's hands. "You all right? When we got separated in the caves I was worried about… well, I'm just glad you're okay."

She gave a subtle smile. "I worried about you too. But we should get going before those men start to question my illusion."

Bree took an uneven step, then stumbled to her knees. I knelt beside her, holding her steady.

"What is it?" I said.

She shook her head. "Nothing. That was the biggest illusion I've ever tried. It took a lot out of me."

"Here." I put her arm around my shoulder and helped her up. "I'll help until you get your strength back."

She nodded and we headed further into the woods.

"You're lucky my friends picked up your scent." Elrick motioned to our wolf escort. "Otherwise we never would've found you. This is a big forest."

"Yes," I said. "Good timing as well. I nearly got roped into life as a forest bandit."

Elrick nodded. "Maybe they needed a bard for campfire songs. Forests are pretty lacking in entertainment."

I chuckled. "No thanks."

The wolves led the way through the shadowy trees. Bree's illusion had worn off and thankfully their eyes no longer glowed white. They padded soundlessly through the darkness, their heads glancing to the side whenever a forest creature scurried among the trees.

After we'd gained a healthy distance from the clearing, Bree's footing grew steady once more. Thankfully, she made no move to take her arm off my shoulder as we continued forward, side by side.

"So." I looked over at Bree. "How was your trip through the caves?"

"Surprisingly uneventful," she grinned. "Not that I'm complaining."

"Yeah," Elrick jumped in. "After all those rumors, I expected at least one creature to attack us. I guess it was just a lot of tavern legends."

"Oh no." I shook my head. "Believe me. It's all true. Much worse, actually."

Bree patted my chest. "Very funny, Jonas."

"No, really. It was awful. I was captured by cave grabbers. Then, I fell through a hive of mammoth spiders. There were hundreds of them. And there were rock giants. Tall as a castle wall. They wanted to keep me as some kind of musical pet."

Elrick laughed. "You see? Bards are natural storytellers. Who else did you meet? Unicorns? Faeries?"

"You should write a song about it," Bree said.

"I'm not kidding," I said. "I barely made it out alive."

"Don't worry," Flyngard said. "I believe you."

Elrick pointed to me. "Check his temples. Maybe he fell in the caves and hit his head. I'd have dreams like that too after all the stories we heard."

Bree touched my head. "You know, I think I do feel a bump."

"That's from Sir Graelcin. His punches are like a horse kick."

"Be glad my enchantment protected you," Flyngard said. "Or you'd have a broken jaw and a concussion after that encounter."

I spent another minute or so trying to convince them of my horrific adventures in the caves. Bree finally said she believed me but patted me on the shoulder as if trying to calm a raving lunatic. After all I'd been through, I just didn't have the energy to keep arguing. Besides, what did it matter? My friends were safe, and we were free from the Chellusk Mountains. And that alone seemed like a miracle.

CHAPTER 20

DAWN CREPT THROUGH the forest, brightening the surroundings and chasing away the deep shadows. The bitter chill of night retreated as the sun warmed my skin. Thanks to the wolves' innate sense of direction, we reached the edge of the forest after only a few hours of travel. The bright rays of the mid-morning sun shone through the tree line, hinting at the green valley beyond. The pines thinned out to reveal the gently sloping green foothills of Kroth. At the other end of the valley, the sprawling farms at the outskirts of Calladia were visible in the distance.

Calladia was spread out over miles of grassland and wildflowers, and hemmed in by the surrounding mountains. The trees in the valley provided a rich palette of colors. Deep red and yellow maples dotted the landscape, mingling with flowering white dogwood trees. A winding river ran along the east side of town, fed by Calladia Falls at the north end of the valley.

Bree took a deep breath. "Is it just me, or is the air sweeter here?"

Elrick sniffed. "And someone's cooking bacon nearby. Anyone else's mouth just fill with saliva?"

"You might not want to stroll into town looking like that." I motioned to him. "And it's probably best for your pack to wait for us here."

He nodded and turned to the wolves. "All right, you know the drill. Stay near the forest edge. You know how people are about wolves."

A gray wolf with dark eyes yapped.

"Yes, Snarlbite, I know it's not fair. Listen, I'll talk to the townspeople. Get you in their good graces. But you can't just keep howling in the middle of the night and expect them to like you. Meanwhile, find as many wolves as you can and bring them here. A war is coming. If these soldiers win, it's bad news for all of us."

The wolves howled in unison and trotted back into the forest.

Elrick shrank back to his human form and turned to us with a smile. "Aren't they the best?"

Bree and I nodded.

To the southeast rose the mountains that separated us from Witchpaw Canyon. Rothman's Pass was visible in the distance. The Pass was nearly two hundred yards across, and it cut through the mountains like the winding track of a giant serpent. Less than a day's travel could bring the king's armies through that pass and into Calladia. I could imagine an endless stream of soldiers pouring through the gap and descending upon the helpless town.

"Rothman's Pass seems closer than I remember." Bree spoke in a quiet voice, almost as if she didn't want to admit how vulnerable the situation was.

I wanted to offer some reassurance, but there wasn't much to say. I was just as overwhelmed at the sight. "Come on, we don't have much time."

A handful of simple houses fashioned from the thick trunks of pines dotted the foothills of Kroth. The highest of the hills had tall wooden towers where archers were stationed. One of the towers showed evidence of a recent fire. The wood and a wide circle of grass surrounding its base were blackened. Wisps of smoke still rose up from the structure. A few of the rooftops nearby showed similar signs of a fire.

"Ah, Kroth!" Flyngard said. "At long last. It's good to be back home."

Crops and cattle were plentiful throughout the unassuming settlements. As we drew near, the noises of pigs, chickens, cows, and goats blended together in their disjointed farm symphony.

We avoided the farmlands and settlements on the outskirts, walking straight toward the largest hill that held the main structures of the community. A thick wall made of sharpened tree trunks surrounded the settlement. There were two guards in leather armor keeping watch at the wooden entrance gate. One of them sat on a barrel with his back against the gate.

"Hold." A portly guard with a long brown beard ambled toward us. "State your business."

"We're travelers from Grandelon," I said. "We're here with a warning. King Mulraith is gathering soldiers nearby to attack."

"Is that so?" He shot a look at the guard sitting on the barrel. "They say they're from Grandelon. News of soldiers nearby."

The other guard looked like the taller, leaner version of his counterpart. His heavy eyelids suggested he'd had a long night. He let out a lazy yawn, then pointed away from the gate. "Move on to Calladia. We've got enough problems."

"Who is this sluggard?" Flyngard said. "A disgrace to the warriors of Kroth."

"The king's armies come for this whole land." I spoke loud enough for the sleepy guard to hear. "You need to prepare for battle."

The lounging guard chuckled. "Listen boy, it's too early for this. What game are you playing?"

"It's no game." Bree stepped forward. "The army gathers at Witchpaw Canyon. Once they come through Rothman's Pass, Kroth and Calladia are both vulnerable."

The lounging guard sighed and slowly got to his feet. "Look, I don't know who you are but we've got our hands full with that cursed dragon Baldramorg. He came here last night for revenge on some fool who stole his treasure. I've been up all night preparing for his return. Unless the three of you are dragonslayers, there's nothing to discuss."

I shared a nervous glance with Bree.

"We are dragonslayers," Elrick stepped forward and stuck out his chest. "We've been tracking Baldramorg and plan to kill him."

The portly guard chuckled. "You three are dragonslayers?"

Elrick lifted his chin. "Yes. They are a plague on the land. And we are the cure."

"I thought you said you were here to warn about the king's soldiers," The tall guard said.

"Yes. Right... that too." Elrick tried to maintain his confidence. "You see, the soldiers complicate our hunt. We need allies so we can focus on the dragon."

The tall guard groaned and rubbed his temple. "Fine. Why don't you so-called dragonslayers go spread your news. Make a day of it for all I care." He unlatched the gate and opened it. He gave a lackluster sweep of his hand. "Welcome to Kroth."

Elrick took confident strides forward through the gate. Bree and I caught up with him on the other side.

Dozens of townspeople milled around on the dirt lanes between the wooden buildings. Their rugged, drab clothes had that distinct imbalance of durability over comfort.

"Dragonslayers?" I raised my eyebrows at Elrick.

He smirked. "Quick thinking, right?"

"Are you crazy?" Bree said. "We didn't need some ridiculous claim to get past those two oafs. Now you put us on the hook."

"Don't worry," Elrick waved her off. "We're here to spread the word about the soldiers, then we leave. We needed something to get us through the gate."

"And what happens if Baldramorg comes back?" Bree said. "They'll expect us to do something. Then what?"

"Relax," he said. "We'll be long gone by then."

"I believe his lycan strength is clouding his judgement," Flyngard said.

"Tell me about it," I said.

"Head for that long building to your right," Flyngard said. "That's the barracks."

The guards at the barracks were more receptive than those at the front gate. They listened to our warnings, but the gravity of the situation didn't seem to sink in. They received our news with stoic nods, but confirmed that their primary focus was on preparing for the dragon. This, of course, sent a wave of guilt through me since we were responsible for his presence. Of course, we decided not to mention that bit of information.

Despite their lack of response to the serious threat from Mulraith's army, we continued to plead our case until they assured us they'd do what they could. We said our goodbyes and walked back into the town square feeling a bit underwhelmed.

"What now?" Elrick said.

"I guess we head for Calladia," Bree frowned. "This isn't quite what I'd hoped for."

"Aye," Flyngard said. "Kroth has become fat and lazy. In my time, we would have seen scouts on horseback, riding full speed for Witchpaw Canyon to confirm the report."

"Well, we're strangers to them," I said. "They don't know if they can trust our news."

"True," Bree said.

"Don't make excuses for these idle guards," Flyngard said. "Head for the tavern. You can find sturdy fighters there."

"Flyngard said we might find some help in the tavern," I said.

Elrick shrugged. "Might as well try as long as we're here."

The tavern was dark, even though it was noon. Every surface

seemed to be made of wood. Small windows on each wall allowed a shaft of light to squeeze through. The aroma of smoked pig and ale floated in the air.

Several clusters of townspeople sat at rough-hewn tables, huddled around pints of ale and roasted meat. Their conversations blended into a low rumble, broken occasionally by short bursts of laughter.

The people of Kroth reminded me of soldiers after a long war. A strange mix of grim determination and despair. I imagined any one of the townspeople could hold their own in a fight, even more so the ones in this tavern. I could see why Flyngard told us to come here.

I tightened my cloak over the chainmail. If there were other battle-ready warriors like Flyngard in here, I didn't want to give off the impression that I was armed and itching for a fight.

"We need to rally as many people as we can," Bree said. "We should split up to save time. If we get the same tepid response as we did from the guards, we'll move on to Calladia. I have family there. They'll listen."

"Let's hope so," Elrick said.

"And please," Bree put her hand on Elrick's shoulder. "Resist the urge to claim we're dragonslayers."

"No promises," Elrick grinned.

Bree shook her head and went to the nearest table.

"How are we going to convince people to join us," I said. "I don't even want to join us."

"Are you kidding?" Elrick said. "This is our chance to change this land. To stop a great evil from happening. And we have abilities now. You and I. Haven't we always wished we could do something? That we could take a stand against the king?"

"Well, yeah, but we're entertainers. I mean, sure we may have abilities now but come on, Elrick. I'm a bard. You're a jester. We're not warriors."

Elrick shook his head. "Don't you get it? After all we've been through? We're not just one or the other. We're both. And more. We're whatever the Eternal One equips us to be. And right now, I'm equipped to fight a necessary battle. And so are you. Now let's gather some fighters and make a difference."

He grinned, gave me a good natured slap on the shoulder, and made his way across the tavern.

"I'm really starting to like him," Flyngard said.

"Of course you are," I said. "He's drunk with wolfish power."

"Perhaps," Flyngard said. "Still, he's got a warrior's heart. I can see why they chose him to be a lycan."

I shook my head and made my way to the bar. There were a few vacant stools near a large man dressed all in gray. He leaned over a pint of ale, his eyes staring blankly into his drink. He was older, with a rounded gut that spoke of many days leaning over pints of ale. But he had about twice the amount of muscle as anyone else in the tavern, and a dangerous looking war hammer strapped to his belt.

"Wait," Flyngard said. "I know him. Or perhaps, a relative of his. He looks so much like my old friend Grunsel."

"Hold that thought," I whispered. "Let me talk to him. See if he'll help."

I took a seat at the bar next to him and gave a friendly nod. "Greetings."

He gave me but a glance, then returned to his pint of ale. Thin scars left discolored lines on his face and neck. He looked to be in his forties, gray hair leaving streaks across his shaggy black mane and thick beard.

"Who are you?" His voice was low and dangerous.

"I'm Jonas. I'm from Grandelon."

He grunted. "My condolences."

"Yeah, well, I don't plan on going back. I'm actually here to warn the people of Kroth about King Mulraith's army. They're gathering at Witchpaw Canyon. They plan to conquer both Kroth and Calladia."

The large man gave me a sidelong glance. "All right… Is that all?"

"Well… Yes, I suppose."

"Good." He flicked his fingers. "Now, off with you before I give you a taste of my boot heel."

I paused, not sure how to respond. "Look, I realize I'm a stranger but war is coming. This whole area will be under attack."

The man gave a lazy nod. "Right… One day it's the dragon, the next it's an army. Tomorrow will bring more bad tidings." He took a long drink and wiped his beard. "Take your war somewhere else. I've had my fill. Go talk to the town guards. That's what they get paid for."

"I did," I said. "They didn't listen."

"Then try again," The man finally turned to face me, his eyes narrowed. "Now, off with you, boy."

"I can't believe the resemblance," Flyngard said. "He looks so much like Grunsel. My old comrade in the Circle of Five. But so much older. Perhaps he's been cursed."

Since I was out of ideas, and this giant of a man looked ready to pummel me, I decided to go with Flyngard's hunch as a last ditch effort.

"Are you Grunsel?" I said.

His jaw clenched. "How do you know my name?"

"No," Flyngard said. "It can't be. I don't believe it."

"I-I heard you were a great warrior," I said. "Part of the legendary Circle of Five."

He leaned back, his brows raised. "Great warrior? Circle of Five?" The anger left his face and he broke into a laugh. "Boy, you've been listening to old tales. Who told you about the Circle of Five?"

"I heard stories from a warrior called Flyngard. He said I might find you here."

"Flyngard?" Grunsel raised his brow. "Well, there's another ghost from the past. You must've been a small lad when he filled your head with those tales. He's been dead for twelve years."

I furrowed my brow. "Twelve years?"

"That's impossible," Flyngard said.

"Aye," Grunsel said. "He went after the sorcerer Rastvane like some reckless fool. That's the last we saw of him."

"He lies!" Flyngard said. "It hasn't been that long."

"Are you sure it was twelve years ago?" I said.

Grunsel nodded and took another drink. "On my honor. And with the chances he took, he was fortunate to live that long. Always running headlong into battle and dragging the rest of us with him. Paying no mind to those who got hurt along the way. Nearly got me killed more times than I care to remember. If he was here, no doubt he'd join you in battle. Probably try to take on that whole army by himself."

A middle-aged barmaid with brunette hair and a kind face walked up to refill Grunsel's drink. "Who'd take on a whole army?"

"Flyngard," Grunsel said. "Your old betrothed."

Flyngard gasped. "Serenia! Great heavens above, it's her. It's my love!"

Her eyes narrowed and she stared at Grunsel for a moment. "And, pray tell, why are you speaking ill of the dead?"

"Whoa." Grunsel leaned back, putting his hands up. "No harm meant, Serenia. This poor lad had his head filled with Flyngard's old tales. You know how he liked to go on. All fight and valor, no mention of the scars and pain left in the wake of battle. I'm just setting the record straight so Jonas here won't end up the same way."

She frowned and took his pint away. "Perhaps you've had enough. Why don't you go walk it off."

"Hey, I'm just saying that–"

She pointed at the door. "Out."

Grunsel let out a heavy sigh and pushed off his stool. "Fine. I'm tired of talking about the past anyway." He trudged out of the bar, looking as though he'd just finished a long journey.

"I can't believe it," Flyngard's voice sounded far away. "Twelve years. How could I have lost all sense of time? This is poison in my bones. Jonas, tell Serenia I'm sorry. Tell her I love her. Tell her… No. Never mind. Don't say a word. There's nothing to say. Eternal One, help me. The damage is done. Say nothing, Jonas… Nothing at all."

The chainmail felt cold and heavy, as if it suddenly weighed twice as much.

"So? Jonas, is it?" Serenia wiped down the rim of a glass. "You knew Flyngard?"

"Yes. I do," I said. "I mean, I did."

She gave a soft smile, the thin wrinkles around her eyes the only sign of age on her youthful face. "You must've met him long ago."

"Well, I suppose I was younger than I am now. But it feels like I met him just the other day."

She nodded. "I know what you mean. His memory is still fresh in my mind. And don't listen to Grunsel. He's had it rough the last few years and ale brings his bitterness out."

I nodded, not sure what else to say.

Serenia put the glass down, a faraway look in her eyes. "You know, back then, they did great things together. Flyngard, Grunsel, the Circle of Five. They stood against impossible odds. Defeated many evils. Saved countless innocents. I know, I was there."

"From the tales he told me, he sounds very brave," I said.

"That's an understatement," she smirked. "He was born for the battlefield. Fearless and deadly. Few could stand against him. And yet, he was kind-hearted. Especially to me."

A few seconds of uncomfortable silence passed. Flyngard was quiet as a mouse, but I knew that for his sake, I couldn't just leave.

"He spoke of you often," I said.

She smiled, looking down at her hands. "Did he now?"

I nodded. "I don't think I've ever heard anyone so in love. Did you know he wrote poems about you?"

She gave a glassy eyed look toward the window. "He said as much. Though I couldn't coax a word out of him."

"He told me one of them," I said. "It was actually quite beautiful. I even turned it into a song."

She raised a brow. "A song?"

I nodded. "I'm a bard. Music is my trade. When I find words from the heart, I can't help but compose a song… would you like to hear it?"

A warm smile spread over her lips. "I would love to."

I retrieved the lute from my bag and cleared my throat. The melody and words of the song I'd worked on with Flyngard came rushing back. I couldn't remember a time when a song I'd composed felt more important to play. I plucked the strings with a careful touch in honor of Flyngard.

I've seen the gold mantle of sunrise on the mount,

the great oaks of Havenshore with green as deep as time,

the endless blue of the Trenarrian sea,

but none, my love, none compares with one glance from you.

One touch of your hand.

One word from your lips.

There is no palace so grand, no journey so glorious, no victory so sweet as my love for you.

You, my love, are the greatest adventure.

I let the strings ring out their final note as the song came to an end.

Tears streamed down Serenia's face. She was quiet for several moments. "Flyngard wrote that?"

I nodded. "He wrote it about you. He told me he wanted to share it with you when he was able."

Serenia reached out and grabbed my hand. "Thank you, Jonas. Thank you so much." She wiped away a tear and rushed into the back room.

I took a deep breath, wondering if I'd done the right thing. "Flyngard?"

There was no response. The chainmail remained cold and heavy.

I returned the lute to my pack. "Flyngard. Talk to me."

Still no response.

A lean man with a bald head slid up next to me. "Excuse me. Did I hear right? Is your name Jonas?"

"Yes," I said.

He gave a broad grin revealing a few missing teeth. "Great heavens, you're my hero. You're the assassin that killed Archinlanks."

I looked over my shoulder to see where Bree and Elrick were. Both were speaking to townspeople on the other side of the tavern.

The bald man put his hands up. "Oh, don't worry. I'm with you. Any attack against Mulraith is a victory for me. The sooner that tyrant meets his end, the better. At least, as far as Beckwich and I are concerned."

"Who?" I said.

"Oh, sorry." The bald man shook his head. "I'm Keltrek. That's my friend Beckwich over there."

At the far end of the bar, a stocky man with an eyepatch smiled and waved at me.

"We heard all about you. Jonas, the bard assassin." Keltrek spread out his hands like he was reading from a banner. "We thought it was just rumors, but here you are, warning townspeople about an attack from the king. You're kind of a legend to us."

"Well, um, thank you," I said.

"And we want to help. We can fight. I mean, maybe we're not the strongest in the land but we have connections. We're part of the bandits' guild." Keltrek put up his hands as if I had an objection ready. "I know what you're thinking. The bandits' guild is not to be trusted. But we want a temporary alliance. The king's soldiers are bad for business. We want to stop them as bad as anybody else."

"Listen," I said. "I'm not the leader of all this. We're just trying to rally people together. I can't promise you or your guild anything."

He pointed at me. "Nor would I expect you to. But the thing is, word has gone out about you. There's a reputation building. You've earned the respect of the bandits' guild. They'll listen to you."

"Well, if you'll join us in the fight, I'll talk to whoever you want." I slid off my chair and stood up. "Can they meet us in Calladia? We're headed there next."

Keltrek nodded. "Of course. Thank you. We'll wait for you there." He turned away, then quickly turned back. "Oh, I almost forgot. Would you mind saying hello to Beckwich? I sort of fibbed and said I knew you and I'd introduce you to him. Sorry."

I shrugged. "Sure, I guess."

Keltrek led me to the end of the bar. Beckwich stood up, his stocky frame looking much taller now that he was out of his seat, standing head and shoulders above me.

"Greetings, bard assassin." Beckwich opened his hand, revealing a small, angular metal device.

A flash of white shot out of the device and hit my cheek, creating a puff of white powder. A soft cloud swirled around my face, and the room began to spin. My limbs felt light as air and all my cares melted away. A small voice screamed at me to run but I was far too relaxed. Firm hands led me to a door at the back of the tavern, and sunlight hit my face right before I fell asleep.

CHAPTER 21

THE CREAKING OF old wood brought me back around. My hands and feet were bound with coarse rope. I was lying on my back in a sunken cavity, in a wagon filled with hay. Branches passed by overhead, revealing the deepening grays of an evening sky. The wagon jostled over uneven ground, rocking me against the prickly hay.

Mumbled conversations came from the front of the wagon. I leaned forward to see the backs of two men sitting on the driver's bench. It was Keltrek and Beckwich, the men I'd met in the tavern. Everything came flooding back. The story of their bandits' guild. The promise of help. The white powder that had put me under. Obviously, it had all been lies. Or at least, most of it. Maybe they were bandits. Only, instead of wanting to help, they just wanted to capture me and turn me in for the reward. Which probably meant we were on our way to the king's soldiers.

Bree and Elrick must've missed the whole thing. Perhaps they were out searching for me right now. Hopefully they were hot on the trail of these wretched bandits.

I strained against my bonds, but I was held fast. Thick coils of rope were wrapped around my forearms as well as my calves. They weren't taking any chances with my escape.

The crickets were out in full force tonight. The hypnotic rhythm of their chirping mixed with the creaking of the wagon in a strange, percussive beat. The noise made for a good cover to make quiet plans of escape with Flyngard.

"Flyngard," I whispered.

A few moments of silence passed.

"Yes, Jonas." Flyngard spoke in a subdued voice.

"I can't move. I'm bound tight."

"Aye." Flyngard sounded weary, as if just waking up. "This is a dark day for both of us."

"Yes. I'm really sorry about earlier. I can't imagine what you're going through."

Flyngard stayed quiet.

Finally, I spoke up. "Flyngard?"

"Aye."

"Listen, I want to help you. However I'm able. I'm here to listen and offer whatever advice I can. But that's going to take a while. A longer journey, if you will. But we'll never get there if I die today. Can you help me escape?"

"I don't think so, Jonas... I'm afraid I just don't have the strength."

I strained against the bonds with all my might, hoping to find some weakness. The ropes only dug deeper into my skin.

"Listen," I said. "You've got to help me get out of here. If they kill me, they'll take my chainmail. You'll be stuck with someone else. One of Mulraith's top soldiers. Maybe Mulraith himself. Is that what you want?"

"Perish the thought. I can't imagine any more loss on this cursed day. If it came to that, I would simply let go. There is a constant struggle in this enchanted world that I've fought for years now. Far more years than I realized. If I surrendered to it, I suppose I would cease to exist. At least, in this world."

"Don't start talking like that. You told me that despair was the end. You said never to give in to it."

"Aye. That was before today, lad. The world weighs heavy upon me. So very heavy. I can't bear the weight of it."

"That doesn't sound like the Flyngard I know."

"He's awake." Keltrek craned his bald head back. "Who are you talking to back there?"

"Forest spirits," I called out. "They're angry at your intrusion. Very angry."

Beckwich turned to Keltrek with raised eyebrows. "Forest spirits?"

Keltrek waved him off. "Save your tales, boy. You're gonna need 'em for the king. He waits with his army nearby."

"Mulraith is here?" I said.

Keltrek smirked. "Yes. And he's quite eager to see you. He wants revenge for his son. Not wise to anger a man like that. Can't imagine what he's going to do with you."

Mulraith rode out with his army on very few occasions. Generally he let Archinlanks or his other knights lead the battles. With Archinlanks gone, perhaps he was taking things into his own hands. Either that or the conquering of Calladia was high on his priority list. With his powerful sorcery backing his soldiers, the battle would be worse than I'd thought.

I strained against the bonds. "Let me go. Mulraith will destroy this land. Why would you help him?"

"I owe nothing to Mulraith," he said. "Nor to anybody else. I go where the money is. And the reward for your capture is substantial."

"Flyngard," I whispered.

"I'm very tired." Flyngard sounded far away. "I'm going to sleep for a while."

"No. I need your help."

"Keep yer mouth shut," Keltrek glared back. "Or I'll shut it for good."

"I'm sorry," Flyngard said. "I have to sleep."

"Flyngard," I hissed.

There was no response.

"Flyngard. Wake up!"

"All right, that's it." Keltrek handed the reins to Beckwich and hopped over the driver's bench, landing in the hay by my feet, my staff clutched in his hand. "The next time I tell you to shut your mouth, you'll remember the beating I'm about to give you. And I'll use your own staff just to drive home the point."

"Whoa!" Beckwich pulled back the reins.

The wagon stopped, the sudden halt throwing Keltrek off his feet. He slammed his head against the wagon bench, landing in a crumpled heap in the hay.

"Idiot!" Keltrek stumbled to his feet, rubbing the back of his head. "What's wrong with you?"

"I thought it was forest spirits," Beckwich said. "But it's worse. Much worse."

"You fool. You're imagining things." Keltrick turned to see what lay before us. "Oh… Oh no."

"Tell me why I should let you live." A low voice with gritty undertones called out.

I strained to lean forward, which wasn't easy considering how tight my bonds were. Finally, I was able to prop my head up on a lump of hay, granting a partial view through the braces of the drivers' bench.

Although I didn't have a clear view of the scene ahead, I could make out a handful of figures clothed in form-fitting, dark green and brown outfits. They all wore deep hoods to conceal their faces. Each of them had bows trained on my captors.

Part of me was ecstatic that my captors were now the captives.

The other part of me wondered if bad had just gone to worse and I was about to be killed right along with them.

Keltrick put up his hands, moving closer to Beckwich. "We're just travelers passing through. Looking for work. We mean no harm to anyone."

"What are your allegiances?" The dark figure said.

"We have no allegiances," Keltrek said. "We're simple merchants. Hay merchants."

"I thought you said you were travelers looking for work," the figure said.

"Yes, I mean, travelers that work in hay. We're merchants traveling to find work elsewhere… with hay."

I cringed at Keltrek's poor attempts at bluffing.

A sharp whistle split the air. Keltrek cried out and grabbed his shoulder. Thin rivulets of blood flowed over his fingers.

The dark figure lowered his bow and drew two curved daggers from his belt. "That was a light graze. Just enough to make you honest. The next strike won't be so kind. Now, once more, what are your allegiances."

"We're in the bandits' guild." Keltrick sounded desperate, grasping at his shoulder. "That's it. We work the land from Calladia to Nillestown, doing what we can to survive."

The dark figure seemed to relax a little. "I see. And who's in the wagon?"

Keltrick gave a quick glance back at me. "Nobody. A business partner that double crossed us."

"He's lying to you," I called out.

Perhaps it wasn't the smartest move but I had very few cards left to play, and Flyngard wasn't talking. I had to do something.

"Is that so?" The dark figure said.

"Don't listen to him," Keltrek said. "He'll say anything to get free."

"Silence. I want to hear him. You. Prisoner in the back. Who are you?"

Since I had no idea how to talk my way out of a situation like this, and judging from Keltrek's attempts at lies that quickly led to wounds, I decided to be honest.

"I'm Jonas," I said. "I'm a bard."

"Jonas?" The dark figure said. "As in, Jonas, the bard assassin?"

Maybe it was time to accept my false reputation. "That's what they've been calling me."

The dark figure pointed his dagger at Keltrek. "You dare take an assassin hostage? You were taking him in for the reward, weren't you?"

"No, no, I promise." Keltrek put his hands up. "I was, um, taking him away from the king. Far away. To freedom."

"No, he wasn't," I called out. "He wanted the reward."

The dark figure gave a nod of his head, and two sharp whistles split the air. Keltrek and Beckwich slumped over, arrows lodged in their chests.

The dark figure leapt onto the wagon with an agile bound. He dropped into the back and sliced through my bonds with such reckless speed I was sure he'd cut me.

He offered me his gloved hand. After double checking that my body was free of fresh knife wounds, I graciously accepted and he pulled me to my feet. He removed his hood, revealing close-cropped black hair, broad features, and three deep scars that ran across his cheek like some bear had nearly taken his head off.

"I'm Trestican," he said. "High assassin, level seven, of the Lynx Collective. Sir Archinlanks was a target for some time. We lost three brethren contracted for his demise. Thank you for avenging their blood."

I nodded, trying to match the intensity in his steely blue eyes. "You're welcome."

"I only recently heard of your deeds. You must have been underground for some time."

I tried to imagine what a secretive assassin would say. The only thing that came to mind was a lame taunt Elrick always used when we played goblin bones in the tavern. "Well, they say the best foe is the one they never see coming."

"Indeed. But now you are known. And with a large reward on your head. It is good we have found you." He put his hand on my shoulder. "The brotherhood of assassins protects their own."

"Thank you. I appreciate that."

His eyes narrowed. "Do you not offer your ranking and collective? Even to brethren?"

"Ah, yes." My head swirled, trying to remember what he'd said. Something about a Lynx and level seven. There was no way I could bluff my way into a legitimate title and since lies brought out Trestican's daggers, I tried to thread the needle of truth as close to deception as I dared. "The thing is, Archinlank's soldiers cudgeled me. I blacked out and could have died. The mind can sometimes lose things with a blow to the head like that. All I know is, I'm Jonas the bard, and my next target is King Mulraith. He rides with his army to attack Calladia and I will stop him."

A wry smile spread across Trestican's face. "Spoken like a true assassin. Even when the mind falters, the mission remains intact. Your target is close, and not even an army will dissuade you. That is the code of the assassin, aye?"

I nodded. "Aye."

Trestican turned to the assassins standing nearby. "Ready the horses. We ride for Calladia!"

CHAPTER 22

WHEN ALL THE hooded figures had emerged from the shadows, I counted about twenty men and women. They appeared to work in pairs.

They all wore dark green and brown from their boots to their gloves. A patchwork of thin leather armor was barely visible beneath their clothes. The deep hoods added a nice finishing touch.

Their clothes were worn and unassuming, and most of their weapons were concealed, save their bows and arrows. In a crowd of townspeople, they could probably pass for simple hunters.

I retrieved my staff from the fallen bandits and leapt out of the wagon to join Trestican and his group of assassins. They led me to a clearing nearby. Horses were tied to trees, saddled and ready to ride.

Trestican explained that they'd spotted the bandits' wagon and knew they had a captive in the back. They'd followed for several miles, remaining out of sight. They thought it might be the runaway prince of a local kingdom they'd been hired to bring back dead or alive. Which, from what I'd seen, probably meant dead. Trestican said that saving a fellow assassin was a far better outcome, but I got the feeling it pained him to miss out on a big payday.

"Archinlanks is slain," Trestican said. "A difficult target, to be sure. But with Mulraith, you seek one of the most formidable ones I've seen. You need to return to the code. Without support, an assassin fails. That is the purpose of the guild, is it not?"

"I suppose so," I said.

"Then we must initiate the code of the mirror," he said. "You shall walk alone no more."

"Right." I nodded, trying to look as if I understood. "The code of the mirror."

"Indeed." He looked toward the group of assassins. "Kellwith. Over here."

A shapely assassin walked over to Trestican and me. She removed her hood, revealing high cheekbones and deep brown eyes. Her smooth black hair was done up in a tight braid. Her beauty was like that of a jungle cat. An elegant symmetry that you stopped to admire just before it leapt out and mauled you.

"Kellwith lost her mirror in the raid at Havensham last month," Trestican said. "She is ready to rebond. As a high assassin, level six, I believe she will be a good match for your skills."

Kellwith put out her gloved hand. "Greetings Jonas. I admire your success with Archinlanks. I look forward to seeing you in action."

I put out my hand to shake hers, but Kellwith grasped my forearm instead, our handshake turning into the arm clasping type of greeting common among warriors.

"Greetings." I gave a tight nod that I hoped would resemble that of a confident fighter.

Trestican wrapped a thin leather strap around our arms, then put his hands on our shoulders. "The code of the mirror. The bond of assassins. We walk together."

"We walk together," Kellwith repeated.

They both turned to me, expectant looks on their faces.

"Oh," I cleared my throat. "We walk together."

Trestican nodded and continued. "Our bond is safety. Our bond is deadly."

I fumbled to repeat the words along with Kellwith.

"We fight together," Trestican said. "We survive together."

We repeated the words, this time in perfect synch.

"The mirror multiplies the assassin. The mirror reflects every slash of the blade."

We repeated once more.

"The mirror will only be broken through death."

I repeated the phrase with Kellwith up to the word death. My voice trailed off at that point. Luckily, neither of them seemed to notice.

Trestican removed the strap from our arms. "A dangerous match. May you drive the dagger through Mulraith's heart together."

Trestican walked into the center of the clearing. "Mount up. We ride for Calladia."

"You ride with me," Kellwith said. "The bandit's horse is too feeble to match our pace. When we stop to rest, we will train. There is little time to prepare, so there is no room to be cautious. We will train with vigor until our attack is united."

My mind conjured an image of getting stabbed multiple times by this woman. "Sounds good."

She took a step forward, her eyes narrowing. "And do not lay a hand of affection on me until I say otherwise unless you wish to lose that hand."

I nodded quickly. "Understood."

The assassins were on their horses and ready to ride in seconds. I joined Kellwith on the back of her horse, and without another word, we set off at a frightening pace.

We rode for an hour, the dark horses weaving through the trees in a thunder of hooves. The assassins communicated in silent gestures. I tried to decipher them as best I could, but the only thing I was fairly certain about was that a flattened hand lifted skyward meant "stop". Obviously I wasn't the best at symbol interpretation.

When we finally stopped to rest, I slid off the horse and headed for a nearby tree. My legs ached from the ride, and all I wanted to do was lean against the trunk and sleep for a while.

Kellwith dismounted and grabbed some daggers from her pack. She walked over and tossed them to me before I even had a chance to sit down. "Here. We must train."

The daggers were finely curved blades that looked sharp enough to shave with.

"Actually, I don't use daggers," I said. "I use a staff."

She frowned. "All assassins are skilled with the dagger."

"I do just fine with the staff, thanks."

"Is that so?" The corner of her mouth turned up and she readied her daggers. "Show me."

"Um, all right, but first, I need to relieve myself. It's been a long ride."

Her shoulders slouched. "Fine. Make it quick."

I headed deeper into the forest wondering if I should just run and never look back. Since my thighs were already sore from the long ride and there was no chance of outrunning their horses, escape wasn't an option.

Once I got out of earshot, I looked down toward my chainmail. "Flyngard?"

There was no answer.

"Flyngard!" I raised my voice. "I need you."

Still no answer.

"I'm about to fight an assassin with a chip on her shoulder and really, really sharp daggers. I need your help."

Flyngard remained silent.

"She's a high assassin, level six," I said. "I don't know what that means, but it can't be good."

I thought I heard a soft mumble.

"Flyngard?" I said. "Please, is that you?"

"I'm very tired," Flyngard whispered. "I need to rest."

"Fine. First, can you help me not get killed? I'm about to go up against a deadly assassin. I think the only time she smiles is when she's standing over a slain enemy. If I don't hold my own, they'll know I'm not who they think I am and they'll probably kill me."

"Assassins," Flyngard spoke as if in a dream. "I remember them… seems so long ago… be careful."

"Flyngard," I said. "Help me fight. Wake up!"

"So sleepy," he trailed off. "So very sleepy."

I tried a few more times to get Flyngard's attention but he wouldn't respond. My heart ached for his turmoil. It felt like we were both slipping into dark pits we didn't know how to climb out of.

After several minutes of trying to come up with a brilliant plan for getting out of this fight, I gave up and headed back. There was nothing to do now but hope that my skills with the staff were enough to keep me alive.

Back at the clearing, most of the assassins sat in close-knit circles, eating or speaking in quiet tones. Trestican spoke with two assassins on horseback who rode off at a full gallop right after I arrived.

Kellwith was close by, practicing fighting moves on her own. She sliced at the air with her daggers in smooth, graceful arcs of death. I swallowed hard, intimidated by the obvious display of skill.

She turned at my approach and beckoned me closer with a flick of her dagger. My muscles tensed at the thought of impending pain. I retrieved my staff and walked over to her, trying to calm my nerves by taking deep breaths.

Trestican made his way closer. He leaned against a tree and folded his arms, watching us. Apparently, I'd have an audience for my defeat.

I stopped a few feet away from Kellwith, anxiety making my stomach churn. "Perhaps we should select a tree and attack it from opposite sides. Coordinate our efforts. Maybe we could use bird calls to indicate—"

Without a word, Kellwith spun toward me, her hand lashing toward my shoulder like the strike of a cobra. My staff was a hair late at deflecting the blade, the sharp tip tearing through my cloak and glancing off the chainmail. Instead of hitting her dagger, my staff struck her hand. A blast of white energy flared over her forearm and she cried out, dropping the blade.

Kellwith took a step back, rubbing her hand. "A strange weapon for an assassin. Bright magic will announce your presence. How can you slip through the shadows unseen?"

She had a good point. I tried to imagine how Flyngard might answer her.

"The more enemies that see me, the better." I gave a cocky grin. "Let them come after me. I'm ready."

She frowned. "That is not the path of the assassin. If I am to fight with you, you cannot be reckless. You will endanger us both."

I didn't have much choice but to go all in on my foolhardy assassin speech. Maybe I'd be fortunate and it would scare her away.

"I'm going after Mulraith, one way or another," I said. "Join me or stand aside."

She held my gaze and gave a small nod. "Very well."

Kellwith dove for her fallen blade, rolling back to her feet before I knew what was happening. She flung her arm forward and a flash of metal shot at my face. I dodged a little too late, feeling a sharp sting across my jaw. There was a soft thud as her dagger sank into the tree behind me.

Before I could recover, Kellwith rushed me, slashing across my chest with her second dagger. The blade found its mark but the chainmail deflected it, almost as if I'd knocked it aside. Her dagger left a long tear in my cloak, exposing the mail underneath it.

Her eyes widened as she focused on the chainmail. "What type of mail is this? Is it magic?"

Since there was no way I could explain Flyngard and the strange enchantment that went with the mail, I decided to add an air of mystery to my reckless assassin persona.

"That is none of your concern." I kept my face impassive. "My secrets are my own."

She frowned. "You seem to have many secrets, Jonas."

A few other assassins had joined Trestican to watch our fight, and now all their attention was focused on me.

Trestican walked over, his eyes studying my chainmail. "You use bright chainmail rather than the leather armor common among the guild. Why?"

"I stay alive by living on my own terms." My assassin persona was getting out of hand. I was speaking out of instinct, hoping I could convince these deadly fighters not to kill me.

Trestican's brow knitted. "Chainmail will catch the light. You will be noticed. And Kellwith speaks truth of your staff as well. These things call attention to you. And therefore, to all of us. This is not the path of the assassin or the guild. You're still bound by oath to the guild, are you not?"

My hunch was, breaking your oath to the assassins guild would get you assassinated. Since everyone around me was flush with knives, I had to think quickly.

"I do not wish to dishonor the guild." I tried the respectful approach. "But I had to adapt to stay alive. Archinlanks now lies dead while I live on. I walk my own path now."

Several assassins gathered behind Trestican. None of them appeared to like what I was saying.

A frown hung on Trestican's face. "If you wish to be careless, you are free to do so on your own. But when you journey with us, you will live by our code." He put out his hand. "Give me the staff and the mail. I will provide you with suitable leather armor and daggers in exchange."

My heart pounded. All I wanted to do was run. What was I supposed to do? Fight them all off?

Trestican's eyes narrowed as he waited for me to comply. "Do not make me ask again."

"I must refuse." The words just came out. As much as I didn't want to upset a man like him, I couldn't remove my armor if I tried. I was bound to the enchantment.

Three assassins formed a tight circle around me, their hands resting on the hilt of their blades. Adrenalin flooded through me, making my limbs feel light.

Trestican stepped forward. "I'm afraid if you will not give them willingly, they shall be taken."

CHAPTER 23

TRESTICAN REACHED FOR the chainmail. The other assassins followed suit, closing in around me. As they did, an idea struck me.

He grabbed the mail around the neck and arm and pulled upward. A warmth spread through the mail and a wave of energy flared outward. I moved with the energy, spinning and sweeping my staff around me. The blast sent all of the assassins to the ground.

I ended my sweeping move with a dramatic, fighting pose. I glared at Trestican as he found his bearings.

"I do not wish to hurt you," I kept my voice low and steady. "That was a warning. I'm capable of greater things."

Trestican got to his feet, locking eyes with me. "So, you are a mage, then? A mage assassin?"

"Call me what you will. Just do not lay a hand on me again." I was really getting the hang of this assassin talk.

He nodded. "Very well. I see that you follow a solitary code. It is not the path of our guild and I find it reckless. But I now see why you target Mulraith. It would take a mage assassin to eliminate a dark sorcerer."

"I will stop him one way or another," I said.

At that moment, I wished I really was a mage. The thought of going up against Mulraith's sorcery with no powers of my own felt like an impossible task. But there was no use dwelling on it, my course was set. I just had to hope that I'd come up with some brilliant plan of victory between now and then.

"Your method may be strange but your mission is sound," Trestican said. "We will form a temporary alliance. But when the mission is complete, we go our separate ways."

"Agreed," I said.

Trestican clenched his jaw. "But do not think for a moment that we fear mages. Magic does not stop the assassin's guild. We have ways around it. The graves of countless magic users that have fallen by the guild's hands testify to that truth."

"Understood," I said.

The assassins went back to their low-talking huddles, leaving me by myself. Kellwith stared at me, her lips pursed. Finally, she turned away without a word and moved to the far end of the clearing. Frankly, I was happy for the break, since I'd had my fill of anxiety for the day. I slumped against the nearest tree and closed my eyes, allowing my body some much needed rest.

I'd barely drifted off to sleep when Trestican gave the call to mount up.

I joined Kellwith on her horse. She gave me a quick glance of acknowledgement before she spurred her horse and we galloped into the forest. Getting the silent treatment from an assassin was enough to send chills down my spine. Who knew what was going on in her head?

After we had ridden for about half an hour, Trestican brought the company to a stop. Everyone went silent as he made a few hand signals, the meanings of which were a complete mystery to me.

A second later, I heard galloping hooves approaching. The fact that Trestican had heard them in the distance over the sounds of our own horses was an incredible feat. The assassins silently drew their weapons, waiting for the arrival of our unfortunate guests.

Two riders emerged in the distance, and I realized it was the same two assassins who had ridden off while the remainder of the party rested. The other assassins put their weapons away as the two riders slowed their approach.

The riders spoke with Trestican in hushed tones.

Trestican turned to the rest of us. "King Mulraith's soldiers are on the move, nearly seven hundred strong. They have marched through Rothman's Pass and are advancing on Calladia under the blanket of night."

The news struck me like a knife. "What? Already?"

Trestican gave me a glance, then continued. "Forces in Calladia prepare for battle, but their numbers are few. We will reach them soon, but the clash of arms will most likely have already begun. I have given many of you targets among the king's knights. The rest of you are free to dispatch as many soldiers as you wish. Mulraith's kingdom has done a great deal of damage to our brethren through the years, and this is our chance to avenge their blood. They are vulnerable without the protective walls of their castle, and their focus is divided. Today the assassin's blade will leave a wound not soon forgotten. For the guild!"

"For the guild!" The assassins shouted together as one, which seemed all the more powerful in contrast to their typical silence.

Trestican turned and urged his horse forward. We followed close behind, faster than before. I glanced at the serious faces of the assassins riding nearby and felt relieved to be on the same side of the fight.

We rode for about half an hour before the forest thinned and the path wound through the foothills surrounding Calladia. From the hilltops, I could see a massive army marching through the outskirts of the town. The glint of moonlight on their armor shone like stones in a river.

The sheer force of the army was overwhelming. My stomach felt hollow at the sight. I wondered where Bree and Elrick were at that moment. Did they stand ready for battle inside Calladia? Were they assembled with the meager forces soon to be trampled by the king? The very thought of it made me sick with anger.

The foothills emptied into the valley, and still we rode on like dark shadows, surging toward the army's back. Trestican turned, making a series of hand signals to the riders. The assassins responded at once, several horses breaking from the group and heading in separate directions.

Kellwith veered right and rode for the hills along the east side of the valley.

"Where are we going?" I called out.

"To finish your mission," she said.

We continued forward at a renewed gallop. Kellwith took the horse through a large outcropping of rocks, their jagged formations stabbing toward the stars. She weaved between the boulders with wild abandon, urging the horse on. I hung on tight for fear of being thrown head first onto a rock. Was it possible she wanted that to happen?

By the time we emerged from the outcropping, we were riding within sight of the rear flank of the army. Whether they noticed us or not, they made no sign that we were of any concern to them.

"There!" Kellwith pointed to the top of a hill overlooking Calladia.

A lone figure stood there, his outstretched arms reaching toward the sky. Glowing red energy pulsated around his hands, and a swirling wind surrounded him. Even from a distance, there was no doubt that it was Mulraith. Seeing him fully engaged in his sorcerous power made me wonder why I'd been so eager to go after him. What would I do when I got there? I might as well be riding toward a cliff.

Kellwith craned her neck back. "The hill is guarded. I count three soldiers nearby. I will take them. The mirror must be broken. You must continue to Mulraith alone."

Scattered fields of rock and sparse trees peppered the hillside. Kellwith rode straight for the base of the hill. I peered toward the trees ahead but didn't see any soldiers. I wondered if she was just assuming there was a guard.

Kellwith handed me the reins and crouched on top of the saddle, preparing to jump off. She drew her daggers and looked back at me. "Drive your staff through his skull for me. Farewell."

She wasn't a poet by any means, but at least her deadly intentions were fixed on someone other than me.

She leapt off at the base of the hill, just as a soldier emerged from the shadows, his sword drawn. He had about half a second to realize his dire fate as Kellwith hit him with the full force of her momentum and a sharp blade.

I assumed her place in the saddle and continued up the hill, through the sparse trees.

Boulders and fields of rocks scattered along the hillside made travel difficult. The horse clambered and surged forward through the obstacles, threatening to unseat me as I clung to the saddle with all my strength.

I expected more soldiers to emerge from behind a boulder or a thick bush at any moment and attack. A small part of me hoped that would happen. I had a far better chance of surviving against a soldier than I did fighting Mulraith.

As I neared the top of the hill, my mind spun through plans of attack. Maybe I should follow Kellwith's example and charge him at a full gallop. Perhaps he'd be so focused on his sorcerous rituals that I'd be able to catch him off guard.

The trees directly before me ignited into a wall of white fire.

My horse skidded to a stop, rearing up and filling the air with a high-pitched whinny. I fell back, the ground knocking the wind out of me, and the horse galloped away.

I lay on my side, gasping for breath. Footsteps approached from behind me. Panicked, I felt around for my staff. It lay on the ground several yards away, out of reach.

CHAPTER 24

"JONAS?" A FAMILIAR voice said.

I rolled onto my back to find Bree and Elrick staring down at me.

Elrick shook his head. "I thought that rider looked a little scrawny for a soldier."

"Yes, but he has a nice face," Bree smiled.

Elrick leaned over and offered a hand up. "Good to see you again, friend."

I took his hand and stood up, giving him a tight hug. "It's good to see you too."

I turned to Bree and gave her a warm embrace. "I'm so glad you're all right."

She kept her arms tight around me for several moments. "You disappeared. We feared the worst."

"I was taken by bandits," I said. "Then rescued by assassins and brought here."

"Assassins?" Elrick said.

I nodded. "Long story. Apparently I'm bonded to one of them now. She's fighting soldiers at the base of the hill."

"She?" Bree raised an eyebrow.

"And you're bonded to her?" Elrick said. "Like a marriage between assassins?"

I waved my hands quickly as Bree's eyes narrowed. "No, no. It's like a fighting bond. I watch her back, she watches mine."

"How close have you been watching her back?" Bree said.

"I'm afraid of her, not attracted to her," I said. "I promise I'll tell you all about it if we live through the night. How is Calladia? Can they survive this?"

"Our warning was heeded in Calladia," Elrick said. "Everyone took up arms. They're sorely outnumbered but they fight for their lives."

"Warriors from Kroth came as well," Bree said. "Many listened to our warning. And when others in Kroth see these soldiers in the valley, more will join the fight."

"And the wolves are readying to attack from the hills," Elrick said. "The soldiers won't know what hit them."

"Is it enough?" I said.

Elrick frowned. "The army is seven hundred strong. Even with help, I don't think we're ready for those numbers."

I nodded, wondering if this night would come to a dark end.

"We spotted Mulraith on the hilltop preparing his sorcery," Bree said. "The situation was already dire, so Elrick and I set off after him. We've taken out most of the soldiers on the hill, but we have to stop his sorcery or all is lost."

"All right." I nodded. "Do you have a plan?"

Elrick looked at Bree. "Not really. We're kind of winging it."

I sighed. "Sounds like my plan… Well, let's get closer. Maybe inspiration will hit."

We stole forward through the rocky hillside, weaving through the thin trees and boulders. The top of the hill was bare, save for scattered mounds of rock that ringed the area like a broken crown.

Mulraith stood at the apex of the clearing, his glowing red hands still outstretched. The wind swirled around him, carrying thin wisps of his magic into the sky in spiraling lines of red. I felt a thrum of energy under my feet as the corruptive forces of dark magic traveled through the ground to join with the gathering sorcery.

Dark lines of upturned earth marked crooked paths toward Mulraith. A trail of dead insects and rodents lay within their wake. A rotting scent hung in the air.

An arc of red energy erupted from Mulraith's hands, curving down toward Calladia like a bolt of lightning. Several trees just outside the center of town burst into flame, their bright orange fire illuminating the nearby buildings.

Witnessing his power up close did nothing for my confidence. I felt like a mouse about to rush a lion. Any strength or ability I had didn't stand a chance against such power.

Elrick transformed into a lycan. He felt his powerful, hairy arms as if bolstering his courage. "This is terrifying. Any ideas?"

"I could distract him with an illusion," Bree said. "You could sneak up behind and attack."

Elrick nodded. "Potential. Of course, if he doesn't buy the illusion, I'd be out there on my own against a dark sorcerer. Not the best odds for ol' Elrick. Jonas, you got anything?"

"What if we use multiple distractions?" I said. "Bree creates an illusion, then I charge from the front and you from the back. Maybe one of us will get through."

"You're going to rush him head on?" Elrick said.

I shrugged. "I've got my chainmail. Maybe it'll protect me."

"Maybe?" Bree said.

I looked deep into her eyes, wishing I had something more reassuring to say. "It's the best I've got."

She stared at me, her eyes misting up, then nodded. "All right. We have to try."

"Right," Elrick said. "Make sure the illusion is a good one. I wish you both luck. Jonas, if we make it out of here alive, you'd better write one fantastic song about this."

I smirked. "If we survive, I'll write a hundred songs about this."

He gave a wolfish grin and rushed nimbly through the rocks.

Bree turned to me, cradling my face in her hand. "Tell me we're going to survive."

I gave her my best look of confidence. "We will. Mulraith will not."

She smiled and leaned in, her warm lips pressing against mine. Her fingertips caressed my hair as she kissed me softly. The world and all its cares melted away for a moment and the great ball of swirling anxiety in my chest dissolved. My thoughts drifted to my stone cottage on a hillside surrounded by pines. I stood under the thick boughs of a tree with Bree at my side, watching the sun dip behind the mountains.

Bree pulled back, a gentle smile on her face. "Be careful, Jonas."

I nodded. "You too."

She placed her hand on my chest. "Protect him as best you can, Flyngard. We're in this together. We fight for our friends and family in Kroth and Calladia."

A subtle warmth spread through the chainmail.

"Flyngard?" I said. "Have you returned?"

"Returned?" Bree knitted her brow. "He can leave?"

I shrugged. "Sort of an ethereal sleep kind of thing. Flyngard? Can you hear me?"

"Yes, Jonas," Flyngard said. "Tell Bree she has a noble heart and I'm glad to know her."

"He says you have a noble heart and he's glad to know you."

Bree smiled. "I'm glad to know you as well, Flyngard. Perhaps today we will strike back against the same vile sorcery that enchanted you."

Flyngard paused. "Perhaps."

"I'm going to move closer." Bree kissed my cheek. "Good luck."

CHAPTER 25

BREE STOLE THROUGH the rocky outcroppings, moving closer to Mulraith. I headed the other way, positioning myself between Calladia and the dark sorcerer.

I weaved through the rocks, the memory of Bree's smiling face giving me the strength I needed to carry on.

Since I was still out of earshot and Bree had broken through to Flyngard, I decided to make one final attempt to rouse him from defeat.

"Flyngard," I whispered. "This is it. I'm going up against Mulraith."

"Madness," Flyngard said.

"Yes, I suppose so. Any thoughts?"

"Turn back before it's too late."

"That doesn't sound like the Flyngard I know."

"The Flyngard you know went up against a sorcerer and wound up imprisoned in chainmail. My old friend Grunsel was right about me. I was reckless. I led people into battle and they got hurt. And now I'm imprisoned, and my old friends are either dead or wounded. Do yourself a favor, don't follow my example."

"That's not what Serenia said about you."

Flyngard was quiet for a few moments. "Perhaps her thoughts are clouded by kinder memories."

"Or maybe she knows you better than some bitter old warrior in a tavern. She said you protected innocent people. Stopped the forces of evil. Saved countless lives. Have you forgotten all that you accomplished?"

"Perhaps, Jonas… But it came at a price."

"As do most things in life worth doing. And right now, we're about to do another good thing and save the towns below. Including Kroth where Serenia lives. You can't give up while she's in danger, can you? Are you with me?"

Flyngard gave a soft chuckle. "Rallying the troops to battle? My young Jonas, you are not the simple bard I met not so long ago."

"Aye. And I'll make you a deal. If you fight with me today, I will compose songs about your past exploits in battle."

"On your honor?" Flyngard said.

"On my honor."

Flyngard sighed. "I wish to help, Jonas. I sincerely do. But my spirit despairs after what I have learned. My strength of will wavers."

"That is not the code of the warrior," I said. "Come on, you remember the words don't you? Heart of fire. Mind of steel. Will of iron."

He paused. "I must admit. Those are powerful words."

"Then let's hear it. Come on. Say it."

"Heart of fire." Flyngard's voice steadied.

"Yes, that's it. Keep going."

"Mind of steel." Flyngard raised his voice. "Will of iron!"

"There it is," I grinned.

He repeated the words once more, his voice returning to its former strength.

"Yes," he said. "You are right. I cannot forget the code. I cannot forget who I am. I cannot leave my Serenia to these dark forces."

"That's the Flyngard I know! Now are you ready to fight with me?"

"Aye!" He shouted. "Let us slay this foul sorcerer and place his vile head atop a spear for all to see!"

"Yes. Except for the head on the spear part."

"Oh, please?"

"I'll think about it."

I traveled in silence as I neared Mulraith's position. Thankfully, a group of boulders stood before him, a mere ten yards away. I sneaked up to the rocks, letting them shield my approach from his view.

"I feel the thrill of battle through you," Flyngard said. "I must admit, I haven't felt this energized in a long while. Thank you, Jonas. I'd nearly let myself slip away, and for that, I apologize."

I nodded, patting the chainmail at my chest.

My breath came in quick, shallow gulps. At any moment, Bree would create some illusion, and I'd have to rush out of my hiding place. My legs felt light, waiting for the moment I would sprint forward, hoping it wouldn't be the last moment of my life.

A sharp crackle split the air, and a bright flash of red lit the sky above. A jagged bolt of red energy slashed through the night and descended toward Calladia. Mulraith was going to just stand here and rain down his sorcery upon the town. Countless lives would be brought to an end just so his power could spread over the land.

The fear that dominated my thoughts fell away. All I wanted to do at that moment was stop this evil man. My life seemed a small price to pay for striking him down and putting an end to the misery he'd poured out on others. I gritted my teeth and gripped the staff, waiting for my chance to attack.

A thunderous screech came from overhead, and a fiery shape

drew my eyes skyward. A huge bird covered in flames lit up the night sky. Its massive wings contracted and it dove toward the hilltop in a streak of orange, as if descending toward prey. I froze at the sight, realizing it was a phoenix. I knew little of these creatures, but I knew enough to stay clear of them.

The phoenix let out another screech, and a burst of fire flared toward Mulraith. At that moment, I realized the truth. The phoenix was Bree's illusion. An illusion so convincing I'd nearly missed my signal to act.

I bolted from the cover of the boulder and ran toward Mulraith. A swirling wind still circled around his thin, towering frame, and his hands still coursed with clouds of red energy. But his attention was fixed on the approaching phoenix. Bree's plan was working. He didn't even see me coming.

From behind him, I spotted Elrick already leaping forward, his sharp claws raised to attack. Elrick landed on the back of the sorcerer, his claws sinking deep into his shoulders. Mulraith cried out, the red energy on his hands dying away.

"Strike him down, Jonas!" Flyngard shouted. "With all your might!"

I lunged forward, sweeping the end of my staff across Mulraith's narrow jaw. There was a flash of white, and he spun sideways, his balance faltering. Elrick clung to his back, raising one hand and sinking his claws in a second time. Mulraith staggered, blood streaking down his crimson robe. I came in for another strike, this time aiming for his temple.

Mulraith lifted his arm with a shout, his voice echoing over the hillside with inhuman power. A thick wave of red energy burst out of him. My body was hurled backward. I flew through the air, my back finally slamming into the ground a dozen yards away.

I rolled to a stop, black splotches swirling before my eyes. My head spun. I resisted the urge to lay down and rest. I propped myself up on an elbow, trying to get my bearings.

Elrick had already recovered. His movements were a blur as he leapt toward Mulraith for a second attack. At the same time, the phoenix illusion descended toward the sorcerer, a blast of orange fire consuming his body.

Mulraith shrieked. A bright pulse of red energy obliterated the phoenix illusion and sent Elrick crashing through the trees at the edge of the clearing.

Mulraith's chest heaved with deep breaths. He glared as he looked around the clearing. "Fools! You think you can destroy me with tricks and feeble attacks. I am Mulraith the great sorcerer of Grandelon. And you will pay dearly for coming against me. You will beg for death before the night is over."

I stumbled to my feet, leaning on my staff for support. Rushing forward for another attack was pointless. The only option was to run for cover and try to come up with a better plan.

Before I could take a step, a sphere of red energy surrounded me like a blanket of fire. My body lifted off the ground and levitated toward Mulraith. A burning sensation coursed through me, the intensity building as I floated helplessly forward. There would be no second attack. This was it. He had me and I was powerless to resist.

"Flyngard," I strained against the magic. "What can I do?"

"I know not," Flyngard said. "For all the victories I achieved on the battlefield, sorcery is the power that overthrew me. At this point, seek the Eternal One's favor and perhaps deliverance will come."

I took a deep breath, my skin prickling with fear as I hovered ever closer to the dark sorcerer.

"If you see a chance to attack," Flyngard said. "Any chance. Take it. Don't despair while you still have breath in your lungs."

The hovering red sphere slowed to a stop before Mulraith's outstretched hand. His gaunt face was tight with lines around his focused eyes. "You?" His eyes opened with surprise. "Murderer of my son! You dare come for me? You vile little worm!"

He clenched his fist and the red energy tightened around me like a constricting serpent. I gasped, unable to breathe. My body felt like it was being crushed under a wall.

"I'm fighting against it," Flyngard spoke in a strained voice. "I'm trying. It's just... it's too strong."

Mulraith opened his hand, and the pressure stopped. "I see you have some protections of your own. Apparently I've underestimated my old bard... Perhaps it's for the best. Your death should be long and slow after what you did."

He twisted his hand and the red energy flashed brighter. A great heat swirled around me and there was a terrible sensation of needles stabbing all over my body. I screamed out in pain. Tears streaming from my eyes.

"Hold on, Jonas!" Flyngard cried out. "I'm fighting against it with all my strength."

Suddenly the pain ceased and I heard Mulraith cry out. The red energy around me dissipated and I fell to the ground.

An arrow stuck out of Mulraith's chest. He gritted his teeth and yanked it out, blood spurting from the wound. His eyes scanned the area and he thrust his hand forward, a red sphere of energy shooting forth.

Bree levitated into the clearing, her body surrounded by the red force. She was frozen in place, still holding a crossbow in front of her. A shiver went through me at the sight. He might be able to destroy me, but I wasn't going to let him take her too.

I rolled to my feet and lunged toward Mulraith, bringing my staff in a perfect arc toward his head. My staff was inches from his face when my body froze. The red energy surrounded me once more, and I was stiff as a statue.

My helpless body lifted in the air, floating away from Mulraith, until I was right next to Bree. I glanced over at her. She was held in place just as I was. We were captured. Our plan had failed.

"Fools!" Mulraith glared at us. "You thought you could kill me with your feeble weapons? You know nothing of my power."

He waved a glowing red hand across his body and the wounds we had inflicted closed up and appeared to be in the final stages of healing.

Mulraith studied Bree. "I should have known. My son's former concubine. The barmaid who thought she was too good for royalty, teaming up with my son's assassin. Well, you shall pay a high price for your insolence as well."

Mulraith tightened his hand and Bree screamed out in pain.

"Stop!" I shouted. "Stop it!"

Mulraith laughed. "Nothing stops! This is only the beginning of your torment."

The red energy pulled me forward until I was face to face with the dark sorcerer. His bloodshot eyes stared into mine. Red waves of energy rolled across his sharp features, giving him a devilish glow. "You killed my son. Now you shall feel the pain of watching someone you care about die. And don't worry, I'll take my time. I'll make sure to savor every moment of anguish it brings you."

"I didn't kill Archinlanks," I strained against the energy but I could barely move. "It was the dragon."

He sneered. "And I suppose it was the dragon that broke a lute over his head the night before he died. I saw the hatred in your eyes. You wanted him dead."

I paused, unsure how to answer.

"Yes, I see the truth," Mulraith said. "Soon you and your barmaid will know pain like never before. But first, let me show you something."

Mulraith levitated high in the air, his outstretched arm bringing us with him.

We floated about thirty yards above the top of the hill, an expansive view of the valley spreading out before us.

"Look there." Mulraith pointed to the battle below.

Hundreds of the king's soldiers poured into Calladia. There was a clash of swords and the distant echo of voices raised in battle. My heart sank at the small handful of forces resisting the soldiers' advance. The situation was hopeless. There was no doubt they'd be overtaken. The numbers were just too unbalanced.

"This was already a day of triumph," Mulraith gave me a crooked smile. "But now, my victory is even more complete. By tomorrow, Calladia and Kroth will be mine, and I will bring the two of you home in chains."

Mulraith descended back to the hilltop, and flung his hand forward. Bree and I were thrown against a boulder several yards away, the sharp impact knocking the breath out of my body. I gasped for air as tendrils of red energy wrapped around us, holding us tightly against the rock.

"By tomorrow's first light, you shall be beaten and broken," Mulraith said. "I'll let my soldiers teach you some manners. Of course, I'll give them strict orders not to kill you, but you'll long for death after they're through. And I shall enjoy bringing you home to the dungeons for a long and painful stay."

He raised his hands to the sky, red energy building around them. "But for now, I have work to do. I will rain terror down upon Calladia until the town is in ashes."

CHAPTER 26

THE WHIRLWIND GREW strong around Mulraith. A low rumble went through the ground. I couldn't imagine the level of power he was gathering to make the ground shake.

The trembling under my feet continued to build, small cracks forming on the hilltop around us. Something beyond Mulraith's power was at work. The hill itself seemed to be coming undone.

"What's happening?" Bree said.

"I don't know," I said.

Mulraith looked toward the ground, his brow knitting. The whirlwind around him subsided and the red energy around his hands diminished.

He glared at me. "What is this? Another trick? Do you wish to see your barmaid writhe in pain once more?"

Before I could answer him, the ground exploded beside Mulraith and jagged rocks burst forth. The sorcerer was thrown back, huge boulders and chunks of earth falling toward him as the ground continued to explode.

At first, I thought the hill was being torn apart. That some great underground force of nature was breaking through and we would all be the unwitting victims of its power. But gradually the rock took shape and moved. The arms and legs of a great rocky beast emerged and I recognized Migmulk, one of the rock giants I had met under the Chellusk Mountains.

Migmulk rose from the gaping hole in the hilltop and stood to his feet, the ground trembling with his movements. The red tendrils of energy holding us in place faded away. We were free once more.

Mulraith was barely visible under the pile of rocks and earth around him.

Bree fell to her knees, holding her arm.

I knelt beside her. "You okay?"

"Just a bit bruised." She stared up at the stone giant. "Let's get out of here before he sees us."

I chuckled. "Don't worry, I know him. I told you I met giants in the caverns."

"I thought you were kidding."

Migmulk raised his massive stone foot and stomped on the pile of rubble covering the dark sorcerer, the force of his efforts shaking the ground. He looked at the pile for a moment, then turned toward me.

He leaned over, his massive stone body towering above us. "Jonas. The great wizard warrior bard. It is good to see you again."

"It is great to see you Migmulk!" I said. "I can't thank you enough for coming when you did."

"You are most welcome." He turned his starry eyes on Bree. "And who is this? Part of your mighty band of warriors?"

"This is Bree." I motioned to her.

"Hello, little one," Migmulk said.

"Greetings," she said. "And thank you. Thank you so much for coming."

"Of course," Migmulk said. "After we left the caves, I asked Guntrick and Brindel where we should travel. But no one knew where to go. We'd been trapped under the mountain for so long, it was hard to even think of going anywhere. Then I remembered you talking about a battle in Calladia and about Mulraith's army, and that sounded good to all of us. We thought we could help. So, here we are."

"Thank you Migmulk," I said. "You just stopped Mulraith."

"Ah, yes," he nodded. "The foul apprentice of the evil Rastvane. How I do hate sorcerers. And as far as his puny soldiers, Guntrick and Brindel are attending to them as we speak. Here, I'll show you."

Before I could object, Migmulk swept Bree and me up in his hand and lifted us high in the air. The battle in the valley below looked far different than it had a moment ago. Guntrick and Brindel resembled men stomping on mice as they trampled across the battlefield. The once organized ranks of the soldiers were now a wild group of screaming men, fleeing for their lives.

Migmulk chuckled at the sight. "It's good to be out from under the mountain once more. I'd forgotten how enjoyable it is to join the battle."

A resounding roar broke out from the sky above. A dark figure approached, growing ever larger and revealing the shape of a dragon. My heart dropped.

"Oh no," I said. "It's Baldramorg. He's found us."

"You fight against dragons, little bard?" Migmulk said. "Are you sure your wizard powers are that strong?"

"No," I said. "They're not. Can you help us?"

Migmulk shook his great, rocky head. "Alas, I am too slow for dragons. His fire cannot hurt me but with his speed and powerful tail, I'd soon be little more than rubble if I stood against him. Perhaps I can protect you? I'll hold you in my hand and keep you safe."

"Okay," I said. "Just don't squeeze too hard."

He chuckled. "As if I could hurt the great bard wizard."

A sudden explosion came from below and Migmulk fell to his knees. There was a rush of wind, and my stomach dropped as we plunged downward. Migmulk staggered and braced the fall with his free hand.

"My leg!" he cried out.

His fallen body spread across the hilltop like a broken tower. His right leg was smashed into small pieces of rock up to his knee. Mulraith stood beyond the fragments of rock, his glowing red hands outstretched.

Bree gasped. "How can he still be alive?"

Migmulk placed us safely on the ground. "Don't worry, little ones. I will stop him." He turned toward the sorcerer, shifting his weight on his knees which sent another rumble through the earth.

"Bree! Jonas!" Elrick came jogging up to us. Several bloody gashes streaked his fur. He clutched his rib cage, wincing.

"Elrick!" Bree grabbed his shoulder, looking concerned. "Are you all right?"

He nodded. "Just scratches, really. I heal fast, remember?"

Migmulk brought a huge fist down toward Mulraith. The sorcerer created a protective dome of red energy, and the rocky fist glanced off of it.

"Thank the Eternal One this rock giant came around," Elrick said. "Let's get out of here."

Migmulk raised his fist high for another strike. Judging from the size difference, it looked as though he could smash Mulraith like an insect.

A bolt of red light flashed from Mulraith's hands and the rock giant's fist exploded into a shower of rocks.

"He's going to destroy him," Bree shot me a nervous glance. "Then us."

I wanted to grab Bree's hand and run as fast as we could away from this place. After all, what was left to do? We didn't stand a chance against this kind of power. Plus, Mulraith had a personal vendetta against me that promised a lifetime of pain.

The sorcerer sent another blast of red energy into Migmulk's chest. A shower of rock burst forth and the rock giant cried out in pain. My heart twisted inside of me. How could I just leave when Migmulk was only here because of me?

Bree grabbed my hand. "We have to go. He's too powerful."

Still, I resisted her pull. My feet were rooted to the ground. Leaving now would ensure Mulraith's victory. How many would die today from his sorcery?

"Look for any path to victory, however narrow," Flyngard said. "Otherwise, seek reinforcements. Perhaps greater numbers will prevail."

I wavered. The only paths I could see led to my ruin.

Another tremendous roar came from above. Baldramorg would reach us in moments.

"Baldramorg!" Elrick grabbed a handful of gold out of his pocket. "Curse my greed. I wish I'd never taken this."

Migmulk let out a deep bellow and swept his other hand across the ground, lifting the earth beneath the sorcerer along with him and hurling him toward us. Mulraith flew through the air in a shower of rocks and dirt and rolled to a harsh stop only a few yards away, half buried in rubble.

"Wait!" A wild thought struck me. "Take off your cloaks. Elrick, get the gold from your pockets. Throw them all at Mulraith. Quickly!"

Without a word, Bree and Elrick set to work. They knew what I was thinking. If the dragon's treasure and the scent from our cloaks were close enough to Mulraith, maybe it would be enough to send Baldramorg after him instead of us. Like Flyngard said, it was a narrow path. But at least there was a path.

We threw what we could toward the fallen figure of Mulraith, then sprinted for the forest.

I turned to Bree. "Can you create an illusion of another rock giant?"

"Yes," she said.

"Mask the approach of the dragon," I said. "Make sure all Mulraith sees is another giant coming."

Bree smiled. "Yes. I understand."

We hid behind a group of boulders nearby and Bree shut her eyes. The white stone in her circlet glowed white.

A rock giant with glowing white eyes marched up the side of the hill, coming toward Mulraith. The dragon flew right behind him.

Mulraith staggered to his feet, swaying with the effort. He turned, his eyes widening when he saw the approaching giant. "Enough of you cursed giants! Back to the ground from where you came!"

A red bolt of energy shot from Mulraith's hands. It obliterated the giant illusion and hit the dragon square in the chest with a bright flash of red.

Baldramorg faltered, his flight dipping as if he might plummet to the ground, then he recovered, sweeping back up into the air. He craned his neck back around as he circled the hill, his green scales gleaming in the moonlight. "Foul sorcerer! You dare attack me. I smell my treasure all around you. You steal from me and then think you can defeat me with your cursed magic?"

Mulraith's eyes went wide and the color drained from his face. He stood there, hands hanging at his sides as if he didn't know whether to run or fight. I'd never seen him look afraid of anything before this moment.

Without warning, the dragon dove toward the hilltop, heading straight for the dark sorcerer. Mulraith snapped into action. He raised glowing red hands and shouted at the top of his lungs. A huge wave of red energy shot from Mulraith into the dragon. Glowing red lines spread across Baldramorg's green scales as if he were cracking apart. The dragon let out an earth-shattering roar and surged downward. A thick stream of orange fire shot from Baldramorg's mouth, consuming Mulraith where he stood and igniting the hilltop around him. Thin rays of red energy shot out from the dragon's scales like sunlight breaking through thick branches. The dragon trembled and roared as he descended at full speed on the sorcerer.

A thunderous boom echoed over the hill, and a flash of light burst forth. I shut my eyes tight and turned away. The ground heaved and I fell to my side.

CHAPTER 27

THE GROUND TREMBLED and a rush of hot wind washed over me. A thick cloud of gray smoke billowed over the hilltop, masking the aftermath of the powerful clash.

Bree and Elrick looked around. Their wide-eyed expressions matched my feelings exactly.

"Everyone all right?" I said.

They nodded.

"That was a thrilling sight," Flyngard said. "Clever thinking, Jonas."

"Thanks." I peered into the gray smoke. "Let's hope it worked."

We waited in the shadow of the boulder as the smoke cleared. A large shape moved in the dwindling smoke. At first, I thought it was the dragon, but it turned out to be Migmulk, kneeling over the bloated and unmoving body of Baldramorg.

I crept out from our hiding place and moved closer. "Migmulk? Is it safe?"

The giant turned, the rocks on his face curving into a smile. "Little bard wizard. Look what happened. Is this your doing? Did your magic pit them against each other?"

"Let's just say it was a group effort," I said.

"You are a humble little wizard," Migmulk looked back at the fallen dragon. "I can't believe my eyes. I thought I was about to be destroyed, but instead two powerful beings lay dead before me."

"They're dead?" I said. "Both of them?"

He waved me over with his still intact hand. "Yes. Come see."

I joined Migmulk near the fallen bulk of Baldragmorg. The blackened ground looked as though a forest fire had scorched the hilltop. The dark green scales of the massive dragon body had lost their former luster, the life force having drained from the great beast.

"You sure he's dead?" I said.

Migmulk nodded his great head.

Now that I was close, I could see the giant's right leg was missing below the knee, his left hand was gone, and a cavernous hole hollowed out his chest. "Are you going to be all right?"

Migmulk nodded. "Yes. In time. I will have to return to the earth for a while but all will be fine after a few seasons. A small sacrifice for this glorious outcome."

Bree and Elrick walked up to us, their mouths slack as they took in the strange sights.

"Is this a new warrior friend?" Migmulk looked at Elrick. "This furry beast?"

"Oh, yes," I said. "Elrick."

Elrick gave an unsure nod. "Um, hello."

"Thank you for your help," Bree said. "You saved us."

Migmulk chuckled. "As if the great bard wizard and his warrior friends needed saving. You are all far too humble."

"No, you did," Bree pressed. "Mulraith nearly killed us all."

"Well, he will kill no more." The giant motioned to what looked like a pile of burnt clothes. "See for yourself."

Mulraith's body lay burnt and withered within his charred crimson robe. His skeletal hands were clenched into blackened fists. I stared at him in silence for a long time. It was hard to believe that this dark sorcerer who had held my life in his hands only moments ago was actually dead.

Bree put her hand on my shoulder. "It's over. Mulraith is gone."

Somehow her words made it seem more real.

Migmulk looked toward the battlefield. "The enemy is routed. The battle is won."

"Already?" Elrick said.

"What's happening down there?" Bree said.

"There's not much that little soldiers can do against rock giants," Migmulk said. "Especially without a sorcerer to help. Those that still live flee back to Rothman's Pass. Although they are being pursued by the townspeople. I doubt they will ever return."

Tears fell from Bree's eyes. "Calladia is safe."

Bree took me in her arms and we shared a warm embrace. A large, hairy arm draped over my shoulder as Elrick joined us.

A loud snap brought our attention back to Migmulk.

"Here, little bard wizard." The giant handed me a dragon tooth. "The mark of a dragon slayer. This will make a great ornament for your home."

"Oh." I took the large tooth in my arms, a thick coating of green blood still dripping off it. A stench like old cabbage filled my nostrils. "Thank you."

"You're welcome," Migmulk said. "Say, when you head down the hill, can you tell Guntrick and Brindel to come up here? I might need some help getting down."

"Of course," I said. "And thank you Migmulk. I owe you a great debt."

"You freed me from the mountain," the giant smiled. "Perhaps we can call it even."

We said our goodbyes and headed down the hill toward Calladia.

CHAPTER 28

T HE SUN ROSE over the mountains as we made our way down the hill. Golden light poured into the valley, ushering us into town.

Calladia was a mix of celebration and tears that day. Thankfully, casualties were few, and the fires that Mulraith had ignited with his sorcery had been quenched before they'd gotten out of hand. Other than a few blackened rooftops and walls, and several scorched trees, the damage was minimal.

The farms on the outskirts of town had received the worst of it. Their fields were burned, most of their homes were destroyed, and their cattle had been killed or escaped. Other than the animals that had wandered back on their own, there was much loss. The townspeople rallied around the downcast farmers, promising to work together and rebuild.

Even in the aftermath of destruction, Calladia was a beautiful town. Cobblestone streets were flanked by one and two-story cottages and shops. Wooden signs hung over door frames announcing everything from the town cobbler to the apothecary. Green foothills cradled the northern edge of the town leading to the majestic mountains beyond. Yellow maples and flowering white dogwood trees were spread liberally along the streets and around town.

A deep sense of relief flowed through me as I walked down the stone streets. The thought that I had been a part of saving this place from destruction was something that would stay with me forever.

By late afternoon, things had settled down. Some of the townspeople had begun the cleanup effort, others rested at home. Long tables were set up around the town square and laid out with food to celebrate the victory against the king's soldiers.

Bree, Elrick, and I reclined at one of the tables after eating our fill of roast chicken, bacon, sweet potatoes, and freshly baked bread. I couldn't remember the last time I'd had a meal as delicious.

"Ahh." Elrick leaned back, patting his belly. "Now that's a meal fit for a hero."

Bree chuckled. "Hero, huh?"

"Well, aren't we?" Elrick spread out his hands. "I mean, why shouldn't we be acknowledged. I've been spreading our story all around town."

"I know," I said. "People keep asking to see the dragon's tooth. I don't want to carry this thing around anymore. I can't get the stink off of it. Even after washing it twice."

"Just a little while longer," Elrick said. "It's our only proof. Once they climb that hill and see a dragon and a sorcerer lying dead, that'll confirm my story. Then who knows? They'll probably want to build statues of us."

Calladia was one of those towns that liked stone statues. Various past leaders and figures in heroic poses were peppered throughout the main streets and flanked all the main buildings. The mayor even offered statues to be constructed in honor of Guntrick and Brindel for their invaluable contribution to thwarting the king's soldiers. However, the stone giants grimaced at the idea, and left soon after to join Migmulk on the hilltop. Perhaps, since they were made of stone, they took the offer of small stone likenesses as some kind of insult.

"Whether they believe our story or not," I said. "I don't want a statue of me. That would be strange."

"Nothing strange about it," Flyngard said. "I had my likeness carved in the castle walls back in Brennelen Kingdom after I defended them from an ogre raid. It's an honor."

"I don't want a statue either," Bree said. "Let's hope they don't offer it."

Elrick grunted. "Well, they're not going to just build a statue of me. You're going to ruin my chance at greatness."

Bree frowned. "Just be glad you survived. Speaking of which, how are you feeling?"

"Oh, I'm fine." Elrick waved her off. "I'll probably be all healed up by tomorrow."

After Elrick had transformed back to a human on our way down the hill, his wounds seemed far worse than I had realized. Several gashes spread across his back, as well as a few on his shoulders and thighs, and one across his left cheek I imagined would leave quite a scar. A chill had gone through me at the sight, wondering if perhaps the injuries might do permanent damage. However, as the day had worn on, I was relieved to see he was already beginning to mend. His new healing abilities were something to behold, and after what we'd been through, I was truly grateful to be spared such a heavy loss.

"You should take it easy," Bree said. "I mean it. Rest up."

Elrick rolled his eyes. "Yes, mother."

She shook her head and turned her attention to me. "By the way, my mother finds you charming. And father told me he'd be glad to have you around for a while. You made a good impression on them."

"Really?" I said.

I'd met Bree and Elrick's parents briefly when we'd first arrived in town. They wept tears of happiness over their children's safe return and welcomed me in. They fed us and gave us a chance to clean up in their home. Our visit was cut short by the needs of the town, but we promised to stay several days and help out.

"Yes," Bree said. "We have a guest room. My parents said you're welcome to use it."

"Yeah," Elrick said. "They'll probably want to adopt you and send me packing."

"Oh, stop it," Bree said.

Elrick stood up. "Well, I promised I'd help father with the hogs. Apparently half of them ran off. I should get on his good side now. That way he won't get angry with me when I don't agree to stay on forever as his farmhand."

"Farming is not a bad life," Bree said. "It's peaceful."

My thoughts drifted to my imaginary cottage on a hill surrounded by trees, with Bree at my side.

"Boring," Elrick said. "That's not the path of a traveling entertainer, right Jonas? We can't hang around a sleepy town like this. Plus, I'm a lycan watcher now. A warrior entertainer. A slayer of dragons and sorcerers, who should have a statue but probably won't."

"I think being a lycan has gone straight to your head," Bree said.

"Jealous?" He smiled and headed off.

Bree sighed. "What am I going to do with that brother of mine?"

I shrugged. "Well, he is a jester at heart. I'm just glad he's healing up. I was worried when I saw his wounds."

"Me too. Even though he can really get under my skin," she smirked. "But after what we've been through, I'm grateful he's all right."

"Indeed. He's been with me through a lot. I'm fortunate to have a friend like him… And I'm fortunate to be here with you."

I leaned in and kissed her. Her soft lips washed away the lingering anxiety of the last few days. For the first time in a long while, I felt at peace.

Bree smiled and placed her hand on my chest. "Just don't let all this hero talk go to your head like my brother. My heart is knit to a simple bard, not a prideful braggart."

I put my hand over hers. "I promise I'll only write a few songs about our adventure. Although my name may find its way into some of the lyrics. That's not really bragging, is it?"

She narrowed her eyes in a playful manner. "Just don't get carried away."

"On my honor."

Bree stood. "All right. I have to go help my father."

I got to my feet. "Me too. I'll help however I can."

Bree touched my arm and smiled. "Rest a while. Enjoy the town's hospitality. Everyone's grateful for what you did."

"I can't just wander through town without you," I said. "I need you to show me around. Tell me about all your memories here."

She nodded. "That sounds wonderful. I will. Perhaps tomorrow. For now, take it easy. I'll see you back at our place in a couple hours."

"But–"

Bree put a finger to my lips, stopping my protest. "Not another word. See you in a couple hours." She gave me a quick kiss, then headed down the street.

I stood there, watching her walk away. I already missed her.

Flyngard cleared his incorporeal throat. "Is this what I have to look forward to? Day after day of lovestruck gushing over each other. I'd rather hunt for goblins in the swamps."

"I can't help it," I said. "You're free to take a nap if things get too romantic for you."

"I'm sensing an abundance of naps in my future."

A few townspeople came up behind me, offering an avalanche

of hugs, pats on the back, and thank you's. Of course, they all asked to see the dragon tooth. I retrieved it from my pack and showed it to them, holding it close to their noses so the full aroma of dead dragon would wrap up the conversation quickly. After some wincing and recoiling, they excused themselves, and I replaced the tooth in my pack.

After they left, I had a strong desire to get away by myself for a while. I strolled through the side streets, making my way to the outskirts of Calladia, leading up to the end of the valley.

"So," Flyngard said. "How does it feel to finish your first quest?"

"Was that a quest? I don't even remember if I ever agreed to it. I kind of just fell into it."

"Aye. Quite common for a new quester. You'll get the hang of it."

"You make it sound like I'm planning on another one."

"Well, aren't you?"

"Not a chance."

"Don't be so hasty," Flyngard said. "With me at your side we can do great things."

"Or end up dead."

"Oh, stop being so dramatic. By the way, where are we headed?"

"I need to get away for a while," I said. "Gather my thoughts."

"Ah, yes. The warrior's repose. The best thing for you after a quest. Other than another quest, of course."

"I'm not used to all this attention. I just want a nice quiet place to rest. Maybe play some music."

"Aye. And prepare for our next quest against my nemesis. Sorcerer Rastvane."

A shiver of anxiety went through me at the thought of facing down another sorcerer.

"I never agreed to that," I said. "I told you, I'm not interested in more quests. I barely lived through last night. It's not like I'm some sorcerer-slayer."

"But how am I supposed to avenge my imprisonment? His defeat is the only thing that will break my enchantment. I'll finally be able to return to Serenia after all these years away. That is, if she'll still have me. Or if she hasn't found someone else. Did you happen to see a ring on her finger? In all the shock I forgot to look."

"Look, Flyngard. I sympathize with your situation. Really, I do. But if Mulraith was Rastvane's apprentice, that means he was trained by him, so Rastvane is even more powerful. If I couldn't stop Mulraith without the help of a rock giant and a dragon and a fortunate turn of events, there's no way I can stop Rastvane."

"Which is why we have to find a place to rest and strategize. Let the creative battle plans flow."

I shook my head. "I just want to rest and play music, all right?"

"All right. I understand. I won't bring it up again… at least today."

"Good."

A low group of hills covered in maple trees bordered the mountains beyond. Their red and gold leaves carpeted the grass like a natural tapestry.

A long stroll took me deep into the cover of the lush trees. Sparrows trilled in the branches, flitting away when I walked too close. There was a peaceful-looking spot under the golden leaves of a large tree just ahead. I retrieved my lute and settled against the thick tree trunk.

I plucked the strings for a while, allowing my body to relax into the music.

"What tune is that?" Flyngard said.

"Nothing in particular," I said. "I'm just letting my fingers play."

"I like the notes. You should put words to it. Perhaps a battle song."

"A battle song, huh? And I suppose you already have something in mind."

"Indeed I do. There's a fantastic story of a group of adventurers that defeated a sorcerer and a dragon and saved two towns, all with the help of a great warrior trapped in enchanted chainmail."

"Hm, I don't know. Sounds like a tavern tale to me."

"I swear it's all true."

"Well, perhaps I'll compose a few lines," I said. "It might make for a catchy tune."

"Aye," Flyngard said.

The notes of the lute floated on the soft breeze, rising up through the golden maple leaves and fading away in the afternoon sun.

THE END

Did you enjoy this book? Please consider leaving a review on Amazon. Every review helps to promote this book series and supports my efforts as an author.

Thank you so much for reading my story. I sincerely hope you enjoyed it!

OTHER BOOKS BY PAUL REGNIER

The Luke and Bandit cozy mystery series

A Tail of Mystery | BOOK ONE
A Scent of Mystery | BOOK TWO
A Star of Mystery | BOOK THREE

The Paranormia series

Paranormia | BOOK ONE
Paranormia Complex | BOOK TWO

The Space Drifters series

The Emerald Enigma | BOOK ONE
The Iron Gauntlet | BOOK TWO
The Ghost Ship | BOOK THREE

ACKNOWLEDGMENTS

I'm so thankful to God for the ability and opportunity to write and publish books. Storytelling is the most enjoyable career pursuit of my life. Stories in books, movies, and shows have given me inspiration, laughter, hope, and lifted me up when I was down. I hope this story will provide the same positive impact to others.

Heartfelt thanks to my wife and best friend Jolene for her support and priceless help brainstorming, reviewing rough drafts, catching typos, laughing at my jokes, and encouraging me every step of the way.

The wonderful editing skills of Nicole Shultz really got this story in shape and I'm so grateful for her help. Special appreciation goes out to Teddi Deppner for her story feedback and encouragement.

Lastly, thank you to the team at Damonza who created a book cover that filled my eyes with tears of joy as well as making the interior pages look fantastic.

All my love to Jolene, Joshua, and Katie.

ABOUT THE AUTHOR

Paul Regnier is a speculative fiction author. He believes one of the closest things to magic on this earth is imagination. His favorite type of story is filled with adventure, humor, and heartfelt moments between characters. He likes to dream up worlds of fantasy, sci-fi, mystery, and the supernatural. Sometimes they end up in a book.

Paul is the writer of the Luke and Bandit cozy mystery series, the Paranormia series, a supernatural comedy, and the Space Drifters series, a sci-fi/space opera comedy.

Paul lives in Treasure Valley, Idaho, with his wife and two children.

Connect with Paul!
Website: *www.PaulJRegnier.com*
Instagram: *www.Instagram.com/PaulJRegnier*
Bookbub: *www.bookbub.com/profile/paul-regnier*